"It's not just commitment that concerns me," Jeff said. "It's the fact that women simply can't be satisfied. They're constantly flirting, constantly on the hunt. I've heard that it's believed that males think about sex three times as much as females. Bull."

"Are you talking about women in general or me specifically?" Babette asked.

"Both."

"That's not true."

"Prove it, and if you do, then I'll talk to Kitty."

"Prove it—how?"

"For the remainder of the time you're here, you remain focused on the job and you forego the temptation to flirt with every guy on the beach."

"I'm supposed to be at the beach for a whole week and not even flirt? In order to prove to you that woman can commit?" she asked. "That makes no sense."

He stood. "Fine. That was my offer." He started walking toward the door, and Babette gawked at his ass in those pants. Damn piña colada. Definitely would have to lay off of them over the next two weeks, because she was accepting his ridiculous challenge.

"You're on."

*Please turn this page for raves*
*for the novels of Kelley St. John.*

# TO CATCH A CHEAT

# REAL WOMEN DON'T WEAR SIZE 2

*more . . .*

"[A] fun tale . . . Hits the right G-note."
**—TheBestReviews.com**

"Wow! This is over the top, and all the fun of a sweet *Sex and the City*! Fans of sizzling romance will have a ride on cloud nine with this one."
**—MAGGIE DAVIS, author of**
***Hustle Sweet Love***

"Kelley St. John's sexy debut, *Good Girls Don't*, delivers both heat and heart, making St. John an author to watch!"
**—Julie Kenner, author of**
***The Givenchy Code* and *Carpe Demon***

"Original, fast-paced, sexy and sassy . . . For all you chick-lit fans out there, heads up! There's a new kid on the block, and she totally rocks."
**—RomanceDesigns.com**

"One of the most entertaining romances I've read in a while. Kelley St. John brings her characters to life, and readers will find themselves immersed in the story from the first sentence on . . . This is one of those 'Don't Miss' recommend[ations], guaranteed to leave readers wanting more."
**—LoveRomances.com**

# KELLEY ST. JOHN

FOREVER

NEW YORK   BOSTON

The characters and events in this book are fictitious. Any similarity to real persons, living or dead, is coincidental and not intended by the author.

Copyright © 2009 by Kelley St. John

*Book design by Giorgetta Bell McRee*

Forever
Hachette Book Group
237 Park Avenue
New York, NY 10017
Visit our Web site at www.HachetteBookGroup.com

Forever is an imprint of Grand Central Publishing.
The Forever name and logo is a trademark of Hachette Book Group, Inc.

Printed in the United States of America

First Printing: February 2009

10 9 8 7 6 5 4 3 2 1

**ATTENTION CORPORATIONS AND ORGANIZATIONS:**
Most HACHETTE BOOK GROUP books are available at quantity discounts with bulk purchase for educational, business, or sales promotional use. For information, please call or write:

**Special Markets Department, Hachette Book Group**
**237 Park Avenue, New York, NY 10017**
**Telephone: 1-800-222-6747 Fax: 1-800-477-5925**

To Linda Howard.
You're the most amazing writer on the planet,
and you're an even more amazing friend.
Thanks for everything, always.
—Kelley

# Acknowledgments

My thanks and appreciation to:
Beth de Guzman and Frances Jalet-Miller, for editing
during the initial stages of
*Flirting with Temptation*;
Selina McLemore, for really understanding
Jeff and Babette's unique relationship
and providing the editorial guidance
to make their story shine;
and Caren Johnson, my incredible agent.

# Flirting
## with
# Temptation

# Chapter 1

Babette Robinson's breath caught, her stomach knotted, and her heart did that whole shall-I-keep-beating-or-shall-I-stop thing when Ethan Eubanks glanced across the reception hall, held up his glass of champagne and smiled toward her table. He was smiling at his wife, Babette's sister, but that didn't matter. Babette simply couldn't control the typical response to seeing him, not because she had any feelings for Ethan *that* way, but because he was the spitting image of his twin, and whether she liked it or not, she always had some form of Jeff's image tickling the back of her brain. It was such a nice image, after all. And seeing Ethan brought it right up front and center.

Sandy blond hair, turquoise eyes, sexy smirk. Jeff's skin was more golden, due to his full-time beach residence, but other than that, the two were identical. Either one of them could double for Jude Law and totally be convincing. But it wasn't Jude that Babette saw when she looked at her brother-in-law; it was Jeff. And her current vision of Jeff had him in the buff.

Again, not a bad image.

"Hellloooo. Earth to Babette, and a gentle reminder—that's Ethan," Clarise said, leaning forward and snapping her fingers in front of Babette's face.

"Trust me, I know."

"Yet you still see Jeff when you look at him. You realize that it's somewhat uncomfortable to watch my sister's eyes glaze over every time she looks at my husband."

"Right. Sorry."

"I realize that I should take it easy on you, since it's your birthday," Clarise said, "but I'd like you to at least attempt to remember which brother is attending Richard and Genie's wedding."

"Jeff should be here," Babette mumbled against her glass, then sipped more champagne. "Richard is his friend, and Jeff was with me when I first realized that he still loved Genie. It's because of us that they worked things out last year, and that now they're married."

"Exactly what did Jeff have to do with it?" Clarise took a bite of the chocolate groom's cake, then hummed her contentment. "Sure, he introduced you to his friends, but you're the one who made it your mission to learn the story behind the tension between them and get them back together."

"Well, I wouldn't have met them without Jeff, now would I?"

Clarise swallowed another bite of cake, smirked. "Jeff has been swamped with work lately. Plus, it isn't like he lives right down the street. It's a six-hour drive from Destin to Birmingham."

"His family owns the company. He can take off when he wants, and you know it. And I know how far it is."

She'd driven it, plenty of times, when she'd visited him at his condo on the beach. *Visited.* Such a light word for everything they experienced in that condo, and on that beach, for that matter.

"For someone who hasn't even spoken to him in months, you seem mighty disappointed that he didn't show. And you've hardly spent any time at all with your gorgeous date." Clarise scanned the reception hall. "Where is he, anyway?"

"Probably with Jesilyn."

"With Jesilyn?" Clarise's brows hitched beneath her bangs. Jesilyn was one of their dearest friends. Babette had spotted the sparks between her and Robbie immediately, so she left them alone. Or rather, she'd nudged them along. Didn't matter that he'd come with Babette; she'd only brought him on the off-chance of making Jeff jealous anyway.

"Yes, with Jesilyn," Babette said dismissively. "And that's fine. Now, what were we talking about, again?" She knew, of course, but she didn't want to be the one to bring Jeff back up. And she also knew that Clarise wouldn't disappoint.

"We were talking about my brother-in-law," Clarise answered. "You've hardly mentioned him since your split in the summer, and suddenly you can't stop talking about him. Wouldn't have anything to do with that announcement in the society section of today's paper, would it?"

"Announcement?" Babette turned her eyes toward the dance floor and wished that the band would start back up. The current lull in music wasn't affording her any opportunity to feign more interest in the dancing than the conversation.

"Nice try, sis," Clarise said, and Babette glanced back to see her grinning as she took another bite. "But I know you too well. You read the announcement that he and Kitty Carelle are engaged, and you're wondering if I know the details."

Babette started to answer, but was halted by the sudden appearance of their grandmother.

"Whew, I've got to sit down for a breather. The twins are adorable, but they're running their great-grandmother ragged." Gertrude Robinson dropped into an empty chair at the table, placed a big slab of white wedding cake in front of her and grinned at Clarise and Babette. Her bold platinum waves were a little less exuberant than they had been at the wedding service, kind of flopping in toward her face and shielding her eyes, but nothing could shield the sparkling pink glitter on her cheeks. "Don't you just love a Christmas wedding?" she asked, plucking a swirl of icing off the side of her cake and popping it in her mouth. "All those poinsettias and candles. Really something."

"Granny," Clarise said, looking behind her grandmother as she spoke, "Where are Lindy and Little Ethan?"

"Oh, don't worry, child." She picked up a cloth napkin from the table and used it to fan her flushed face. "I left your little angels in good hands. They're currently going through the dessert line with their Grandma Olivia."

Babette hadn't realized Jeff's mother was attending the event, but it made sense, since Richard worked as an executive for Eubanks Elegant Apparel. "I didn't know Olivia was here. I haven't had a chance to talk to her," Babette said, gazing toward the dessert line to see if she could spot her niece and nephew, and Jeff's mother.

"And what, I wonder, would you and Olivia discuss, if

you happened to talk to her?" Clarise glanced at Granny Gert before adding, "I mean, after you saw today's society pages and all."

Granny's focus turned from Clarise to Babette. "I wondered if you read it, but you didn't say anything, and I figured you might not want to talk about him today, on your birthday, and especially at a wedding. Kind of always thought we'd be attending a wedding between you two, you know, instead of him planning one with that uppity society queen. Personally, I think you should call him up, or drive down to see him in Florida, whatever it takes for you two to work things out. He isn't married yet. I've told you about how I hooked your grandfather, haven't I, the first time I found him alone in his barn?"

Before Babette or Clarise could answer, Granny barreled on. "He was nineteen, I was seventeen, and he had my heart, same way he did the rest of his life, God rest his soul." She winked. "I had to give him a bit of a push in that barn, but it was worth the effort."

"And how was it you gave him a push?" Clarise asked, as though she couldn't recite Granny Gert's famed story by heart. Babette leaned forward to hear, even though she'd heard it just as many times.

Granny Gert grinned, excited. "I told him I had a mind to kiss him and a mind to marry him. And then I did both." She turned toward Babette. "I used gumption, and I think you should use some too, with Jeff, if you want to know how I feel about it."

Babette never had to wonder how Granny Gert felt about anything. Granny never made any bones about telling her, in detail, and quite often. And since they lived next door to each other, with Granny occupying the other half of Babette's duplex, Granny's opinion was always readily available.

The band started back up playing *Shout!* and every person on the dance floor shot their hands in the air and chanted the lyrics. Genie, still in her wedding gown, shimmied up to the stage and danced with the lead singer, while her new husband cheered.

Babette took advantage of the increased noise level to ask what she really wanted to know. "Okay, I'll admit it. I saw the announcement, and I want details."

Clarise shrugged. "I don't have any. In fact, we just learned about the engagement this morning. I think Jeff had planned to tell the family in person, but then he learned that the news had leaked to the paper, and he called."

"And?" Babette asked.

"He said that he was getting married, and he'd tell us all about it when they come home in a few days for Christmas."

Genie's voice, horribly off key, suddenly boomed over the microphone as the song reached its climax. "Now, *wai-a-ait a minute*," she sang, while Richard, and every other guest, burst out laughing.

"Clarise, I'm taking the little darlings out to the foyer to see the big Christmas tree." Olivia Eubanks's voice was louder than Babette had ever heard it, with her trying to pitch it over Genie's shrill singing and over the four-year-olds, both begging to go see the "big tree."

"That's fine," Clarise said, ruffling Little Ethan's hair as she spoke. "As long as both of you are good for Grandma Olivia."

They bobbed their heads, while Olivia's attention moved past her daughter-in-law and to Clarise's sister.

"Babette, I almost didn't recognize you with the long blond hair. It's quite stunning, dear."

"Thanks." Babette noted the crisp winter white suit that perfectly accented Olivia's classic creamy white waves. The look was something totally befitting Meryl Streep's character in *The Devil Wears Prada,* except where Miranda Priestly's face always held a hint of disdain toward the world in general, Olivia's shone with kindness.

"Last time I saw you, you had a black bob, didn't you? Actually, that looked very nice as well," Olivia said with a smile, while Clarise gave the kids additional instructions on what to touch, or not to touch, when they saw the Christmas tree.

"I thought she looked like Jackie Kennedy then, didn't you?" Granny Gert asked Olivia.

"Yes, I did," Olivia agreed. "Oh, Babette, I wanted to compliment you on the work you did for the Fall catalog. Preston went on and on about the photos you took at the last shoot, and when I saw the finished product, I could see why. You really are an excellent photographer."

"It helps that all of the Eubanks clothes are so incredible," Babette said.

"Well, I'd agree with you there, though I know that the models help, too. However, I also know it takes a photographer with a good eye to capture the look my husband and his boys want for the business."

His boys. Ethan and Jeff were thirty-eight, but still "boys" in Olivia's eyes. Babette mentally willed Olivia to say something about Jeff's engagement.

Didn't happen.

"Preston mentioned you'd taken a new job at an assisted living center, but he said you'd still be able to shoot our catalogs," Olivia said. "If we put out more than two catalogs a year, maybe your work with us could be something more than part time. Anyway, I'm glad to know that you can do both."

Babette swallowed, nodded. Maybe Olivia wouldn't ask for details about the new job. Thankfully, Lindy and Little Ethan chose that moment to grab her hands and begin tugging her from the table.

"Come on," Little Ethan urged.

Olivia laughed, said her goodbyes, then let the twins lead her away, before Babette learned anything at all about Jeff and Kitty Carelle.

She turned back to Granny and Clarise, while the music died to a whisper as the group got to the *"a little bit softer now"* part.

"Oh, honey, you were fired again, weren't you?" Granny asked, loudly.

Babette prayed that the *"little bit louder"* portion of the song got here soon, before everyone at the reception heard her job woes.

"It just happened yesterday. How did you hear already?" She really hadn't wanted to discuss yet another job loss on her birthday.

Granny's mouth curled in a bit, not quite a frown, but not far from it. "Oh, honey, no one told me. I could see it on your face when Olivia mentioned it."

"I missed it, but I was looking at the kids," Clarise said. "What happened?"

"Basically, I caused a fight between two guys in wheelchairs, then received a pink slip with yesterday's paycheck."

The corners of Granny Gert's pink glossed lips gave

up the fight and tugged all the way down in a full frown. "I don't get it. You were doing great at the assisted living center. All of my friends there loved you. They said so, all the time. Why, Maud Lovett said just this week that they'd never had more fun with an activities director than with you."

"So how, exactly, did you cause a wheelchair fight?" Clarise asked, and she had the good manners not to smile or laugh when she said it, quite a feat, when considering the image those words created: silver hair, slinging fists, and wheelchairs. An odd combination, for sure, but one that Babette had seen firsthand. Not pretty.

"Remember how I told you I thought Lambert Wiggins had his eye on one of the ladies from the quilting class?"

Clarise shook her head. "No, I don't."

Granny nodded. "You told me, dear, when you were explaining the whole body language thing. And you know, I'm learning to spot some of the signs myself, when I'm at the center and out shopping and all. It does come in handy."

"'The body language thing?'" Clarise asked.

"Babette has been studying up on body language," Granny said.

Clarise rubbed her eyes, then squinted toward Babette. "Studying up? Oh, Babette, are you going back to school again?"

"Don't worry, I'm learning about it on my own. I'm done with degrees. Heaven knows I can't handle any more student loans."

Clarise sighed. Babette couldn't blame her; the whole family knew she'd dug herself in deep with all of the debt she owed to three different universities, because she simply couldn't make up her mind about what she wanted to do. Too bad she didn't realize she liked trying to figure people out before her job at Shady Pines. Maybe she could've gotten a degree in psychology or something like that.

"Babette has a knack for reading folks," Granny said, her train of thought apparently in line with Babette's. "Why, she told me after her first day at the center who hung out with who, who despised who, and even who the denture thief was."

"The denture thief? Someone was actually stealing dentures?" Clarise wrinkled her nose disgustedly, while Babette laughed.

"Not exactly stealing. Borrowing. And that one really didn't involve any body language. I'd noticed that Ms. Mulhaney was on a soft diet, since she didn't have teeth. Then I saw her munching on an apple at lunch. Later on, she was all gums again. And in the meantime, the denture thief had stolen Ms. Fenton's dentures, for about an hour."

"Long enough to eat an apple," Clarise said, smothering her laugh.

"Yep."

Granny Gert wasn't as subtle with her laughter, and actually snorted. Thankfully, all of the wedding guests at the tables surrounding them seemed involved in their own conversations and didn't notice. "Poor Ms. Mulhaney."

"Anyway, at Shady Pines, I started noticing that I'm pretty good at reading people, their body language, even interpreting what they're really saying when they speak. Most of the time, I'm spot on. And lately, I've been reading up on body language and researching it on the Internet, and I've bought a few books on intimate behavior, that kind of thing." She shrugged. "You know me, always wanting to learn something new."

"And getting bored with the things you already know," Clarise said, grinning.

"Show Clarise how you do it," Granny urged. "Why don't you read Clarise?"

Clarise sat back in her chair and raised her brows speculatively. "Okay, I'm game. Read me, sis."

"Read you?"

"Sure. What is my body language saying, right now?"

Babette realized that she had, in fact, surveyed Clarise's actions throughout this conversation and had a good idea exactly what her sister was thinking. "It isn't all that difficult, once you figure out the signs."

"Okay, so read me."

Babette narrowed her eyes a bit, focusing on her sister. "You're trying to act interested in this conversation, but your hands are busy fiddling with your fork. However, your eyes are still paying attention to me." She paused, recalling something else noteworthy, then added, "But when Granny mentioned I was studying how to read people, you rubbed your eyes."

Clarise smirked. "And that tells you, what?"

"The fact that you're fiddling with the fork but looking at me tells me that you understand what I'm saying is important, but you've got half a piece of chocolate cake left and you're wanting to delve back in. But you don't want to seem rude."

Granny Gert laughed, and Clarise joined in. "Okay, I do want more cake, and I'm assuming it's okay with you for me to have it while you discuss your latest dilemma."

"Knock yourself out."

"Is that all you can tell about me now?" Clarise asked, then took a big bite of cake.

"You rubbed your eyes," Babette repeated. "That means you couldn't believe what you were hearing. It's a sign of disbelief, and in this case, I'd say you couldn't believe that I was possibly going back to school again. Which I'm not, as I said."

"Not bad," Clarise said.

"It's kind of fun, once you start learning how to do it. And I am still learning—certainly not an expert or anything."

"She got the idea from Dr. Phil," Granny said. "You know, he talks about body language and such a good bit, and Babette heard him mention it, decided that she might be able to use body language to help her figure out what the folks at the center were thinking, and then she started putting it in action." Granny sounded quite impressed.

Babette was too, right up until her new technique cost her another job.

"Okay, so what does your learning how to read body language have to do with you getting fired from Shady Pines?" Clarise asked.

"Something to do with Lambert Wiggins and the lady from the quilting class? And I know Lambert, of course, but you'd better fill Clarise in," Granny said.

"Okay. Lambert Wiggins, an eighty-two-year-old with a sweet smile, signed up for the quilting class. That was odd to begin with, because he was the only male in the class, but he said his mama used to quilt and he'd always had an interest in it. However, he wasn't just interested in quilting. He was interested in Joslyn Peal, a sixty-nine-year-old lady in the same class. Reading the two of them wasn't hard at all. They held eye contact a little longer than they needed to, gave those sideways glances, smiled, you know, the easy signs. So I asked Lambert if he'd like me to formally introduce them. Kind of funny that they're the age they are and still shy, don't you think?"

"It's sweet," Clarise said, while Granny shook her head.

"Oh, child, you didn't."

Apparently, Granny knew the story behind the story, but Babette had been clueless. "I did. I talked to both of them, found out they were interested in having a date, and then I brought in all of the necessities for a candlelight dinner, music, good soft food—he has dentures—and everything for a night of elderly romance."

Clarise grinned. "How sweet! So what went wrong?"

"Joslyn was married, and her husband happened to be Lambert's canasta partner. The dinner never happened, because Roy Peal found out and took after Lambert in his wheelchair. He had one of those battery-operated state-of-the-art models and nearly put Lambert in the grave when he ran him down. Lambert's in a wheelchair too, but he's got the plain old-fashioned type. He didn't stand a chance against Joslyn's husband's motorized chair."

"So *that's* how you started a wheelchair fight." Clarise smothered her laughter, but it still caused a few glances from the surrounding tables, primarily due to the band's break between songs.

"Oh, child, I could've told you Joslyn's married. I swear, that woman needs to stop that flirting. Honestly, still trying to make Roy jealous, after all these years. She's lucky he didn't have a heart attack."

"I was lucky Lambert didn't have one, the way Roy came after him. But he didn't, just a few cuts and bruises. And I, naturally, got that pink slip with my paycheck. They said I should pay attention to details, particularly wedding rings, but I haven't grown accustomed to checking left hands of the eighty-plus crowd."

"Well, sis, I've gotta hand it to you. No one loses a job the way you do." Clarise, still giggling, stood from the table. "I'm going to find my husband and sneak in a dance while the twins are occupied with Olivia." She started to walk away, then turned back toward the table. "Babette, don't you think you should go spend a little time with your date?"

Babette and Granny Gert followed Clarise's line of sight until they spotted Robbie and Jesilyn talking on the other side of the room.

"No, I'd rather him spend time with Jesilyn. Maybe *they'll* even make it to a third date."

Clarise sat back down. "You know, I'm sure the twins are going to be looking at that tree for a while. Ethan and I will have that dance later."

"Tell you what, I'll go out to the lobby and check out the big tree too. That way I can help Olivia entertain them a little longer." Granny stood hurriedly. "I'm sure we'll keep them occupied long enough for you two to have a sisterly chat, and probably long enough for you to have a dance or two." She winked at Clarise, then turned and left.

"She thinks we're going to talk about sex," Clarise said.

Babette nodded. "I figured that much, but she should've stuck around, since I haven't got anything to talk about anyway." She reached for Granny's mostly untouched piece of cake. "You think she'll mind if I finish this?"

"You know Granny; she'll go get herself another piece if she wants one." Clarise grinned. "And she was probably willing to let the cake go to let us talk about how long it's been since you've had a third date."

Clarise—and evidently Granny Gert—knew Babette's typical rules for dating. Regardless of the fact that she never denied her enjoyment of great sex, she also never had sex with a guy before the third date. Well, except for Jeff, and that baffled her. Lots of things about Jeff baffled her, if she wanted to get right down to it. Which she didn't. Not now, anyway.

"Granny's right, that hottie you brought is mighty pleasing on the eyes. You sure he isn't third-date material?"

"Not for me, but I definitely see sparks between him and Jesilyn."

"I don't know. They're talking and all, but lots of people talk and dance at weddings. And I thought I heard you tell him earlier that you didn't feel like dancing earlier, and that he should dance with Jesilyn, since she's here solo. He could just be waiting for you to decide to dance."

Babette scooted her chair closer to her sister. "Come here. I'll show you." She indicated Jesilyn and Robbie, now sitting at a table across the reception hall with their glasses of punch in hand. "Okay. See how they're sitting?" Babette smiled, her point proven.

Or so she thought.

"They're sitting by each other," Clarise said, unconvinced. "I'm not sure that qualifies as anything more than the fact that the reception hall is crowded, and they need a place to sit."

"You honestly don't see it?"

"See what?"

Babette sighed. "Okay, for starters, in the past two minutes, they glanced at each other at least twice, with Jesilyn looking down and away afterward, because she's wanting him to extend the gaze."

Clarise's brows dipped down, and her mouth quirked to the side. "They glanced at each other because they're being polite, and I don't get how her looking down and away is telling him she's interested in him. Seems like that'd mean she wasn't."

"If she wasn't, she'd just look away and keep her eyes level."

"You seriously believe that?" Clarise shook her head. "Sorry sis, but I can't buy into this one."

"The eye glance isn't all I've noticed," Babette said, surprised by how much fun she was having showing Clarise how telling body language could be.

"Okay, I'll bite. What else do you see?"

"One, they're both sitting open, relaxed in each other's company and receptive to the other's ideas."

"Open?"

Babette turned toward Clarise and draped one arm over the back of the chair, then she leaned slightly forward and raised her brows as though waiting to hear whatever Clarise said. "This is open posture." She then pushed her back against the chair, folded her arms against her chest and looked away. "This is closed."

Clarise looked at Robbie and Jesilyn. "Okay, I agree. They're open. Anything else?"

"Look at the way they're sitting, turned toward each other and almost mirroring their positions, one leg crossed over the other."

Clarise nodded.

"That says they're in the same place emotionally. And now look; Jesilyn is touching her cheek while she talks. That means she'd like him to touch her there—not necessarily now, but sometime."

Clarise tilted her head as she studied the pair. "So now, she's rubbing a finger over her lower lip . . ."

"Ooh, they're definitely getting along. She's thinking about being kissed."

Maybe, if Babette nudged things along, Robbie might even give Jesilyn a ride home from the reception. Then Babette wouldn't have to worry about trying to explain why she didn't want to go out with him again.

"He might not be the third-date guy for me, but their body language says maybe he is for Jesilyn."

"Not trying to be too nosey, but you haven't gotten to the third date with anyone since Jeff, have you?" Clarise may not be able to read other people's body language, but she had an uncanny knack for reading Babette; now, unfortunately, was no exception.

Babette stabbed her cake with her fork, then popped the big chunk of cake and icing in her mouth, chewed and swallowed. She really needed more sugar for this conversation. "You know, now that you mention it, I *haven't* had a third date with anyone since Jeff." Might as well lay it all out there for her sister to dissect, since she was bound and determined to do it anyway.

"I'm surprised you ended things with him, if he still has this kind of effect on you. It's been a year and a half."

Clarise leaned forward, obviously studying Babette's re-action to her words.

Babette focused on her cake, took another bite.

"I know you said you didn't want to talk about what happened, but have you seen him at all since then? Or at least talked to him?"

"No, and just so you know, I'm not sure I was the one that ended it."

"I thought you told me that you were talking on the phone, the two of you were fighting, and you hung up on him. That's all you said about it, and of course, he never said anything at all, so I have to wonder—what were you arguing over?"

"I'd tell you, if I could remember. I honestly thought we were having one of our typical fightfests, and that we'd have fun making up. I know that we were talking, then I told him I was going to hang up, and then he said if I did, he wouldn't call me back."

"But you thought he would."

"Sure, eventually." Babette did remember a bit of the conversation, and oddly enough, she recalled that they were talking about Clarise and Ethan and the kids. That's why Jeff's weird attitude really threw her off. She didn't think it was all that big of an argument, but apparently it had been, at least on his end, and by the time she realized that, he wasn't calling.

And Babette—being Babette—didn't call him either. Two stubborn souls does not a good relationship make. However, they did have good sex. Great sex. Superb sex. But besides missing their notable tangos beneath the sheets, she couldn't deny that she also missed sparring with him, chatting with him, and laughing with him, for that matter.

"Neither of you were seeing anyone else, right?"

"Well, we never said we were only dating each other. It wasn't that kind of relationship."

Clarise cocked a brow.

"Okay, I wasn't seeing anyone else, but I sure wasn't going to tell him that."

Babette's tiny beaded purse started quivering on the table, and she fished out her vibrating phone, then eyed the caller ID. "It's Mom," she said, smiling, and a bit thankful that her mother had literally saved her by the bell. Or rather, the vibration.

Her mother, father, and his sister Madge all lived in a retirement community in Fort Lauderdale. They'd sent Babette a birthday card with a check inside. No matter how much she needed the money, she wouldn't cash the check, but it was the thought that counted.

"Happy birthday, dear," her mother said as soon as Babette answered. "How's your day?"

"Everything's great." It wasn't completely a lie. The cake was good, and her mother had just saved her from having to delve into her feelings for Jeff with Clarise. Not bad. "Daddy and Aunt Madge there?" Babette asked, assuming that they were probably, as usual, calling her via the speakerphone.

"Yes, we're here. Happy birthday, honey," her father said, and Babette grinned.

"Happy Birthday," Madge echoed. "So, you found a guy yet? Or maybe a job?"

Babette rolled her eyes, and Clarise, leaning close enough to the phone to hear Madge's yell, stifled a giggle.

Babette was used to her aunt's teasing, and typically added fuel to the flame by announcing whatever her latest job venture, date, or degree choice happened to be, but she wasn't in the mood to mess with Aunt Madge today. So she simply said, "Thanks."

"Are you having a good birthday?" Babette mentally translated her mother's question—*have you met a guy yet, and is he there with you?* Janie Robinson was many things, but subtle wasn't one.

"I'm having a terrific birthday. Matter of fact, I'm eating cake, right now." No, it wasn't birthday cake, and it wasn't even a cake made for her, but it was cake. And good cake too. She fingered another dab of icing.

"How old are you, Babette?" This came from Aunt Madge.

"Thirty-four." No use lying.

"Wow, next year, you're officially midlife, right?"

"I don't believe midlife is thirty-five now, Madge," Babette's mother corrected.

"Well, if it isn't, it's mighty darn close," Madge snapped.

Clarise's hand moved to her mouth while she only marginally controlled her laughter.

Babette glared at her, and Clarise merely shrugged.

"Anyway, how's the job situation going? You still at the retirement center?" her father asked.

Babette shook her head at Clarise. No way did she want to divulge that she'd lost job number twenty-three. She'd tell her parents later, when it wasn't her birthday and when Aunt Madge wasn't listening.

"I just finished my third week," she said, holding back that she'd also just finished her last day.

"That's some kind of record, isn't it?" her aunt asked, then she grunted, and Babette had a sneaky suspicion that she'd been elbowed.

"Not yet. My current record is eight weeks." Babette silently dared Aunt Madge to respond. Smartly, and probably with the threat of another elbow to the belly, she remained silent.

"Well, have you met anybody interesting?" her mother asked, as Babette had expected that she would.

"No, Mom, I haven't."

"Well, that's okay, dear," her mother said consolingly. "You still have plenty of time."

Plenty of time. She could almost hear her biological clock ticking. *Tick, tick, clunk.* That clock was breaking, and she wasn't all that certain how much she cared.

"Mom, Dad, Aunt Madge, I've got to let you go. I'm actually at a wedding reception, and the groom is getting ready to make a toast." Richard was, in fact, moving to the stage with a flute of champagne in hand. "Love you." She waited for them to say bye, then gladly disconnected from the uncomfortable conversation.

"Oh, good, we made it back just in time for the toast," Granny Gert said, as she and the twins shuffled toward the table. "Olivia went to find Preston."

Ethan also made his way over, brushing a kiss across Clarise's cheek before scooping up Lindy in his arms.

"Let's see what Mr. Richard has to say," he said to Lindy, while Little Ethan squirmed his way into Clarise's lap to get closer to the last bit of cake on her plate.

Richard cleared his throat into the microphone, then eloquently thanked everyone for attending the most important event of his life. He smiled at Genie, toasted her, and then proclaimed his endless love for his new bride. It was a beautiful speech, and the entire crowd cheered and applauded when it ended. But then, Richard cleared his throat again, raised his voice a bit more than before, and turned his attention toward another woman in the room.

Babette.

"And I need to add a special thank you to one guest in particular, because without her help, Genie and I would still be denying our love. Please join me in toasting Babette Robinson, my personal love doctor." The crowd turned toward Babette. Every glass lifted and then toasted her accomplishment.

Granny Gert sipped her champagne and then poked Babette's arm. "He's right, you know."

"Right?" Babette questioned.

"He called you a love doctor, said that he wouldn't have worked things out with Genie without you. A love doctor. Don't know why no one has thought of that before. I mean, it isn't something you'd traditionally think of, when you're thinking about employment, but given your gift for reading people, I think you could do it. And you are between jobs now," she added with a wink.

Truth was, Babette had spent most of her adult life between jobs. But she was still itching to know what Granny was talking about. A love doctor?

"Oh, I see what you're saying, Granny," Clarise said. "People pay for matchmaking services, don't they? Just look at eHarmony and Match.com." Then her mouth quirked to the side. "But Babette didn't actually match-make Richard and Genie."

"She wouldn't be matchmaking, she'd be match-*mending*. She'd mend relationships that have gone off to the wayside. Heaven knows everyone has someone hiding in their past that they'd like to know . . . what if things would've happened differently? Or something like that. Babette could help them find out. Sure, there's lots of people out there matching people, but there isn't anyone mending old fences."

"You think I could actually *be* a love doctor?"

"People pay real doctors big bucks to fix them when they're sick," Granny said. "Why wouldn't they pay a love doctor big bucks to fix a love gone bad?"

"Clarise," Ethan said, and Babette sensed the voice of reason about to make an appearance in this bizarre conversation.

But Clarise had other plans. She looked pointedly at her husband. "Yes, Ethan." Her look said plenty, but mostly, don't mess with my sister, or you won't be messing with me tonight.

Evidently he got it, and he grinned. "I think I'll take the kids over to get some rose petals. Richard and Genie should be leaving soon, and I don't want them to miss out on tossing them at the bride and groom."

Clarise returned his grin. "Great idea."

"A love doctor, huh?" Babette said, after Ethan left.

"I can totally see you doing it," Clarise said. "You'd be terrific. And you could use your new body language skills."

Babette thought about it. She'd been through twenty-three jobs with no success, but never had she created her own position. And they were right; she did like helping people get together. Just look at Richard and Genie. She glanced across the room where Jesilyn was standing near Robbie but looking at Babette. Jesilyn waited for

Robbie to look in the other direction, then held up the okay sign, obviously questioning Babette on whether she had a problem with the two of them together.

Babette smiled, reciprocated the gesture, then looked back to her sister and grandmother. "Babette Robinson, the love doctor," she whispered softly, but inside she was cheering. She likened the idea to Will Smith's character in the movie *Hitch*, except where he used technique (and a bit of deception) to get people together, Babette would simply use the feelings and emotions that already existed, but were hiding beneath the surface. She'd need to get as many books as she could find on body language and intimate behavior. If she was going to do this right, she'd need to hone her skills.

How about that, four degrees and she was trying out a career where she was basically her own instructor. Excitement bubbled through her.

"What do you think?" Granny Gert asked.

"I think," she said, "that it just might work."

# Chapter 2

Isn't it something that the *Birmingham News* ran that article about the Love Doctor by the wedding announcements? And right next to the photo of your most recent success story too!" Granny Gert sounded almost as excited as Babette felt. She'd only been officially in business six months, and she already had a feature story in the paper. Not bad.

"It's definitely something," Babette said, still scanning the paper, even though she knew she should get back to paying her bills.

"Um, did you happen to see the other article of interest in today's paper? The Gossip column," Granny asked, leaning out of the kitchen to catch Babette's reaction.

Babette didn't try to hide the fact that she knew what Granny was talking about. "The article mentioning Jeff and Kitty's breakup?"

"That's the one. I'm really surprised it took them this long to find out and report it, aren't you? Clarise told us about it at least a month ago. I'm betting the paper picked it up now because of the wedding date and all. Wasn't it supposed to be around now?"

"It would've been this past Saturday," Babette said. Two days ago, to be exact. "I wish Jeff would have told Ethan the details, then we could have at least found out what happened from Clarise."

"Well, you can't fault the boy for refusing to kiss and tell, or break up and tell," Granny said. "I think it says a lot about his character that he hasn't." She waited a beat, then asked the same thing she'd been asking for the past month, ever since Clarise had told them that Jeff's wedding was off. "Have you called him? He's officially available again, you know. And if you ask me, you two shouldn't have ever broken up in the first place." She turned back toward the stove and mumbled, "Don't know what he ever saw in that uppity thing anyway."

"I haven't called him, Granny. You do realize it's been nearly a year since we've even seen each other, let alone talked. Don't you think it'd be kind of odd for me to call him up now?"

"Have I ever told you about when I cornered your Grandpa Henry in the barn?"

"Yes, Granny, you have."

"Well, that's the problem with relationships nowadays. No one out there has any gumption, or if they do, they simply aren't using it. If you ask me."

Babette smiled, knowing better than to argue with Granny on her favorite subject. Gumption.

Granny continued moving around the kitchen, and Babette put the paper aside and powered up her computer. Eventually, Granny peeked back out to glance at Babette's usual spread of bills next to her laptop on the table. "Getting better? Your money situation, I mean?"

"Yes, getting better." Babette divided her bills into her typical three stacks—paid, need-to-pay, and wish-I-could-pay. Thankfully, there was only one remaining in that last category, but it was her biggest student loan. She'd knocked off her other debts one by one over the past few months, ever since she'd started The Love Doctor, and after that last monstrous-sized student loan was gone, she'd really be, as Granny Gert said, "living in high cotton."

"Well, I've got a new client for you," Granny said, stirring the spaghetti sauce while she spoke. "That'll add some more money to the pot."

Babette took her attention away from the bills and focused on her grandmother. "A new client?"

Granny Gert's bold platinum waves shifted as she nodded. "She's a bit beyond her prime, but she's feisty and she's got a lot of sass, so I don't think she'll be too difficult to fix up. See, she's wanting to reconnect with an old flame. Or maybe 'old flame' isn't the correct term. It's an old *friend*, who could potentially turn into an old flame. Or I guess I should say new flame. Anyway,"—she paused, shrugged a little, then continued—"well, she's been thinking about giving the dating scene a try again for quite a while." Her top teeth grazed her lower lip, and her brows eased up a notch. "What do you think? Will you help her out?"

It didn't take a rocket scientist to know exactly who her grandmother was talking about. Babette's eyes widened, and she couldn't control the fact that her voice pumped up the volume on her reply. "Granny, are you wanting me

to fix *you* up with someone?" Last year, when Babette
had been working at Shady Pines, Granny Gert had said
she was thinking about dating again, but then she'd never
said anything more about it. Babette had assumed she'd
changed her mind.

Obviously, she hadn't.

"I called my friend Sally Mae Lovett the other day.
See, Sally Mae and I went to high school together, and
every now and then we call each other and chat and catch
up on our old classmates, folks that we've seen around, or
lately, the ones who've passed on." She paused. "Kind of
sad when you stop talking about who got married, or had
kids, or had grandkids, and start talking about who's still
living. It kind of goes through stages, you know, keeping
up with the folks in your past. This last stage isn't much
fun, most of the time."

Babette nodded. She'd noticed lately that her own conversations with friends from high school had changed as
well. Used to be, they'd talk about who married who, but
lately, that talk had turned to who had children. Apparently, she was running a stage behind the remainder of
her group.

"Anyway, I remembered the last time we talked that
Sally Mae mentioned someone, and I wanted to see what
all she knew about him."

"What's his name?"

"Rowdy Slidell, and he still has all of his teeth,"
Granny Gert said above the boiling water hissing on the
stove. Turning from Babette—but not before Babette noticed her cheeks were slightly flushed from the current
subject—she dropped a fistful of spaghetti noodles in the
pot. "He's got a bit of a nose, but I don't really care about

that. The main thing is the teeth, and Sally Mae said she saw him at the Super Wal-Mart in Tuscaloosa and that he definitely has his own chops. She said he's lost all of his hair and has a head that's slick as a baby's butt, but in a Bruce Willis kind of way."

"I've never thought of Bruce Willis's head as anything remotely resembling a baby's behind," Babette said to Granny Gert, who was cooking enough pasta for an army, even though they were the only two dining. She often insisted on cooking for the two of them, claiming that she'd eventually, somehow, put some meat on Babette's bones. Hadn't happened yet, but Babette sure didn't mind letting her try. Granny Gert could seriously cook, and Babette seriously couldn't. Granny turned the knob on the stove to adjust the heat. She looked . . . relieved, and Babette suddenly wondered how long she'd been trying to get up the nerve to tell her about this Rowdy Slidell.

She bit back the urge to laugh at the idea of her grandmother as flustered as a teenager and pulled her laptop toward her to put her mind on something that would keep her from giggling. Yep, her last student loan's balance was the perfect solution. No reason to laugh there, even though it was way better than it'd been in the past.

"But you've got to admit," Granny Gert continued, "Bruce is slick. Hair or not, he's one nice package, and according to Sally Mae, so is Rowdy. He was a looker in high school, even if I never took much stock in it back then; I was smitten with your grandpa Henry. But I'm fairly sure Henry wouldn't have wanted me all by my lonesome forever, you know, and he always liked Rowdy."

"Rowdy," Babette repeated, while she clicked the keys and continued paying her bills online.

"That isn't his real name," Granny Gert explained, then tasted a spoonful of her thick red sauce. "Needs more basil." She located the green spice container and dashed a surplus of leaves in the pot, then spooned another bite. "Mmm, that's better."

Granny Gert set down her spoon and turned to face Babette. "So, are you going to take my case and hook me up with him?" She tore the white paper off the long loaf of French bread Babette had picked up from the Kroger bakery, then she inhaled deeply as the yeasty smell claimed even more attention than the garlic and basil previously overpowering the kitchen.

Babette turned from her computer screen to view her grandmother. Big, bold waves framed her round face in a Marilyn Monroe style that, according to Granny Gert, was timeless. Babette agreed. In her shiny peach dress, matching lipstick and glittery blush, she radiated spunk and sass. No wonder she was interested in hooking up with an old high school buddy who still had his own teeth. Granny Gert didn't deserve to spend all of her remaining years alone, and she was right; Grandpa Henry wouldn't have wanted her to.

"I'll try to help you hook up with Rowdy, but like I've told you before, finding people isn't exactly what I do. I meet with them, read their emotions by what they say—or don't say—and guide them toward the relationship that both parties typically want, but are either too afraid or too stubborn to admit."

"Oh, I know, child. You're a fence-mender, and I don't exactly have a fence that needs mending, but I still think you could help me locate him." She stirred the sauce. "It'd add to your repertoire, you know, if you started lo-

cating long lost loves as well, or lost friends who potentially could be more, in my case. I just need you to tell
me where in the world he's living, what he's doing now,
that kind of thing. It must be near Tuscaloosa, if he was
shopping at the Super Wal-Mart there, don't you think? I
figure I can plan some, you know, coincidental meeting or
something." She winked. "Maybe you can even give me
some pointers on how to do that. I'm afraid I might be a
bit rusty on that kind of thing, flirting and all."

"I highly doubt that," Babette said, grinning as her
grandmother slathered gobs of garlic butter across the
sliced bread.

Granny Gert finished with the garlic and slid the pan
in the oven, then dusted her hands over the sink before
slapping them together in a when-do-we-start move. "So,
how much do you charge? And don't give me some cheap
family rate. I want to pay full price, and I know you need
the money."

"I'm doing fine on money, and I'm not charging you."
Babette held up a palm when Granny Gert inhaled to
argue. "I mean it. I'd love to help you find this Rowdy
guy. It really shouldn't take more than keying in his name
on Google. I'll need his real name, of course."

Granny Gert clicked her tongue against the roof of her
mouth, then frowned. "That's the hard part. I can't *remember* his real name, and neither can Sally Mae. She
went with me to the fortieth reunion, since I didn't want
to go by myself and all, after Henry passed. I talked to
Rowdy, and I remembered her chatting him up a spell too,
so I thought she might have gotten his real name."

"But she didn't?"

"No. Well, she might have, but she said if he told her,

she'd already forgotten it. That's probably the case, since none of our memories are what they used to be."

"What about your high school yearbook? That'd have his real name, wouldn't it?"

"In our yearbooks, it says Rowdy Slidell. I did an Internet search for Slidells in Tuscaloosa, but there are fifty-seven, and none of them ring a bell." Granny tasted another spoonful of sauce. "Lord help me, that's good stuff," she said, smacking her lips. "Okay, on to the particulars. I'm going to pay you, young lady, so don't even try to argue with me about that. Think you can find him?"

"I'll give it my best shot, and you can pay me by teaching me how to cook."

Her grandmother's mouth fell open, then slowly closed and curved into a grin. "Well, I'll be. You really are starting to settle, aren't you? Paying off your bills, getting a real job, one that has lasted longer than any of the others, I might add."

"Six months," Babette said with pride.

"And you want to learn how to cook. Shoot, maybe I'll get a little meat on your bones after all."

"Maybe so," Babette agreed, though she doubted it. She was doomed to be skinny and shapeless, and while men didn't seem to mind the Paris Hilton look, she dreamed of the kind of curvy frame Clarise and Granny Gert sported so well. She hadn't been blessed with what Granny Gert termed the Robinson Treasures, aka big boobs, or the Robinson Rump (no aka necessary). Then again, you always want what you don't have. Case in point, her hair. Right now, it was blond and straight, giving even more prudence to the Paris resemblance. She typically only changed the color when life circumstances changed, but her life had been uncommonly stable since she'd started the Love Doctor bit, and consequently, she'd been a blond for over half a year.

As if following Babette's thoughts, Granny Gert chimed in. "Do you realize you haven't changed your hair in ages? You really are settling down. In fact, maybe it's about time you considered finding a nice man and settling down that way too. Or maybe calling up an old flame and doing a little match-mending for yourself."

Babette hadn't confided that she'd been thinking about that very thing. She'd thought about it a lot last month, in fact, when Clarise told her that Jeff and Kitty hadn't tied the knot after all. She'd made it as far as picking up the phone and dialing his number, but when the answering machine picked up, she simply hung up. Besides, if he still thought about her and wanted to talk to her, then he would've called her.

He hadn't. And since then, she'd kept herself busy with her business and with trying to pay off bills. She rarely ever thought about him.

But she was thinking about him now, and all because Granny Gert had said the "s" word.

*Settling.* Unfortunately, the word had dual connotations. She *wanted* to settle, to be committed and all of that. It'd worked out pretty well on the job front so far. But with a man, another "s" word seemed to go hand in hand with settling. Or make that two "s" words. Smothering and stifling.

"I know that look," Granny Gert said. "What's his name? Or would I get it right if I guessed?"

"No one." Sure, she'd momentarily envisioned Jeff, waves of sandy hair teasing a tan face, and a sexy smirk

that made her insides quiver, but it wasn't because she
was thinking about him in *that* way. Not in a settling down
and sticking together forever way. She was just thinking
about him because he'd been the only guy she dated who
didn't want to smother her, stifle her. Jeff had understood
the impulsiveness that had her switching jobs, hairstyles,
degrees. And he *hadn't* tried to get her to commit to their
relationship long-term. She'd liked that. Really.

When Granny looked suspicious, Babette added, "Seriously. I haven't even been out on a date since I started the
Love Doctor business, haven't been looking and haven't
got anybody in mind." She winced. She did have someone
on her mind, but that wasn't necessarily the same thing as
someone "in mind."

"Well, it's high time you started looking. And while
you're looking, you can locate Rowdy too. I'm not sure
whether I could get the nerve to call him up, or anything
like that, but if I find out how he spends his days and all, I
could manage to bump into him sometime."

"Accidentally, of course."

"Naturally," Granny agreed, dumping the noodles in
a silver colander in the sink. "Oh, by the way, I bought
some golf shoes today."

Babette squinted toward the kitchen. "Golf shoes?"

"I used to golf with Henry, you know," Gert said, as
though she hadn't swapped subjects from finding Rowdy
Slidell to purchasing golf shoes in record time. "Or rather,
I used to ride in the cart when he golfed, but I believe I'm
going to take it up and give it a go."

"O-kay," Babette said slowly. "Does Rowdy Slidell
play golf or something?"

Her grandmother shook her head. "Heavens, how would I know? I've only seen him at reunions."

"Do you even know where to go? I mean, is there a golf course near here? I know about the one at Inverness, but isn't that one for more,"—Babette hesitated, not sure how to continue.

"Advanced golfers?" Granny supplied, then nodded. "Yes, it's definitely not a place for beginners, but that isn't where I'm going. I'm thinking about going back to the course at Mirror Lakes. It's near the house where Henry and I lived when the kids were little, and it's the course where your Grandpa and I used to go. Even when we moved from that old house and lived closer to other courses, he always drove back to Mirror Lakes." She paused, sighed. "It's a special place to him, and to me."

Babette knew there was more to this than Granny was telling. She'd carefully averted her eyes as she spoke to Babette, and she'd slid her hands in the pockets of her dress. Babette read her easily; hiding something. But Babette had no idea what.

"I believe dinner is about ready," Granny said, and before Babette could determine exactly what question she wanted to ask about Granny's rejuvenated interest in golf, of all things, the buzzer sounded by the door.

"I've got it." Babette stood and crossed the room while the square panel continued to blast its annoying sound across the small space. She punched the button and called to the guard station. "Yes?"

"Ms. Robinson, you have a guest," Milton said.

*Ms. Robinson?* Babette and Granny Gert looked at each other, both of them knowing this wasn't Milton's typical tone, or salutation. Usually, he said, "Babette, so-and-so is here. Want me to send 'em in?" But not this time.

"A Ms. Kitty Carelle is here to see you, ma'am," Milton added, enunciating the words as though he suddenly had gone British.

"Have mercy, did he say what I think he said? *Who* I think he said?" Granny asked loudly. "Kitty Carelle? Here? To see you?"

The same questions reeled through Babette's head too, except hers were embellished with an additional name. *Jeff's ex, Kitty Carelle? Here? To see me?*

"Is Ms. Carelle with you now, Milton?" she asked, using a professional tone.

"Nope, Babette," Milton said, lowering his voice and switching back to good ol' boy mode. He really enjoyed playing guard dog for the neighborhood. "She rolled her window back up. Guess those uppity folks don't like to sweat in this blissful late April heat. Been a hot one today, hasn't it? Guess she can't take it," he said, then added a sarcastic, "Bless her heart."

"Any idea what she wants, Milton?" Babette asked, while Granny swiftly turned off the stove, withdrew the bread from the oven and left the kitchen to stand by Babette.

"Yeah, what does she want?" Granny echoed.

"She said she wanted to see Babette Robinson about a business matter. She also said she didn't have an appointment, but that she didn't think you'd mind."

Babette nodded, swallowed. Two weeks ago, she'd helped Lenora Maxwell, head of the Birmingham Welcome Committee, reconnect with an old flame. Ms. Maxwell had promised to tell her friends of Babette's talents. Evidently, one of those friends must've been Kitty.

Granny Gert gasped. "Oh, Babette. You don't think . . . He's the only guy she's ever been engaged to," Granny spouted, adding insult to injury. "But doesn't she know about you two?"

"Probably not." Jeff wasn't the type to kiss and tell, and since Babette had never been in the society pages—and since that was probably the only way Kitty Carelle would have ever seen her with Jeff or anyone else—then no, the woman most likely had no clue whatsoever that the Love Doctor was Jeff's ex-ex-flame, sort of.

Then again, there was a chance that Kitty wasn't here to talk about Jeff. Or that she wasn't here to talk about her own relationships. She could be asking about Babette's services for a friend; that'd happened a few times, particularly with women who were well-known in the community. They didn't want people knowing there were any problems in their love lives, so they had someone else ask Babette about her services.

Yeah, that could be it.

"Lord have mercy," Granny whispered, "What are the odds?"

Babette silently repeated the sentiment. Who was she kidding? Kitty wasn't here for someone else, or for some other relationship. She'd been engaged, not so long ago, and Babette knew that more than likely, that'd be the relationship Kitty needed to mend. Or correction, the relationship she needed Babette to mend.

"Hell," Babette mumbled, and Granny nodded.

"That's the word I'd use," she said, "if I used that word."

Babette glanced down at her tank top, khaki shorts, and bare feet, then she pressed the speaker button. "Milton?" she whispered.

"Don't worry, Babette, her window is still up and she's talking on her cell phone. What you want me to tell her? Want me to tell her you're not in?"

"No, but thanks for the offer," she said to the sweet old man. "However, can you stall her a couple of minutes and give me time to change?"

"You got it."

"Kitty Carelle," Granny said, shaking her head. "What are you going to tell her, if she's wanting you to get her back with Jeff?"

"I don't know." Turning down Kitty Carelle's business wouldn't exactly secure Babette's staying power as the Love Doctor of Birmingham, but helping her get back with Jeff . . .

"Well?" Granny prompted.

"I don't know," Babette repeated numbly.

"Okay, we haven't got time to worry about it now. I'll clean up the kitchen. You put on that new red dress you bought at Marshall's. It's sophisticated, but not too flashy. You've got to look professional, you know."

"But it's red," Babette said, thinking it wasn't all that professional.

"Red for love, my dear, and you *are* the Love Doctor. That's why she's here, and that red dress will keep your mind on that, hopefully." She pulled the pot of spaghetti sauce off the stove and placed the lid on top, then continued neatening the kitchen while Babette headed down the hall to change.

In record time, she swapped the tank and shorts with

her new red dress and matching sandals. Blessedly, she'd taken the time to give herself a pedicure this afternoon, so every toe was tipped in red. How about that, they matched her dress, and she hadn't even planned it! Maybe it was a sign that this meeting would go well. Babette certainly hoped so, because there were oh so many ways that it could go badly. Very badly.

The doorbell sounded, and Babette's pulse catapulted.

"I'll get it," Granny called, her voice all cheery.

Babette checked her appearance in the bedroom mirror while Granny Gert welcomed Kitty into the tiny apartment. Funny, it didn't seem so tiny a few minutes ago, when she hadn't been trying to impress a socialite. But, Babette reminded herself, Kitty had come here seeking the Love Doctor's help, so tiny apartment or not, Babette had already made a good impression. And it definitely wasn't because she used to sleep with Kitty's ex.

Spotting a gold barrette on the end of her dresser, Babette brushed her hair and gathered it sleekly back, holding it in place with the barrette at her nape. She produced her professional, confident smile for the mirror, tried to forget the fact that the client—the very wealthy client—in the front room had been engaged to Jeff merely a month ago and envisioned that last student loan disappearing.

Nice vision. Nice enough to give her the courage she needed to get Kitty Carelle's business, no matter who the other person in her relationship woes happened to be. She took a deep breath, then started down the hall toward the front of the apartment.

"I live next door," Granny said to the pretty woman who looked even more like Heather Locklear in person. They turned toward Babette as she entered, then Granny continued, "I'm going home, Babette. Call me when you're ready for dinner." She grinned congenially at Kitty, took the lady's hand and patted it appreciatively. "Pleasure to meet you, Ms. Carelle."

"The pleasure was mine," Kitty said, her crystal blue eyes sparkling at Babette's grandmother. She waited until Granny Gert had left, then turned to Babette and visibly swallowed. "You're the Love Doctor, right?" she asked hesitantly, as though *she* were actually nervous. Babette noticed her body shifting ever so slightly, rocking almost imperceptibly from one foot to the other. Definitely nervous.

Babette smiled brightly. This woman didn't know her from Eve. In her mind, Babette was a professional love-fixer and successful businesswoman. And *she* was nervous.

Worked for Babette.

# Chapter 3

With her heart racing, Babette completed her trek across the room and shook Kitty's hand. "Babette Robinson," she said, "And yes, I'm the Love Doctor." She felt good about the confidence in her tone, the self-assuredness that filled her when talking about her business venture. With Kitty Carelle calling for her services, she was doing even better than she'd realized, and she was very, very pleased about that.

"I'm sorry that I didn't call for an appointment," Kitty said, holding up a business card that Babette immediately recognized. She'd had the cards, glossy white with red lettering, printed a few weeks ago. "Lenora Maxwell told me how you helped her reconnect with Vince Collins, and I thought you might be able to do the same for me."

"Well, I can sure try." Babette waved her hand toward the small table in her breakfast nook. She casually combined the three stacks of bills, slid them into a file folder and then pushed it aside. "Come on in and sit down. I'll get some information from you, and we'll define a plan for helping you mend fences."

"That sounds fine," Kitty said, her voice soft yet poised, extremely proper. She sat at the table, while Babette gathered her standard information sheets from her desk. Thank goodness she'd taken the time to generate professional forms for one-on-one meetings. Before Lenora, she'd simply used a spiral notebook to keep up with client information. After Lenora, though, she'd thought she should look more official, in case Lenora actually did send her friends Babette's way. Babette was suddenly quite glad she hadn't skimped on the quality. The creamy linen paper with her Love Doctor logo across the header was topnotch.

She turned to see Kitty place her pale peach purse on the table then glance at her manicure. Typically, Babette would see the gesture as a sign of a lack of interest or boredom, but that wasn't the case with Kitty. She was throwing out the wrong signal, but Babette had read enough people now to spot someone who had created their own body language. Kitty's manicure check was an attempt to hide the fact that she was uncomfortable. Being uncomfortable probably wasn't something she was used to. The woman was the epitome of wealth and class. Due to inherit Carelle Pharmaceuticals, she gave the appearance of an intelligent, sophisticated individual who, judging by the professional yet feminine pastel business suit, was very in tune to her sexuality. This was the kind of client Babette dreamed of, one who would help her make her mark with the women of Mountain Brook. Lenora Maxwell was known by some people around town, but Kitty Carelle was the crème de la crème when it came

to Birmingham society, and the potential for more affluent clients.

"So, how can I help you, Ms. Carelle?" Babette asked,
taking the seat across from her then writing Kitty's name
across the top of her client information form.

Kitty's pretty mouth dipped downward and she sighed
deeply. "I lost the love of my life, and I want him back."
She paused, then added, "In truth, I broke his heart."

Babette wrote her words on the paper, not necessarily
because she said something that should be written down,
but because Babette wanted to keep her hands, and her
mind, busy. Plus, it caused her to look at the page, and
it hid her eyes from Kitty momentarily. Eyes and hands
were the biggest giveaways in body language, and Babette didn't want to give anything away on her end. She
mentally willed her pulse to stop racing, took a steady
breath, then looked back up. "Tell me what you have in
mind, Ms. Carelle, and I'll do my best to iron things out
between the two of you."

"I want to get back with him," Kitty said matter-of-
factly. "But he won't even return my calls. I know I
treated him terribly, but in truth, ever since meeting him,
no one else compares. I mean, sure, my head was turned
by Samuel Farraday, but that was merely infatuation."

"Samuel Farraday, of Farraday Suites?" Babette asked,
still writing.

Kitty's perfect heart-shaped mouth quirked into a semi-
frown, and she nodded miserably. Her hair shimmered
with the motion, and Babette silently wondered if there
were any time whatsoever that this woman didn't look
like she was ready for a photo shoot. She was upset, nervous, and yet still somehow looked extremely polished.

"Do you want to tell me what happened?" Babette asked. "So I'll know how to best repair the relationship?" And because she simply wanted to know.

"We were in Florida, and Samuel happened to be staying at the same resort. He saw me by the pool—we'd seen each other at a few charity functions before—and we started chatting. He mentioned he was taking his yacht out for a week or so and wanted some company. I guess I was getting scared at the prospect of getting so serious with one man, so I left with Samuel."

"You left,"—Babette's voice stalled before she blurted out, *"Jeff?"* She wasn't supposed to know who the woman was talking about—"you left the man you love?" She tried her best to make the question sound more factual than accusing.

"Doesn't make sense to me, either," Kitty admitted. "But I want him to know that I realize how stupid I was and that I'd do anything—anything—to have him back." She sighed again. "I worshipped him completely. Then I just let him go, like I do every other guy, except we were about to—about to get—" The lower half of her glossed lips trembled and she shook her head, unable to finish the sentence with the word Babette was expecting—*married*.

"That's okay. If you can't talk about the relationship, I understand."

"No, no I need to. I haven't talked about it enough, because there are always reporters around at all of the functions I attend, and they're always listening. Truthfully, I need to talk about it, and I know it will help you do your job if you know as much as you can."

"Okay. Then take your time," Babette said, offering an

understanding smile, and chomping at the bit to find out why this lady would pick Samuel Farraday, yacht or not, over Jeff. Samuel Farraday, from what Babette had read, was a spoiled, über-rich frat-boy type, who was in his mid-forties, but tried to pass for late twenties.

Kitty sniffed. "The main thing you need to know is . . . he *isn't* like every other guy. He's amazing, and I want him back. I want to marry him."

"I see," Babette said, nodding as though this wasn't a big deal, but knowing that any guy who'd been "worshipped," then dumped in the manner Kitty presumably discarded last year's shoes, probably wouldn't be all that eager to reconcile. With Jeff Eubanks it'd be even more of a boot to the ego.

"I know you're busy," Kitty said, opening her purse and removing her checkbook. "Lenora said you stay booked well in advance."

"I actually have an assistant now," Babette said, referring to Genie, who had recently started helping her with clients. Genie had taken an interest in Babette's business after being half of Babette's first success story. In fact, she'd spent the last six months watching Babette and practicing her own people-reading techniques and was looking forward to having her own assignments.

"Oh, that's wonderful," Kitty exclaimed, her baby blue eyes glistening. "Then you could start immediately?"

"I should be able to," Babette admitted, slightly surprised by the woman's urgency. She wondered if Jeff would be put off if the woman asking him to give Kitty a second chance happened to have been his bed buddy, sex buddy, whatever you wanted to call it, a year ago. She inhaled, then exhaled thickly. Better cover her bases now, just in case Jeff hung up on her the minute she called. "You realize that what I'll do is talk to him, get to know him and attempt to read what he's hiding beneath the surface. I typically try to point out what a person is already feeling but unwilling to admit." She took a deep breath of encouragement, then added, "I can't *make* anyone fall in love. However, if he does still have feelings for you, I'll attempt to convince him to give you another chance. Beyond that, I can't guarantee what happens. That's up to you."

"Oh, I know. Lenora explained the process. If you can't mend the fences, then you don't charge your clients. She also said that's why your services are so expensive, but that you're worth every cent."

Babette didn't know what to say to that. Her services were high because she only took a few clients at a time and spent several weeks on each relationship, ample time to schedule meetings and "read" the couple.

"But I also know that your track record so far is a hundred percent," Kitty said.

Babette nodded, and began to rethink her business plan, specifically the part where she got no money whatsoever if the relationship wasn't mended.

"I'm willing to pay you triple what Lenora paid you," Kitty said, while Babette tried to control her galloping heart.

"Triple?" The word came out in a semi-croak, making Babette's shock unmistakable. So much for controlling her own body language. And then, of course, her mind whispered, *"Kitty knows talking Jeff into seeing her again will be next to impossible,"* but then that was quickly followed by, *"Goodbye student loan, hello cha-ching!"*

"I don't know if you've ever traveled for the job, but I'll need you to. Jeff lives in Florida."

"Jeff?" Babette questioned, her voice remarkably normal, thank goodness.

"Jeff Eubanks, my ex-fiancé," Kitty supplied.

Babette wrote it down, then added, "He lives in Florida?" She forced her facial expression to remain neutral, like someone who didn't know exactly where Jeff lived and hadn't spent a good deal of time in his condo.

"Destin. On the beach," Kitty clarified, gracefully pushing her hair behind her ear with her professionally manicured hand. Each nail was a perfect oval, Babette noticed, and tipped with a frosty peach polish that complemented her outfit beautifully. Babette's nails, by contrast, were shaped square on the ends because that was easier for her to do on her own, and they were painted a color deemed Knock 'Em Dead Red that had been on sale in the Cosmetics section at Wal-Mart.

"But I'm willing to pay you triple your normal fee, plus all expenses for you to stay at the same complex where he owns a condominium. It's on the beach, so it shouldn't be a terrible hardship," she continued, while Babette simply nodded, speechless. "Lenora said you typically require three weeks to contact the old flame, talk with them and smooth the waters."

"That's the average time required and has proven to work well," Babette admitted, glad for delivering a controlled response, instead of blurting it out in *Have mercy, she's paying me triple!* fashion.

And Kitty had done her homework. Three weeks was Babette's average for a relationship repair. She usually took one week to learn as much as possible about the per-

son's current lifestyle, another week to establish a connection with the individual and, most importantly, read
their body language toward the other person, then the last
week to actually meet and discuss the prospect for recon-
necting with their old friend, or in this case, old fiancé. It
was a process that worked, or at least it had worked every
other time. There were always emotions hiding beneath
the surface, and Babette truly enjoyed the task—something akin to an emotional treasure hunt—of unveiling
them. So far, every client had suspected correctly that the
significant other from their past still cared. Kitty obviously suspected the same about Jeff and simply wanted
Babette to help her prove it.

But this assignment would be different, because Babette didn't need the first steps. She certainly knew everything there was to know about Jeff's lifestyle, and heaven
knew the two of them already had an established connection. Or disconnection.

In any case, Babette really wanted to make this fence-
mend between Kitty and Jeff work, even if she were deal-
ing with her own old flame, because triple her normal fee
would give her enough cash to completely pay off that
last student loan. And she really wanted that thing to dis-
appear for good.

"Here's a check for your services," Kitty said, sliding
it across the table. "I've already reserved a beachfront
condo for you in Destin." At Babette's shocked expression, she explained, "I wanted to make sure one was available before I presented the offer to you, and naturally, I'd
hoped you'd take me on as a client."

"You've made the reservation already? When did you
plan on me starting?" Kitty wasn't expecting Babette to

turn her down. Babette wondered if that were part of the woman's techniques for success; she simply assumed she'd get what she wanted, went for it and got it.

Kitty's smile tightened, only slightly, but Babette noticed. She did not want to be turned down. "The reservation starts tomorrow, with check-in at 4:00 P.M., and I have it reserved for two weeks."

"Two weeks?" Babette asked. The woman had already stated that she knew a mending of fences typically took Babette three weeks. Granted, it shouldn't take nearly that long with Jeff, since Babette knew him, but Kitty didn't know that.

"That's why I'm tripling your pay. I don't want to wait three weeks to have him back. I need you to do it in two." She placed both palms on the table as she spoke. Easy body language there; she was taking a position of authority and wasn't open for discussion on the matter at hand. And since she was the one with the big check, and Babette was the one who wanted said big check, Babette swallowed past the urge to tell her what she could do with her money and her demands.

"Your confidence in my abilities is flattering," Babette said. "And I do believe I can accomplish everything in two weeks, if I have a bit of background information from you to get me going. Basically, you can help me with what I would normally do during week one."

"Of course," Kitty said. "What do you need to know?"

Babette held her pen poised and ready to write. "Tell me about your relationship with Jeff Eubanks," she said, glancing at his name on the page as she spoke. "The details about how you first met, your background and all. And the breakup, of course."

"It was at the annual Bruno's charity golf tournament in Birmingham. He was there to represent his family's department stores—they own a department store chain—and I was there for my family's company." She smiled softly. "There were plenty of nice-looking men at the event, but there was something about Jeff that simply made him stand out, and it wasn't just the fact that he was quite compelling in appearance. He also has a presence about him, a confident, strong, sexy quality that simply made my heart flutter. Once I saw him, I didn't even notice anyone else, and I decided right then that I had to meet him."

Babette knew that feeling well. She'd experienced it herself, and she suddenly recalled the man who'd invoked it. Though Kitty sat across from her, Jeff's image clearly overpowered the social queen. And it was such a nice image that Babette didn't have the heart, or the desire, to push it away.

His skin was usually tan, because he loved long walks on the beach, and his hair was perpetually sun-streaked for the same reason. His smile always held a hint of mischievousness, as though he knew a secret, or could make you divulge your secrets to him if he so pleased. And though he and his brother were identical twins, there were subtle differences that Babette adored. Jeff kept his hair longer than Ethan; where Ethan's was cut close and neat, Jeff's sandy waves were neat enough to pass for business, but long enough to capture and emphasize those natural highlights. They teased his brow and curled slightly at his nape. Those curls were perfect for wrapping your fingers in when he was above you, pushing his length deep inside of you, while he drove you over the edge.

Babette cleared her throat and pushed the image, the

delicious image that would probably invade her dreams later, out of her head. "So then you met him at the golfing event?"

"Yes; when I did get to talk to him, he was so quiet and reserved. Honestly, he wasn't anything like what I expected. I guess I thought someone who looked like him, and was as successful as he was, would be more outgoing and more secure about himself around women."

Babette turned her shocked gasp into a cough. Jeff could be classified tons of ways, but quiet and reserved weren't on the list. And insecure around females? Never.

"I had even heard rumors from some of my friends in Atlanta that he was known as something of a playboy there. But those were just rumors. Or maybe something had happened to change that, but I didn't meet a playboy. I met a sensitive guy, who didn't really seem all that keen to even talk to women. He was ignoring practically all of us there, and that fascinated me even more." She lifted a shoulder in a mini-shrug. "He intrigued me so much that I simply had to find a way to be with him."

Babette cleared her throat and prayed she didn't look as uncomfortable as she felt. "How did you do that?"

Kitty smiled. "Basically, I wouldn't leave him alone. I found out which events he was scheduled to attend, learned what places he typically frequented when he came to town, found out that he lived in Destin and made a trip or two down there, then casually ran into him there, and each time, we chatted a little more, and I basically let him know that I was quite captivated by him. It took a while, but eventually, he asked me out to dinner, and then we started dating."

Jeff had been engaged to a stalker.

"After that, we dated regularly and he really came out of his shell, if you know what I mean. I started seeing that playboy that my friends had told me about, but it didn't turn me off at all. Quite the opposite, because while he had the charm of a player, he still only had eyes for me. Probably hard to understand . . ."

"Not at all," Babette said, cutting Kitty off as politely as she could manage. She didn't want, or need, to hear any more. She knew Kitty had finally seen the real Jeff Eubanks when they started dating, though Babette couldn't fathom why she hadn't seen that in the beginning. That was something to concentrate on when she met with him about Kitty, for sure.

"After a couple of months of dating, then we were," she paused, and her brows lifted a little as she added, "intimate. I'm assuming you need to know that, that we had a sexual relationship."

Babette tried not to let the mention of their "intimacy" sting too much. "Two months?" she asked, concentrating on the part that stood out. Kitty had waited two entire months before sleeping with Jeff. And then Babette spouted the next obvious question—"Why?"

"Why did I sleep with him?" Kitty asked, undoubtedly surprised at the question.

Babette gathered her composure. "No, I'm sorry. That's not what I meant. I guess it just seems a little long to wait in this day and age, you know." Did that sound like a question of merit? Because Babette needed it to, and she also needed to find out how any woman could have waited two whole months without getting hot and heated with Jeff.

"Oh," Kitty said, then laughed. "Well, it wasn't easy,

believe me. I mean, he's extremely desirable, and he definitely has his share and then some of sexual appeal, but that's just a rule I've never broken."

"What rule?"

"How long I date a guy before I sleep with him. The relationship has to last at least two months before I go to bed with a guy, because I really don't have any desire for casual sex. If I sleep with someone, then it's because we're making love, not merely having sex, you know? Two months seems to be the amount of time I need to make that decision, whether it's real love, or merely lust. And when we finally got together, it was definitely making love."

Babette's stomach churned. Two months she'd waited. Real love they'd made. Babette had a rule about sleeping with guys as well, but hers didn't seem nearly as conservative anymore. She'd thought the third date should be the deciding factor. But with Jeff, she'd broken even that rule and somehow, at the end of date one, found herself stark naked and panting without any clear-cut reason about why she'd thrown her pitiful excuse for a rule right out the window. Something about being with Jeff made her unequivocally lose her senses. And her panties.

She didn't want to hear anymore about Jeff and Kitty's sex life, or rather, their "making love" life. "Okay, let's move on to the breakup. You said you left with Samuel Farraday. Can you tell me exactly what happened? Did you and your fiancé argue over Farraday, and then you left, or was it something else?"

Kitty's hair shimmered as she shook her head. "I actually wish it had been something like that, but the truth is I never even told Jeff I'd seen Samuel—well, not verbally, anyway. I told him in the note I left."

"You broke your engagement with a note?" Babette did her damnedest to control how appalled she was over Kitty's lack of breakup finesse.

"It was stupid," Kitty said, vocalizing Babette's sentiment.

"Well, I'll do my best to see if I can help, and if the damage is irreparable, I'll let you know." She figured she should throw that out there, since she couldn't imagine any guy in their right mind—particularly Jeff—going back to a woman who broke their engagement via a Dear John letter. But the chance of getting rid of that last student loan and getting a free beach vacation to boot was worth giving it a shot.

"I think I've got everything I need," she said, but then another question tickled the back of her brain, and she couldn't resist asking. "Wait, one more thing. When did the two of you start dating? And how long did it last?"

"That golf tournament was the first week of August last year," Kitty said, "and we ended our engagement a month ago, or rather, I ended it when I left with Samuel Farraday."

The first week of August last year would have been . . . the week after he and Babette had last spoken. Basically, he went from Babette's bed to Kitty's. Well, after two months of dating, that is.

Two months. Babette had barely made it inside his condo after their first date before she was naked and on top of him. As a matter of fact, their first time they hadn't even made it to the bed and had proceeded to have sex against his apartment door, something she thought had been exhilarating and magical at the time. Now, after Kitty's "waiting until we were making love" sentiment, it felt rather cheap.

"Do you need any additional information?" Kitty asked, unaware of the turmoil her little proclamation had created in Babette.

Again, Babette gathered her composure. She needed this woman's business. She needed the Love Doctor to succeed and keep her record at a hundred percent. And she needed to stop comparing her own relationship with Jeff to Kitty's.

Like that was going to happen.

Anyway, she would do what she was supposed to do, attempt to reunite Kitty with Jeff and, if she could pull it off, keep Kitty's money in her bank account. "Ms. Carelle, I'd love to help you resolve things with your fiancé." She slid another sheet of paper toward Kitty. "If you'll provide his pertinent information, I can get started tomorrow."

"Wonderful," Kitty said. "I can't tell you how much I appreciate this. I do love him. I do. I just didn't realize how much until I lost him. He's so passionate, so loving," she continued, as she quickly filled out the information, basically his address, brief description of appearance and general background, on the page. "There. I feel better already."

Babette glanced at the check and all the pretty zeroes on it. "Well, I plan to have you feeling even better soon, when I reunite you two," she said confidently, accepting the information sheet from Kitty as the woman stood.

"Oh, trust me. If you can get me another chance with him, I'll make sure to treat him right this time forever. I only wish it hadn't taken losing him to realize how special

56        Kelley St. John

he is." Digging for her car keys in her bag, Kitty completely missed Babette's thick swallow, or the tiny twitch beside her eye that always happened when she fought tears. She'd already resolved herself to the task of getting Jeff back with his ex-fiancée and prettying up her bank account in the process. But there was something about the words Kitty had said . . .

*"I only wish it hadn't taken losing him to realize how special he is."*

"I mean, he's perfect," Kitty continued, unknowingly twisting the knife. "Sexy and spontaneous and thoughtful and kind. The sex, well, it was the best I ever had, but he's also so warm and emotional, the kind of guy that you could spend your life with. I could never, ever find another man as perfect as Jeff."

"Sure you can," Babette mumbled, her throat parchment dry.

"What?"

Babette looked up from the paper, blinked away the surge of emotions that totally sideswiped her, and smiled. She needed this job. She needed to pay off that student loan. She needed to find out how in heaven's name this high-society feline had managed to capture—and break—Jeff's playboy heart. "I said," she quickly improvised, "that I have the perfect plan."

Kitty cocked a suspicious blond brow, but then seemed to accept Babette's assured smile as genuine. "Wonderful. You'll keep me posted of how things progress in Destin, then?"

"You can count on it. And you have all of my contact information on the business card, if you need me while I'm there." Leading the way, Babette crossed the room, opened the door, then nodded as Kitty left, walking purposefully as though she'd just taken care of a big business deal. Then again, she had. Kitty wanted Jeff back, and Babette had promised to bring him to her.

Jeff. To another woman. To Kitty Carelle.

"Can I really do this?" she asked, snapping the door closed then jumping when it promptly smacked her in the back.

"Who does she want you to find?" Granny Gert asked, bustling through the doorway in full I've-gotta-know mode. "Is it Jeff?"

"You *knew* it would be. I knew it too."

"She's wanting you to talk him into not only getting back with her, but marrying her! You, of all people."

"She has no idea that we dated, or whatever it was."

"It was more than merely dating, and you know it, child. Why you let that one go without a fight is beyond me."

"Go on, tell me how you really feel. Don't hold back."

Granny's cheeks flushed guiltily. "Goodness, I'm sorry. My gumption got the best of me."

"Well, I wish it'd got the best of me back then," Babette whispered. Listening to Kitty talk about how she'd lost the perfect guy hit way too close to home. From everything Kitty said, the limitations of Babette's relationship with Jeff seemed clear: they'd been sex partners, while he and Kitty had been lovers. Babette and Jeff had merely got together, quite often, and burned up the sheets. Or the floor. Or the hallway. Or wherever they happened to be when lust got the best of them. Kitty, on the other hand, had Jeff's ring on her finger when she threw it all away.

Babette couldn't understand how Kitty convinced him

that he should be in it for the long haul, for the whole kit and caboodle, when Babette had never even been able to get him to say that they were dating exclusively. Not that she tried. But what did Kitty Carelle have that she didn't?

Class. Polish. Elegance. Style. Panache.

Babette's throat tightened, and she wished so *many* descriptions didn't come to mind.

*"The sex, well, it was the best I ever had."* Babette could make the same comment . . . about the same man.

A large oval mirror hung on the living room wall, and Babette pivoted to take in her reflection. She squinted as she studied her face, still a tad flushed from her meeting with Kitty. She'd heard there were two kinds of women in the world, those who captured men's hearts with their elegance and class, and those who were merely the playthings they used along the way—until they got what they really wanted.

Her skin grew hot. She was *not* merely a plaything. For Jeff, or anyone else. And she had everything to offer that Kitty did. More. If she'd have wanted to settle down with one guy, she could have. But that hadn't been what she wanted. She blinked. It wasn't what she'd wanted before, but she had found some stability with her job, and she rather liked it. Maybe now was the time to find stability in a relationship too. But first she had to cross the humongous obstacle of getting her ex back with his.

No pressure.

She reached back, unclipped the barrette, tossed it on the couch and let her hair fall free.

"Uh-oh," Granny said, moving behind Babette to dash a glance at her in the mirror. She clucked her tongue against the roof of her mouth then shrugged. "Something big is happening, so you want a new 'do', right? Want me to call Cecile and see if she can work you in?"

Babette smiled at Granny Gert's perceptiveness. They really were alike, after all. "I told Kitty I'd leave tomorrow, so tell Cecile that I'll pay her double if she can squeeze me in late tonight or early tomorrow morning."

Granny picked up the phone and dialed the number. "Cecile? It's Gertrude. . . . I'm fine. Listen, Babette's got a new job that's going to put her working with an, um, young man from her past. She needs a new"—Granny stopped talking and started nodding—"That's right, Cecile. I don't know if I can tell you that or not. Hold on."

"She wants to know which young man," Granny relayed. Cecile followed the traditional hairstylist motto of having to know everything about her clients and everyone else in town.

"You can tell her," Babette said, holding her hair up as she tried to envision what type of look she wanted. The entire three years she'd dated Jeff he'd been specific about what he liked best, and because of that, Babette had never given it to him. It'd been a little game they had played, and she'd enjoyed having fun with him. He'd seemed to like the fact that he couldn't tell her what to do, couldn't control what she did. In fact, he'd claimed he loved her impulsiveness, her spontaneity and lust for life.

Kitty had done the opposite during her "worshipping him" stage and had given him everything he wanted.

Granny Gert's chatting swiftly converted from calm and casual to nonstop and excited. "Yes, that's him," she rattled. "Uh-huh, Clarise's brother-in-law. Yeah, they did date for quite a while, three years, on and off. No, I'm still not real certain why things ended. She doesn't talk about stuff like that all that much. Clarise always told me everything, but Babette's her own person, you know. Strong-willed, that's what we always said about her when she was little. And she tends to keep some things to herself. Yeah, the important stuff," Granny said, laughing, while Babette crossed her arms.

"Hellooo," she said, raising a hand and waving her fingers at her extremely talkative grandmother. "I'm right here, and I can hear you. And just so you—and Cecile—know, I'm not changing my hair for him. I simply want something new for my biggest Love Doctor challenge yet. That's it."

Granny Gert put a pink-tipped hand to her chest and mouthed, "Sorry, child." Then she continued the conversation with their favorite hairdresser. "Yes, Cecile, she can come in an hour." She looked at Babette. "You can, can't you? That will give you enough time to eat some dinner first too. We've got all that spaghetti, you know." She paused, then said, "Sure, Cecile. I'll send you a plate with Babette."

Babette nodded, still a bit miffed. "An hour is fine."

"Hang on, Cecile. I'll ask." Granny grinned, and Babette's irritation dissipated. How could anyone stay mad at this outrageous woman?

"What?" Babette asked, knowing Granny Gert was enjoying this way too much.

"She wants to make sure she's got the color you want," Granny explained. "Let me guess. I bet I get it right."

The laugh that bubbled from Babette's throat was unexpected, but welcomed. "You know me better than most everyone, so *I'm* betting you're right."

Granny nodded approvingly, then winked. "Back to her roots, Cecile. Her natural color. Fire engine red, with lots of wild curls. A spiral perm, I'd say. That's her favorite look for the beach, and that's where she's going." She nodded toward Babette. "Am I right, dear?"

Babette looked back at the mirror, remembered the first time she'd ever seen Jeff. He'd dubbed her "Red" and then he'd never seen her with fiery hair again, though he'd asked for it repeatedly when they dated.

Red. In truth, it was her favorite color, and as Granny said, it was the original hue. And the one that signified confidence and spunk, two things she'd need in spades if she was going to pull off a miracle and get Jeff back to Kitty.

She swiveled and announced with a single, emphatic nod, "Yes, red. Definitely red."

# Chapter 4

Jeff Eubanks hung up the phone after the bizarre call from his brother, stepped onto the patio of his Destin condo, inhaled deeply and welcomed the familiar scents and sounds of the beach. Salty air, crashing waves, laughing kids, giggling females—refreshing reminders that he liked it here, and that he liked where he was in his life right now, enjoying life and freedom and women, each to its fullest capacity. After the one-two emotional punches dealt by Babette and Kitty, it was amazing he was able to, but he was, and he was doing it quite well.

But thanks to Ethan's call, Jeff now knew that his life was about to be turned upside down again by the most prominent women in his past. Babette was on her way to Florida to convince him that he should take Kitty back.

He shook his head, laughed at the absurdity of it all. First, that Babette would begin to think that she was an expert on love, and second, that Kitty would have the balls to think he'd take her back after she sailed away with Farraday. Hell, he must have dated two of the most brazen women in the country if they thought they could pull this off.

Wasn't happening. Not now, not ever.

He glanced out at the beach, specifically at a young couple, probably newlyweds from the look of things, lounging on an oversized beach towel on the sand. The woman rolled onto her back and handed a brown bottle of tanning oil to the guy, who smiled as he took it from her hand. He drizzled the shiny liquid all over her stomach while she stretched on the towel, then ran her fingers through her long, red hair, fanning it out behind her. Taking one palm to her belly, he slid the oil across her abdomen, then slowly eased his hand toward her breasts, while his face moved closer to hers. He didn't even attempt to kiss her, but merely looked at her, drinking her in, while his hand never stopped its seductive perusal of her flesh, and—from Jeff's vantage point on the balcony where he could see—he slipped his fingers beneath the edge of her bikini top and teased the lower curve of her breast.

Jeff swallowed and moved his attention away from the heated exchange to two teen boys, tossing a bright orange Frisbee near the edge of the water. He focused on the orange disk, the way it caught the wind and the way one kid snagged it mid-air, then flung it back. This was what he should be looking at from his balcony, people enjoying a good time on the beach.

But his voyeuristic impulses took over and his eyes turned back to the couple, now lip-locked, with the man's hand no longer visible, hidden within the shadow of his body over hers and apparently paying homage to a lower part of her anatomy now.

Jeff had thought spending a little time on his balcony

before his date arrived would get his mind off the woman currently en route to his condo, but watching the couple's heated exchange only reminded him of a very similar experience he'd had. Except in his case, the female had been the one distributing the tanning oil. Babette had also heightened the interaction by whispering what she'd do to him as soon as they were away from watchful eyes.

He turned his attention away from the couple. No need for reminders of sex with Babette now. Soon he'd see her, and that'd be plenty reminder enough. He hadn't spoken to or seen Babette in a year, and he was fine with that. In fact, from the day Kitty had entered his world, the two of them had been so "into" each other that he'd hardly thought of Babette. Kitty, quite frankly, hadn't given him time to think of anyone else. And, unlike Babette, didn't leave anything to the imagination. Jeff knew from the first date that she was "smitten" and that she could see herself with him for a "long, long time." Her words. Before Babette, he'd have been long gone if a woman came on that strong, but after years with a woman who seemed to forget he was alive, who could take him or leave him, having someone like Kitty dote on him was exactly what he needed.

Of course, the fact that Kitty ended up sailing away with Farraday merely a month before their wedding didn't exactly make for the ending he'd planned. He smirked. At least he was back in the realm of reality again. Women couldn't commit, a fact proven by Babette and Kitty. And he'd finally worked his way back around to the life he'd lived before them, the life where he enjoyed the moment and whatever female happened to be sharing it with him.

No strings, no commitment, no headaches. Or heart-aches.

He left the balcony, returned to the condo and glanced at the clock. He'd left work early, opting to spend the afternoon working at the condo and enjoying the beach scene. Little did he know that Ethan's call would cause his traditional viewing of the beach to be jolted by memories of sex with Babette. At least he didn't have to worry about beach sex memories with Kitty. Kitty was Kitty Carelle, socialite, after all. And while she never minded grasping his arm in public, or smiling at his side, or broadcasting that she'd "love this man until the day she died," she wasn't the type to do anything that would get her name in the paper in an unflattering light.

Ethan had mentioned that their broken engagement had finally hit the Birmingham papers. No doubt Kitty would cringe at the negative publicity. He wondered if that was what had prompted her to enlist a love doctor to mend their relationship. And he wondered what she'd do if she knew that the love doctor she'd selected used to sleep with him.

He laughed. He couldn't help it. To have been a fly on the wall and have watched Babette's face when Kitty asked her to get him back. Surely Babette knew him well enough to know his response to Kitty's request would be something along the line of, "Go to hell." No, he wouldn't be that cruel, but a firm "not interested, not now, not ever," would sum it up.

Turning on the television, he decided to relax for a while. Work would keep, and he had a few hours before his date with Kylie Banks.

Unfortunately, the commercial in progress was advertising

the most notable Day Spa in Destin, and more specifically, the current special they were running for Buff and Bronze sessions.

He flipped the channel, but it didn't matter. In his mind he still saw Kitty on the day of their engagement, when she'd returned to the condo after a celebratory shopping trip.

"After I finished shopping, I went to the spa for a buff and bronze," she'd said.

"A buff and bronze?" Jeff attempted to sound as though he didn't know what was involved with that procedure, even though Babette had described it to him in detail, and that description had led to one of their hottest afternoons ever. He waited, wondering if Kitty would describe it too.

"Yeah," she said, smiling. "So I need a shower, but after I'm done, why don't you meet me in the bedroom and we'll celebrate our engagement properly?" She closed the distance between them, kissed him softly, then turned and retreated to the bathroom.

Jeff had started to ask her to stop, forgo the shower and get started with their celebrating right there in the living room, with the balcony door open, sounds of the beach creeping in, and the slight risk of someone catching a glimpse of the two of them making love. But he didn't want to ruin the moment, and with Kitty, making love with the risk of getting caught wasn't exactly what the doctor ordered.

So while she showered, he went to the bedroom, stripped out of his clothes and waited for her on the bed. Unfortunately, while his body was waiting for Kitty, his mind was recalling Babette's detailed description of a buff and bronze.

Her hair had been short and black, not his favorite, since he preferred Babette with long, red curls, but hell, on her, short and black was sexy too. She'd entered the apartment looking like she had a secret and was dying to share. "There's something I need you to help me with, a little problem with that buff and bronze session," she said, crossing the threshold to the bedroom. She glanced toward the open window and inhaled the Gulf breeze filling the room and causing the drapes to flutter. Then she looked at Jeff and lifted her brows. "You want to help me?" She stepped closer, so close he could feel her breath against his neck.

"What do you need my help with?" he asked, while she unbuttoned his pants, then slid the zipper down.

She pushed them to the floor, moved her hand to his erection and gently stroked it as she spoke. "You see," she said, "while I love the fact that I can get a perfect tan with the buff and bronze, every now and then, the women leave a smudge."

Jeff blinked. "Women?" *Smudge?*

"Yeah, so I thought that maybe you could, you know, check me over and make sure I'm smudge-free," she said with a seductive smile.

"Women?" Jeff repeated, all blood having vacated his brain and headed south.

"Yeah. That's the way they do it, you know," she said, taking her hand from his penis and putting both palms against his chest, then easing him back toward the bed.

"The way they do what?"

"You know, they mentioned to me today that a lot of guys are really turned on by the process, and I wanted to see if it did that for you. And then you can check me over—thoroughly—for smudges." She moved her hands to the top button of her flaming red sundress, slid it through the hole, then pulled it open to reveal the sweet hollow between her breasts.

She slid another button free, then pulled the two halves of the dress apart to reveal her breasts, bare and beautiful. Her nipples were taut little buds, like always. Babette often joked about her small breasts, but Jeff thought they were perfect, incredibly sensitive to the touch . . . to *his* touch.

"So I thought I'd tell you about it. Do you want to hear?"

He nodded. What else could he do?

"They slather this sugary lotion over their hands, and then they rub it in tiny circles all over me," she said, working on the next button. Her skin was so silky smooth that it glistened, and Jeff wanted to kiss it, touch it, lick it. *Sugary* lotion?

"That's the buffing part, they move that gritty lotion all over my skin to make sure it's as smooth as absolutely possible." Her hands neared the button at her waist now, merely two buttons to go, and Jeff was all but drooling. "And they rub it everywhere."

His imagination shifted into overdrive, and his mind did a rapid transition to another image, not of Babette standing before him undressing at the side of his bed but of her in a spa, with two women rubbing lotion all over her and preparing her for . . . what she was doing right now. His cock moved, and she licked her lips.

"That does turn you on, doesn't it?" she asked, eyeing him boldly.

"Yeah, it turns me on." He'd have to be dead not to be turned on.

She'd finally reached the last button, and she undid it, then let the dress fall to the floor. A buffed and bronzed Babette stood before him wearing nothing but lacy high-cut red panties.

"And then, they take me into the shower."

His imagination again overpowered the current scene. "They go with you—into the shower."

"That's part of the treatment, making sure they rinse me clean before they apply the bronzing solution."

He swallowed. Hard. "*They* rinse you?"

"Yes," she whispered. "They run their hands all over me and rub all of the gritty lotion away."

"O-kay." He saw Babette and two women who, in his mind, were almost as beautiful as her, in a rub-fest in a shower, and he wondered how long it was going to take for her to join him on this bed and let him put his current state of mind into action.

"After that, they dry me off, and then they coat me, thoroughly, in bronzing lotion. That part is basically like any massage, except . . ."

"Except?" he asked, while she moved her hands to her hips and then removed the panties—and Jeff realized that she hadn't merely been buffed and bronzed today. She'd been waxed as well.

"Except you have the option to wear these tiny dispos-able panties, nothing more than a wisp of fabric, or . . ."

"Or?" he asked, while she climbed on the bed and straddled him.

"Or you can go nude and let them buff and bronze you everywhere. And since I was already letting them do this"—she motioned to the bare area between her legs, and then to his absolute delight, she guided his cock into her slick, wet heat—"I decided to go nude."

"You knew I'd like that," he said, as her inner muscles clenched around him, and then she flattened her palms on his chest and gripped his pecs as she took her body where it wanted to go, without a care that the window was open and the world was just outside. In this room, at this moment, nothing existed but the two of them, exactly the way Jeff wanted it.

Jeff's heartbeat had still been thudding rapidly when the bathroom door opened and Kitty emerged wearing a long pale blue gown.

She looked at him, then at the window. "Oh, honey, the drapes are open." Without a word to Jeff, she crossed the room and closed them. Then she moved slowly toward the bed. Jeff couldn't see her, his eyes still trying to adjust to the sudden darkness.

"Now," she whispered, easing onto the bed beside him, "everything is perfect."

The shrill ring of the phone snapped Jeff back to reality. Glancing at the caller ID, he answered, "Don't tell me; you've got more surprises heading my way."

Ethan laughed on the other end. "Hell, you don't think your ex-ex driving down there to get you back with your ex is enough for one day?"

"Trust me, it's plenty. What's up?"

"Clarise wanted me to inform you that if you're mean to her sister, she'll kill you."

Jeff grinned. Those Robinson sisters, always protecting each other, even when the hellion of the pair was, once again, causing trouble. "Don't worry. I won't be mean. I'm just going to tell her she's wasting her time and that she can get her cute behind back to 'Bama pronto."

Cute behind. Obviously, Jeff had been thinking about her adorable ass or he wouldn't have mentioned it. He really needed to get onto his date with Kylie, and get his mind off hellions and socialites.

"Well, I told my wife I'd ask you to play nice."

"Tell her you did, and I'll do my best."

Ethan relayed the message on the other end, then said, "So, Babette hasn't made it down there yet? Clarise says she should've been there by now."

"Maybe she wised up and didn't make the trip."

"I highly doubt that. Anyway, take it easy on her. You may not have to see her again, but I have to deal with her on a regular basis."

"Like I said, I'll do my best." They disconnected, and Jeff grabbed his computer and headed toward the balcony. He'd come home to enjoy the beach while he worked, and he wasn't going to let this wild scenario with Babette and Kitty ruin that. He'd simply wait for the "love doctor" to arrive, and then send her on her lovely way.

# Chapter 5

Babette had planned her day perfectly. With Granny Gert's help, she'd been packed and ready to go by nine-thirty. She swung by the bank and deposited Kitty's check and was on the interstate heading south by ten, which would have put her arrival in Destin at four, the exact time she could check in at the condo. But then she'd started through Montgomery, spotted a TJ Maxx just off the interstate and simply *had* to stop. With Kitty's money in her account and a new hair color to boot, she couldn't deny the need to buy a few necessities for the beach, such as new bikinis and beach frocks.

Beach frocks. That was Olivia Eubanks's term for the casual, girly cover-ups so popular for wearing over swimsuits and strolling in the sand. Babette sighed. She really liked Jeff's mother, but since their weird split, she'd only spoken to Olivia that one time at Richard and Genie's wedding. Maybe she should call her up and say hello.

She laughed. Jeff would probably die if she called Olivia. But the truth was, Babette *had* connected with

Olivia, and she shouldn't lose that connection because her son hadn't ever called her back—or because he'd picked a prominent socialite over Babette.

What *did* he see in Kitty?

Attractiveness. Intelligence. Success.

*No*, she wasn't going there again. She and Kitty were night and day, no doubt about it, but she remembered a time when Jeff had liked the night portion of that pair.

She glanced down at the emerald green "frock" that she'd decided to wear out of the store, in case she happened upon Jeff when she arrived in Destin. Everyone knew green was the best color for redheads. If she only had green eyes, rather than plain brown, then everything would be perfect, but hey, she was as close as she could get without colored contacts.

The outfit was meant to be a cover-up, but Babette was wearing the gauzy all-in-one as her main attire. Her only attire, truth be told, since she'd forgone a bra and panties, not wanting strap lines and panty lines messing up the "look." And this was a very good look, if she did say so herself.

Basically it was a top and shorts made together, buttoning up the front and reminding Babette of the rompers that she and Clarise had worn as little girls. It didn't look all that impressive on the hanger, but due to the saleswoman's persistent urging, Babette had tried it on, and she was glad she had. The hanger had disguised the way the sheer fabric played peek-a-boo with tiny pinpricks dotting the cloth. And the waist was tapered, fitted so it created curves that were nonexistent in Babette's usual clothes. Wonder of wonders, she actually had hips. The shorts were extremely short and flared to give the appearance of a teeny, tiny skirt.

A teeny, tiny skirt that would make Jeff's jaw drop.

Exactly the effect she was going for.

She turned off of Highway 98 and made a beeline for Jeff's condo at the White Sands resort. It was six-thirty, due to her shopping spree in Montgomery, but that was okay. The new clothes were a necessity. And the fact that she'd arrived a couple of hours after the check-in time wasn't a huge issue. She'd worn the sexy outfit on the off-chance that the two of them ran into each other when she was checking in, but the truth was she didn't expect to run into Jeff today. She remembered his usual schedule, and at six-thirty, he'd either still be working at one of the Eubanks stores nearby—Panama City, Fort Walton, or Seaside—or he'd be cooking an early dinner while he worked from the computer in his condo. So, chances were he was indoors somewhere and would stay there until the sun set, when he'd go for his usual evening walk on the beach.

Jeff was business-oriented and did his job well, but he rewarded himself by ending his workdays with nightly walks on the sand. Babette had enjoyed those walks too, and the way they'd occasionally take an evening swim.

Babette shook off that image. She so did not need to go there now. Yes, she was glad Jeff was a creature of habit and probably wouldn't be outside when she arrived. She wanted a good night's sleep and a little more time to prepare before she saw him. Walking up and stating, "Hey, I'm here to get you back with the ex-fiancée who dropped you for a sailorboy," didn't quite take the ticket. Sailorboy? Yachtboy? Richboy? Samuel Farraday qualified as all of the above, but it didn't matter; Babette would not use that particular icebreaker.

No problem. She'd figure out what to say, after some sleep. Last night, Cecile had kept her up well past midnight curling, conditioning and coloring the red spirals that now whipped madly around her face due to the breeze blowing through her car windows. They'd attacked her eyes like wild red whips from Birmingham to Montgomery, so naturally she'd purchased a pair of really amazing sunglasses at TJ Maxx; and they did their job, kept her hair out of her eyes while she was driving *and* made her look ultra-cool in the process. Not bad. They also disguised the hint of puffiness and dark circles under her eyes, due to her insistence upon a new 'do.

Tomorrow. Tomorrow she'd see Jeff and start the two-fold progression to one, make him realize he was a fool for not calling her back, and two, get him to give Kitty another chance so Babette could keep her business thriving, taking full advantage of Kitty's extra-healthy chunk of cash and her connections in the Birmingham society scene.

A big gust of wind passed through the window, and she inhaled thick salty air. She really loved it down here and was slightly miffed at herself for not returning since her split with Jeff. A beach vacation would've been nice, but it'd have also taken money, and heaven knew she hadn't had much of that. However, thanks to Kitty, that was changing. And the additional clients that would come because of Kitty could change it permanently.

"Wild ride, lady!" The screaming kid was perched outside of a hut-shaped shop speckled with airbrushed T-shirts and car tags. He held a fluorescent green T-shirt, apparently his item to be painted, since he was standing in line with a horde of other kids waiting for the airbrush artist to embellish their purchases. As if Babette hadn't heard him, he waved the shirt in the air and yelled again, and the remainder of the line turned to see what had caught his attention.

Babette smiled and patted the dash. She'd grown so accustomed to heads turning when she drove Sylvia, her pet name for her CRX, that every now and then she forgot how unique the vehicle was. Sylvia was one of a kind, for sure, but not in the Lamborghini or Ferrari arena. She was more like that car Johnny Cash sang about, made up of a wild conglomeration of pieces and parts.

A teenager who lived next to Babette at her old apartment, the one she lived in before she moved next door to Granny Gert, was a vo-tech student, and Babette had let him and his classmates practice on Sylvia. The only problem was that she had no say in the final product, and they never practiced the same technique on the entire car. As a result, Sylvia was truly eclectic. The body on the driver's side was pale purple. For a couple of years, the passenger's side had simply been primer, but the boys had finally given it a shiny candycoat finish, transparent red over gold. The hood was royal blue with a hot pink swirling flame that looked like something straight off *Pimp My Ride*.

Babette had considered getting a more conservative, or at least more normal, vehicle after she'd started the Love Doctor venture, but Sylvia was paid for, ran great and got a lot of attention. And, God help her, Babette liked attention.

Another surfer dude whistled as she cruised down the street, and Babette whistled back. Damn, she'd missed the beach. And beach guys. She wouldn't have even considered anything more than whistling at the guy (and she did that while her car was moving away from him); he looked nineteen, early-twenties tops, and she wasn't ready to be a cougar. But that was the great thing about Florida and the beach. The guys would flirt, she could flirt back, and that was that. There wasn't any third date consideration, because there wasn't a first or second date to begin with. It was a fun, free-spirited atmosphere with sand and sun and waves, and Babette truly blended well here. Well, maybe "blended" wasn't the right word. She stood out, from her car to her hair to her clothes, but standing out wasn't a bad thing. The locals and the tourists seemed to appreciate it, which was emphasized again when a passing car honked, and then the guy inside whistled.

Babette whistled back. Drive-by flirting. You didn't get safer sex than that.

She saw Jeff's resort, towering several stories above the other condominium complexes along the beach. It was stark white with a royal blue roof and the White Sands logo, a matching royal blue wave along one side. Awnings of the same bright hue extended from the wide windows in the center of the building, and Babette knew from her previous stays that those were the elaborate suites, expansive luxury condominiums that stretched from the front of the building to the back and were the equivalent of four normal-sized condos. Jeff had one of those; the one in the direct center of the building, in fact, and he loved the view that the broad width of the condo provided. The entire back side of his home was wall-to-wall windows.

Babette had thoroughly enjoyed making love to him with those windows open, listening to the waves crash against the beach, feeling the warm breeze against her skin as Jeff undressed her and then distributed feather soft kisses over every inch of her body. She tingled at the memory, almost feeling the tantalizing sensation of that Gulf breeze teasing the damp wake of those heated kisses.

She swallowed. For all she knew, he did the same thing with Kitty. Opened those windows and made love to her like there was no tomorrow, until she thought she'd die from the sheer pleasure of it.

There. That did it. No more reminiscing.

She put on her blinker and started to turn into the resort parking lot, but a blazing red convertible Jaguar whipped in merely inches in front of her, causing Babette to slam both the brakes and the horn. Thank God the brakes worked better than the horn; Sylvia stopped on a dime, but the wimpy excuse for a horn didn't scare anyone, certainly not the woman in the Jag. She merely tossed her head, sending her sleek brunette hair swinging around her bare shoulders, then gave Babette a fingertip wave and a smile, as though that made the near-wreck acceptable.

If Babette hadn't just gotten here, and if she didn't suspect that Jeff's neighbors might notice a little (or big) tirade in the parking lot—or an all-out cat fight—she'd jump out of this car and give the brunette bimbo a piece of her mind. And her fist. And her foot. But given she didn't want to cause a scene before she'd even unpacked, she took a deep breath, counted to ten, then started toward the valet. She pulled close, very close, and nearly let Sylvia kiss the bumper on that Jag, but the rude one didn't even notice. She was too busy sprucing up her makeup while two valet attendants all but fell over each other trying to get to her and her Jag. No one was making any effort whatsoever to tend to Sylvia's needs, or Babette's, for that matter. *Bitch!* Babette merely thought the word, but in her mind, she shouted it with fervor, grabbing a fistful of brunette hair as she did.

She squinted toward the woman in the car and tried to determine whether she'd seen her before. The turnover at White Sands wasn't all that great; people fortunate enough to have a White Sands condo didn't typically sell. Since she had met lots of Jeff's neighbors during her past trips, she was fairly knowledgeable about the residents, and even if she didn't know them by name, she knew the majority of them by sight. But this woman wasn't anyone she'd seen before. And something about her, and the way she'd cut Babette off, put her in a snooty classification that was all her own.

The folks at White Sands might be rich, but most of them were still polite. Babette had the sudden recollection of Kathy Bates in *Fried Green Tomatoes*, when those two girls stole her parking space. If it weren't for loving Sylvia, and for probably not having nearly as much insurance as Kathy Bates's character had in that movie, she'd ram that Jag into oblivion too. Then she'd bet the valet guys *and* the brunette would notice. As it was, she did love Sylvia, and she only had liability coverage, so she simply glared at the woman's back as she exited her car and entered White Sands.

And wouldn't you know it, both valet attendants had suddenly disappeared, one in the Jag and the other with the brunette. So Babette waited for *someone* to notice the fuming redhead growing hotter and hotter every second, not merely because Sylvia had a pitiful excuse for an air conditioner and needed a serious Freon fix and not because the temperature outside was nearly a hundred, but because Miss Rude Jag Lady had thoroughly pissed her off.

# Chapter 6

It was probably a good thing that it took a while before Sylvia was rather reluctantly taken by a valet attendant. By the time Babette had entered the White Sands lobby and checked in, the Jag woman was nowhere to be seen.

"Yoooohoooo!"

Immediately recognizing the owner of the shrill scream, Babette pocketed her condo key and turned toward the voice she remembered so well. "Hey, Ms. Nettles. How are you?"

"Good Lord, I don't care if it has been a long time since you've seen me, you best call me Rose." The elderly woman wrapped her shawl—a shawl, in one hundred degree weather—around her bony shoulders and quickly entered the lobby as though she actually resided at White Sands, instead of at Sunny Beaches, the retirement resort next door. Sunny Beaches wasn't nearly as nice as White Sands, but then again, the places set up for retirement typically weren't. But it was nice enough, and even nicer because of all of the sweeties living within its walls.

Rose's knee-high stockings didn't quite reach the end of her floral skirt, and one was two shades darker than the other. She had a seashell-embellished comb holding back one side of her soft white hair and her eyes twinkled as though seeing Babette had unquestionably made her day.

"Come on, let's take a walk and chat in private," she said, ushering Babette back out the door she'd just entered.

"Wouldn't you rather come up to my room and visit there?" To Babette, an air-conditioned room sounded intriguing, particularly since she'd sat a while in Sylvia waiting for the valet guys to remember there were other customers besides the brunette in the Jag. Plus, Babette was curious to see the room Kitty had provided.

"Wouldn't *you* rather walk on the beach while we're chatting? You haven't been here in ages, and I'm betting you missed it."

Babette grinned. "Good point."

Rose shuffled down the sidewalk, then glanced back toward the valet attendants. She took a few more steps, then cupped one hand around her mouth and whispered, "I was sitting on my front deck and saw that uppity bitch in the Jaguar cut you off. Of all the nerve."

Babette snorted. Rose had to be eighty if she was a day, but Babette had to hand it to her; she was still pretty quick when it came to speaking her mind. Babette had missed her visits to Florida, and now she realized she'd also missed her visits with Rose.

"I thought you'd jump out and take her down, and I was coming to help," Rose continued.

"I appreciate that," Babette said, holding back the urge

to laugh; the woman was dead serious. "But I decided I didn't want to start a fight on my first day."

"We could've taken her," Rose said, lifting one shoulder as she made the proclamation, then readjusting her shawl when the motion caused it to slide down a notch. "I got all excited when I saw your car turning in, kind of assumed that's what you came down here to do, start a ruckus. That is why you're here, isn't it? To finally take back what's yours? But are you just going to start one with her, or are you down here to go after all of them?"

" 'All of them'?" Babette had no idea what Rose was talking about. All of the people at White Sands? No, she didn't plan to start a fuss with the most affluent residents in Destin, because that was who stayed at White Sands, the top dogs. Babette suddenly realized how much more comfortable she had always been at Sunny Beaches than at White Sands. She'd spent quite a bit of time visiting with Rose and her friends. Maybe it was because many of the Sunny Beach residents reminded her of Granny Gert, or maybe it was just because she liked older folks, but in any case, at Sunny Beaches, she was in her comfort zone. At White Sands, not so much.

But being uncomfortable didn't mean she would pick a fight with all of the place's inhabitants. "Contrary to popular belief, I don't think all of the people who stay there are snobs, and no, I don't plan to fight them all," she said with a grin.

Rose shook her head and frowned. "That's not what I meant. I'm talking about her, and I'm talking about all of the other ones."

"All of the other ones?"

"Jeff's dates," Rose said flatly. "She's the most recent,

but he doesn't see any of them for long, so she should probably be gone pretty soon. A different one every couple of days, I'd say, and all of them hanging all over him like he's their last chance to procreate."

Babette's stomach lurched. *All of them.* She inhaled, exhaled thickly. *A different one every couple of days.* There were two main reasons those statements bothered her. One, she was supposed to get Jeff back with Kitty, but Jeff had obviously moved on, and on, and on. And two, the thought of Jeff with *all of them* stung.

"That woman in the Jag," Babette finally said, removing her sandals and opting to carry them, primarily to keep her hands occupied. For some reason, she had the wild impulse to fist them. "She's with Jeff?"

"You'll see in a minute."

"How's that?"

"His balcony, silly. And all those windows. I swear the boy should really use some privacy every now and then." She paused. "But I do enjoy looking."

"Rose!"

Grabbing her shawl at her chest, Rose shrugged. "I haven't seen anything beyond kisses, and I'm mainly just trying to get him to quit." She walked a little faster, scooting her black thick-soled shoes along the sandy wooden planks of the walkway that provided beach access. "He hasn't got any business seeing so many females. I told him."

"What did you tell him?" Babette walked beside the woman who had proven, once again, to be an endless fountain of knowledge regarding all things Jeff Eubanks. Rose really cared about Jeff, and Jeff had an affinity toward the older woman too. He'd told Babette as much on several occasions way back when. His own grandparents had passed on when he was young, and Babette suspected that Rose Nettles was the Granny Gert he never had.

*All of them.* Why did that bother her so much, after all this time?

"I told him that he didn't need the poodle and that he should get over her anyway."

Rose's comment took Babette's attention off how thoroughly Jeff had moved on.

"The poodle?"

"Poodle, kitty, whatever. Always reminded me of one of those show dogs, pretty to look at and able to strut, but no spunk to complete the package."

Babette laughed. Kitty would undeniably have issues with an eighty-plus woman spying on her when she was with Jeff and then referring to her as a real bitch.

"And I told him he needed to get back with the one he should've stayed with in the first place." Rose pointed to Babette, and Babette knew better than to argue. "And then I told him that if he was actually sleeping with all of those floozies that I see on his balcony every night that he better be using protection. And then I bought him some, to make sure he did."

"You—what?"

"Bought him some. I admit that I had a little fun with it, considering I went to the same pharmacy that fills my water pills. You should have seen the look on that young pharmacist's face when I picked up my regular prescription and a case of condoms. Did you know they come in flavors now? And you can get different colors too. They've even got a camouflage one, and you know what it says on the outside?"

Babette was speechless, so she merely shook her head.

"So they can't see you coming," Rose said, then her cheeks flushed and she giggled. "Get it?"

"You bought Jeff condoms," Babette said disbelievingly. She only wished she could have seen his gorgeous face when Rose presented him with her gift. "What did he say when you gave them to him?"

"Well, he said thank you, of course. He's a polite boy, after all."

"Rose, he's thirty-eight."

"Like I said, a polite boy."

The thought of Rose presenting Jeff with condoms—a case of them—was hysterical. Laughing, Babette stepped off the end of the ramp to the beach, but her feet had barely sunk into the warmth of the sand before Rose grabbed her arm and yanked her off-balance, causing Babette's calves to bank against the end of the walkway and her butt to drop to the sandy planks.

"Wait!" Rose said, her voice at an urgent whisper. "I wasn't thinking. We need to go this way." She pulled on Babette's arm until Babette stood beside her, then she tugged Babette away from the walkway and into the shady area between the edge of the condominiums and a cluster of palm trees. "Under here."

"Rose, what are you doing?" Babette asked, and to her shock, Rose put her palm over Babette's mouth to shush her the same way Babette's mother used to do in church, when she was talking too loud during the sermon. The scent of Rose's lilac lotion suddenly overpowered Babette's senses. It might have been pleasant if it wasn't so solidly pressed against her airways. She moved away from the intrusive hand, then sputtered, "I have to breathe, Rose."

"Shh, he'll hear you." Rose, looking every bit the elderly spy woman now, jerked her head to indicate the resort next door, or more specifically, the man lounging on his balcony.

"What"—Babette's words stilled in her throat. It'd been a long time since she'd seen Jeff, and even seeing her brother-in-law on a fairly regular basis didn't prepare her for his twin, sitting on the balcony, a laptop resting on his thighs as he worked with his feet propped up on the rail. The breeze from the Gulf teased his sandy waves, which had a few more sunstreaks than she remembered, and his skin was a bit darker than before too, with a richer, surfer's tan that made those highlights in his hair stand out even more.

He straightened a bit, and Babette wished she could see his eyes, but he was too far up for her to know whether he was looking in her direction or at the computer screen. However, from the way he was sitting, and the way his hands didn't move on the keyboard, she'd guess he was looking right at her.

She backed against the building. "Rose, he's looking."

"Nonsense," Rose said. "He's working. He doesn't know we're down here. Trust me, I do this all the time." She put her weight on one foot and leaned forward. "That is one fine tribute to the male gender. I swear, if I was fifty years younger . . ."

Babette grinned. Rose was right; the only way he could have been looking directly at them is if he were actually watching for them, which he wasn't. He was working. Besides, even if he saw them, chances are he wouldn't recognize Babette. It'd been a while since he'd seen her, and she'd had a black bob then. He wouldn't be expecting her in Florida, nor would he expect the red hair. She was safe to stare.

So she did.

He wore a royal blue pullover with khaki shorts, and his feet were bare. He looked like he'd been plucked out of a Kenny Chesney video, one of the muscled, too-good-looking-for-his-own-good guys hanging out on a sunny day at the beach without a care in the world, except for the laptop saying that this guy was no beach bum; he was a beach businessman, and he was still the sexiest one Babette had ever laid eyes on.

His hands moved over the computer, long fingers tapping against the keys, and Babette relaxed a bit more. He definitely wasn't looking at them, and she undeniably wanted to stare a little longer. His jaw was set as he looked at the computer monitor, and his mouth quirked to the side as he typed, as though he were pondering the next thing to enter on the screen. It was a sexy quirk, and it reminded her of how good those lips had felt, nibbling intoxicating kisses against her mouth, and her neck, and . . .

"Here she comes."

Rose's words coincided with the appearance of the brunette on the balcony. She said something, and Jeff turned toward her. Even though Babette could no longer see his mouth, she had a side view of his jaw, and it relaxed as though he were smiling.

She felt cheated. She wanted to see that smile too. That smile had always held the power to make Babette forget—forget what she was saying, forget what she was doing, forget everything but how much she wanted that smile, and that man.

The brunette moved closer, ran her fingers through his hair, then leaned toward him and whispered something in his ear.

Babette wasn't used to playing voyeur, but she was used to reading people, and the brunette's body language said one thing. She wanted sex. Or, more specifically, she wanted sex with Jeff. Babette didn't like all of the emotions going through her at the moment. Rage at the woman for cutting her off this afternoon. Irritation at herself, for allowing Rose to take her into her little spy hollow. And finally, another emotion that really didn't suit Babette's traditionally apathetic mentality toward relationships. A very green emotion that she couldn't deal with at all, because if she were jealous over the brunette touching him, what would she do when she convinced him to go back to Kitty—for good?

She'd deal with that when the time came.

He turned slightly away from the smiling woman on the balcony, and Babette thought that their free show was blessedly ending.

She was wrong.

He placed the laptop on a nearby patio table and then stood, leaning his back against the railing and simply waiting for her to move toward him, slowly, like a tiger sizing up prey, and smiling as she progressed. Again, Babette couldn't see his face, couldn't even see his jaw now, but she knew he was giving the woman that sexy smile.

"Oh, my," Rose said, as the woman closed the gap between them and then practically crawled up his body, nipping his neck and smiling against his ear as she whispered something, then her hands slid up his back and into those curls at his nape.

Babette's palms tingled, recalling the way those springy curls felt when she used to tunnel her own fingers through them.

The Jag lady kissed him, and it was no ordinary kiss. It was an I'm-going-to-give-you-anything-and-everything-you-want-and-then-some kind of kiss. Her body was moving and rubbing against him, and Babette suddenly grew very hot. Everywhere.

This was not good. She needed to stop staring. She needed to leave this cramped little hiding place between the palm trees and the building.

She needed to breathe.

As if knowing that Babette was watching and simply couldn't take any more, the brunette pulled away, took Jeff's hands and tugged him back inside the condo.

"Whew, alrighty then," Rose said, exhaling loudly as she shook her head. "I've seen him put on many a show on that balcony, but I believe this one takes the cake." She dropped one side of the shawl, gathered it up with the opposite hand and waved it in front of her face like a fan. "I'm not cold anymore."

"As if anyone could be cold watching that," Babette said.

Rose snorted. "Didn't leave all that much to the imagination, did they?" Then she tilted her head, glanced back at the balcony and said, "Well, I guess they did. Or we'd have seen some skin."

Unable to shake the image of the woman attacking Jeff like an animal in heat, Babette glared at the balcony. "I didn't know he was dating someone," she said aloud.

"Dating?" Rose actually cackled. "Honey, you haven't been listening. It's a different one every two or three days. That's why I bought him that case of—"

Babette waved her hand in front of Rose's mouth before she blurted out "condoms" for everyone sitting on their balconies to hear.

"I was going to say protection," Rose huffed.

"Sure you were."

Rose's cheeks pinked, and she smiled guiltily. "You know me too well."

"A different one every few days?" Babette asked. So Jeff had gone back to his old playboy ways after things ended with Kitty.

"Pretty much. I mean, sure, some of them could be repeats, since basically I just notice tall, short, blond, brunette, that kind of thing, but there's so many different ones that I sure can't keep them straight. Doubt he can."

Babette nodded. If he wasn't into just the brunette, then there was still a chance she could get him back with Kitty Carelle and keep Kitty's money, which was the only positive thing about this situation that she could think of at the moment.

"But I'd be shocked if you couldn't get him back," Rose added. "He was his happiest with you. Never did understand why you split up."

"Neither did I," Babette said, more a whisper to herself than a response to Rose. Then before her little peeping tom could continue, she added, "But I'm not here to get him back for me. I do plan to make him regret ever letting me go, but that's mainly to soothe my ego. The real reason I'm here is to get him back with the poodle."

# Chapter 7

Gertrude Robinson should have slept late this morning. She'd been up until nearly midnight, when she finally got in touch with Babette and made sure she'd arrived in Florida okay. Deep down, Gert had known that she was fine; Babette was notorious for forgetting to turn on her cell phone, or forgetting to charge it, or something or other. The girl was definitely old enough to find her way to Florida.

Gert rolled over, glanced at the clock beside the bed. Five thirty-eight. She pushed the covers aside and sat up, knowing that she wasn't going back to sleep and that she might as well start the coffee. What was it about getting old that made you automatically get up with the birds no matter what time you went to bed, and then feel like your day was nearly over by noon? She hated that, hitting the middle of the day and needing a nap, but since she'd barely gotten five hours of sleep, she knew a nap would be in order.

No problem. She wasn't going to the golf course until

tomorrow anyway, if she actually went. The jury was still out on whether she had enough nerve for that one, but she needed to, for Henry. And for herself.

She went to the bathroom, grabbed her robe from behind the door, and slipped it on. Then she paused a moment to look in the mirror. Her hair looked even whiter in the mornings, eyes a lighter shade of brown, though that could be because she wasn't focusing all that well yet. She still had the morning squint that her mama had always called "sunshine eyes." She tilted her head one way and then the other, examined the tiny slivers of wrinkles that bordered the corners of her eyes, as well as the thicker ones that spanned her forehead. When her hair was fixed, those were virtually unseen, and she liked them that way. But she had earned them, after all, and she wasn't going to do anything cosmetically to have them changed. Those were her own version of an officer's bars, each of the three on her forehead standing for milestones in her life. Her marriage. Her children. Her grandchildren. She expected a fourth one to show pretty soon; the great-grandkids were almost five now and due their own place of honor on Granny Gert's face.

She slipped her feet into pink satin slippers that matched her robe, gifts from Babette and Clarise, and then took one more look in the mirror. Standing there in her nightgown and the pink satin robe, she didn't look all that bad for wear. Henry had said she was always a teenager in his eyes. However, now that she was thinking about getting "out there" again, Gert wished she had someone giving her the same encouragement, that little smidgen of an ego boost to let her know that she could do this and do it well.

And more than that, she really needed to make certain that Henry was okay with her dating again. Even though he wasn't here anymore, and even though he'd been gone for over a decade, she knew that he was still around, in his own way. He'd promised her he would be, and occasionally, she could almost feel him near, making her smile, cloaking her with love and approval. She wondered whether he'd approve of her finding Rowdy Slidell.

She made her way to the kitchen and found her favorite mug, one that little Ethan had bought her for Christmas last year.

"World's Greatest Grandpa," she said, reading the side of the mug and smiling the way she always did when she took it down each morning. Little Ethan had never even met Henry, and the darling thought that the picture on the side was an older woman, instead of a man. Gert had to admit, it could go either way. But Clarise hadn't asked him to swap the gift that he picked for Gert, and she was glad that she hadn't. In his own special way, little Ethan had given her a new morning ritual, a way to be reminded of Henry, and that he really was the "World's Greatest."

She kissed the picture on the side of the mug, poured her coffee, then sat at the kitchen table to think. Last night, she'd waited up to reach Babette partly to know she'd arrived safely, but also because she wanted to ask her if she'd started calling the list of Slidells in Tuscaloosa. Babette had printed all of the possible numbers before leaving and told Gert that she felt certain she could find Rowdy and provide her with his number and address.

Gertrude sipped the hot coffee and glanced toward the mantel, and the tall urn in the middle. If she got the number, would she call it? Should she? It'd been a long time since she'd even talked to a man in the way that a couple talks.

Babette had been flustered when Gertrude reached her and hadn't even mentioned the phone numbers. Instead, she'd talked nonstop about the clothes she bought in Montgomery, and then about seeing Jeff but not talking to him, visiting Rose Nettles, one of her friends at the retirement condo, and she'd also mentioned something about hiding out behind a building and being afraid that she and Rose would get caught. Oh, and then she said something about a "brunette bimbo who'd cut her off."

Gertrude laughed, then drank more coffee. There was never a dull moment in Babette's over-eventful life, and there had been too much going on in her life yesterday for her to remember to call the Slidells in Tuscaloosa, which was just as well. Gertrude still wasn't certain she wanted to reach Rowdy.

She stood and took her coffee with her as she padded in slipper-clad feet across the living area to the mantel. Taking another sip, she stared at the urn. It was gray, natural quarried granite, a symbol of strength and dignity, or that's what the gentleman who'd sold it to her had said when Henry passed on. A cast bronze dome topped the granite, and an engraved plate with Henry's name, birth date, and date of death centered the bottom.

Gert touched the urn, the coolness of the granite a mighty contrast to the warmth of the coffee cup in her other hand. "What do you think, Henry? It wouldn't hurt for me to call Babette again this morning, would it? I have been so lonely, you know. I mean, no one would ever take your place, never, but it would be nice to share my life with someone again. If that's okay with you," she added, nodding as she mentally modified what she wanted her granddaughter to do. "I believe I'll get her to find his phone number and address, but I won't have her actually call him. I'll just get it, in case I decide to get in touch with him again. And I won't get in touch with him until you've given it your stamp of approval. So you've got to let me know, somehow. I know. It won't happen here, will it? But I've got an idea that I think might work, a way you can tell me what's what, and let me know what you want me to do."

She bobbed her head slowly as she realized that she'd made her decision. She didn't want to do anything to hurt her first love, even if he were no longer physically here. Glancing at the clock, she decided to give Babette a while longer before she called, in case she slept late.

Then she looked back toward the urn and wondered why she so often found the need to converse with it. Goodness knows Henry wasn't going to give her any answers from there. The gray granite was exactly what the salesperson had said, strong and dignified. But, what Gertrude knew, and what she'd probably have to tell her family members eventually, was that the elaborate piece in the center of her mantel . . . was empty.

"Hello, can I speak to Rowdy Slidell please?" Babette asked, then nodded as yet another Slidell in Tuscaloosa told her that she had the wrong number. She'd been calling the numbers on the list ever since Granny Gert woke her up this morning and informed her that she didn't want Babette to actually talk to Rowdy; she simply wanted her to get his information so Granny could decide whether or not to call him herself.

Babette had been working on the list sporadically throughout the day, between checking to see if Jeff had returned from work and answering phone calls from Clarise, Genie, and Kitty. Clarise had wanted to find out if she'd seen Jeff yet and make sure that her brother-in-law had been nice; Babette had told her that she hadn't even spoken to him, so she had no idea whether he'd be nice or not.

Genie had simply wanted Babette's opinion on the two Love Doctor clients that she was helping out in Birmingham. That conversation didn't last long, since Genie hadn't met the clients yet.

Kitty, on the other hand, was not so easy to get off the phone. In fact, she was another reason Babette had only managed to strike fifteen of the fifty-seven Slidells in Tuscaloosa from her list. Kitty had called all day long. Over and over. And each time, she asked the same things in rapid fire succession.

"Have you seen him? How did he look? How did he act? Did you mention me? Did you talk to him about getting back together? Well, if he isn't there, where is he? Will you go to the store and find him, or will you wait for him to come back home? He usually goes to the Seaside store, you know, but sometimes he goes to the office at Panama City, and every now and then, he goes to the Fort Walton one. You could call the stores and ask which one he went to today. Is he seeing anyone? Do you know her name? What does she look like? Is she pretty?"

Babette had told her, repeatedly, that she hadn't seen Jeff (a lie, but elderly espionage didn't really count as far as what Kitty had in mind), that she didn't know if he was seeing someone (she didn't know that he was seeing *someone*; she knew that he was seeing several *someones*), and that she had no idea whether whoever he was seeing, if he was seeing someone, was pretty (although the girl climbing on top of him last night would fall into the striking category). Bottom line, Babette didn't want to tell Kitty anything, because she didn't really know anything. And more than that, she didn't want to talk to Kitty. Yet. Eventually, it'd have to happen, because she promised regular updates when she worked on a client's case. But she didn't mean minute-by-minute, even if the client did pay triple for her services.

Just thinking about Jeff lip-locked with the brunette made Babette's skin burn, and she knew good and well it wasn't merely because his sexual gallivanting was going to make it harder for her to convince him to get back with Kitty. It was also because his sexual gallivanting was making her want to gallivant with him too. A lot. Kept her up practically the entire night with hot and heated dreams of Jeff against that balcony railing and a woman climbing all over him, except the woman in her dreams wasn't the Jag lady. It was Babette. Naked.

She glanced at the clock and realized she'd been on the phone all afternoon. It was nearly six o'clock in the evening and she hadn't even set foot on the beach all day. The closest she'd come was running down to one of the resort's two restaurants and eating a club sandwich. She'd selected a table on the deck, and she'd enjoyed the atmosphere of the beach while she ate . . . and talked to Kitty. The woman simply hadn't let up. Had she been that relentless with Jeff? And if she was, had he actually liked that?

Obviously he had. He asked her to marry him.

Babette scanned her notes beside each number on her list of Slidells. She'd tried them all. Some had answering machines, and she didn't leave a message. Others didn't have answering machines at all. And the ones where she actually reached a human on the other end didn't have a clue who Rowdy Slidell was. She could call some more later, after people had a chance to get home from work. For now, she was going to make up for all of the beach time she'd missed by staying inside all day. She put the cell phone on the table. If anyone needed her, they could leave a message.

That included Kitty Carelle.

She left the condo and within minutes was enjoying everything she loved most about Florida—warm sand, splashing waves and salty breezes. Completely comfortable with the world around her, she ran straight toward the water like a child seeing the beach for the first time, then laughed when a huge wave soaked her shorts.

She was so busy enjoying the freedom and the beauty of the beach that she didn't even notice that the French doors on the condo that centered the fourth floor had opened, and she didn't see the gorgeous male who'd always had the power to make her heart stand still step onto his balcony and watch the show.

Jeff had spent the entire day on the brink of frustration, courtesy of Babette and Kitty, even though he hadn't seen either of his most memorable exes in months. Ethan's call yesterday had, quite frankly, shocked the hell out of him, with a surplus of information, and none of it good. But that wasn't what had Jeff so frustrated. What had him so perturbed was the fact that Babette hadn't made an appearance yet, and he was ready to get it over with. Last night's date had been horrific due to his feeling that she could show at the most inopportune moment, and he'd consequently sent Kylie home early. Very early, as in before they'd really spent any time together. She'd understood when he said he'd had a hell of a day, but she'd assumed he'd meant his day at work, not his day of learning what his exes were up to.

However, today he actually had had a hell of a day at the office, because he hadn't been able to concentrate on work, thinking that at any moment Babette would appear with her ridiculous request for him to take Kitty back.

Again, it hadn't happened. True to form, Babette was full of surprises, and she was throwing him off his game, both his dating game and his work game. Perhaps that was why today's eternity of conference calls with advertising directors, the Alabama and Georgia store managers, and then his father and Ethan—all discussing typical corporate minutiae—had completely exhausted him.

He entered his condo, dropped his keys on the table near the door and did what he always did upon arriving home, moved to the back of the condo to view the beach. He'd always loved beaches, Florida's Destin beaches in particular. The sand on the panhandle was whiter than that on the Atlantic, the water bluer, and the atmosphere enough to lift his spirits, even after a half dozen tedious conference calls.

Occasionally, he stayed at home throughout the day and worked. Thanks to the Net, he could conduct business practically anywhere, but he typically went to one of his nearby offices, usually the one composing the top floor of the Seaside store, because it made him feel more like he was "at work." Plus, it made coming home even more rewarding, that feeling of leaving work at work.

Right now, all he wanted was to spend the remainder of the day away from the job and have a good time with Kylie Banks, particularly since he'd sent her home last night. Jeff had met the pretty brunette at last month's Destin Chamber of Commerce dinner. She only lived two resorts from White Sands, in a condominium complex much like this one, but due to their conflicting work schedules, he'd never seen her before the Chamber dinner. She'd mentioned that she worked in real estate, and since seeing her that night, he had noticed her photo on several billboards around town. Nice photo. She was an attractive woman with a killer smile, a great combination for selling real estate, or at least for capturing attention with her billboards, and she was easy to talk to. She'd also been extremely flirtatious at that dinner, and had called Jeff last weekend and invited him sailing. The sailing had gone well, with both of them enjoying each other's company, and with both of them knowing there were no strings attached. Jeff, as usual, had made that clear up-front, and Kylie agreed that fun-and-fun-only was exactly what the doctor ordered for her too. She'd gone through a recent break-up with a long-term boyfriend and didn't want anything to do with commitment. Therefore, when she had called Jeff again and asked him about making up for last night and enjoying a date that consisted of "forgetting the jobs and having more fun," he'd agreed.

He liked the boldness of women here; it was different from what he'd been used to in Birmingham, where he'd been raised. And it was nice, given his current non-committal mentality. The women pursued him, and that

made it easier to tell them from the get-go that he was all
for having a good time, but that was it. Most of the time,
they understood, or said they did. If he'd have met Kitty
now, instead of right after the fallout with Babette, he'd
have told her the same thing. She'd come on strong, relentless in her pursuit to not only date him, but get a ring
on her finger. But since he *had* met her right after Babette,
and since he was still stinging from the knowledge that he
"wasn't commitment material," the fact that Kitty thought
he was a commitment kind of guy lured him in and kept
him there until he nearly tied the knot. He would have,
if it hadn't been for Samuel Farraday and his yacht. Jeff
smirked. He should send the guy a thank-you note. In the
end, Kitty was like every other woman he'd dated; none
of them had it in them to commit. And maybe Babette
was right: the reason they didn't was because he simply
wasn't the commitment type.

When Babette hadn't shown at his office today, he
couldn't deny that he'd been somewhat disappointed. Not
because he wanted to hear her plead Kitty's case, but because it'd been a long time since he'd seen her and he was
looking forward to sparring with her again. The two of
them had an odd relationship, with sarcasm and flirtation
working hand-in-hand to keep everything fresh and exciting. One thing was for sure, he'd never been bored when
he was with Babette.

He stepped onto the balcony, inhaled the warm Gulf
breeze and looked out toward the beach. The view always
took his breath away, but this time, this view did even
more.

He didn't have to wonder if the woman standing amid
the waves with wild red curls tumbling down her back

was Babette. It didn't matter that she'd changed her hair, he'd know that body anywhere, and more than that, he'd recognize her excitement for life anywhere.

Throughout their three years of dating, Jeff had made no secret that he wanted to see her as a redhead again. She'd had the vibrant hue the first time they'd met, and he'd been drawn to it—a fiery red flame accenting a woman equally fiery, equally feisty and equally unpredictable. Likewise, Babette had made no secret that she wanted him to grow his hair longer. *Long enough for me to run my fingers through,* she'd said. Even though she changed her hair color practically every time she went to the salon, she'd refused to color hers red until he grew his out; likewise, he'd vowed to keep his short until she colored hers red. And that pretty much summed up their entire relationship, two stubborn souls butting heads with neither willing to budge.

Her rich, throaty laugh carried on the wind and had people all around the beach looking toward her and smiling. Jeff smiled too. She was too damn cute for him not to, charging toward the waves, the water slapping against her thighs and splashing up to douse the ends of those red curls.

Her head turned a little with the slap of each wave against her legs, but then she merely laughed and ventured out a little farther, bending over slightly to let her hands graze the top of the water. That bending caused her heart-shaped behind, in shorts soaked completely, to tease Jeff from his vantage point on the balcony. There wasn't a centimeter on that appealing feature that he hadn't kissed, licked and tasted, once upon a time.

He swallowed, images of making love with Babette

causing his throat—and other things—to tighten. She'd made love the same way she faced those waves, with no fear and complete abandon, lost to everything around her except for whatever currently held her attention. Back then, that had been Jeff. Unfortunately for him, every time he'd been with anyone since Babette, he faced the problem of comparison. No one else compared. And damn if that didn't bite. She was the only woman he'd ever been with who didn't want to cuddle post-sex, didn't want to talk, didn't want to do anything but sleep. He laughed, remembering how spent she'd been after their wild sessions of burning up the sheets, or the carpet, or the wall, or the beach. She put so much into it that she simply had nothing left when it was over.

He'd loved it.

Now she'd returned into his world to convince him to go back to someone else.

He watched as two twenty-something guys prowling down the beach slowed to watch her play. They eventually stopped completely, and Jeff knew both were hoping she'd turn around, notice them and perhaps even offer a sign of encouragement that one of the bastards actually had a chance. It didn't happen. Jeff had known it wouldn't. She was completely absorbed in the waves, in having fun, the same way she'd been completely absorbed in making love with him, and in simply being with him, a couple of years ago.

A knock at his door signaled Kylie's arrival. Jeff took another look at the temptation on the beach, wondered how long it'd be before *she* came knocking at his door, and then went to let his date in.

As usual, Kylie was the picture of a beach beauty.

Straight brunette hair cut blunt at her shoulders with a sexy swirl of bangs teasing her right eye. She had on a hot pink tank top, khaki shorts and sandals, with huge silver hoop earrings dangling from both ears and a bunch of matching silver bangles covering each wrist. Kylie wasted no time rising on her tiptoes and softly kissing Jeff, who maintained his distance; he was still semi-hard from seeing Babette.

"I thought we were going casual," she said, indicating the white dress shirt and navy pants he'd worn to work. He had forgone a tie, as usual, and his sleeves were rolled up to the elbows, but he was still overdressed for a night of checking out the carnival rides on the Miracle Strip, which was what she'd suggested for their "forget work" night.

"Just got in and haven't had a chance to change," he said, deciding not to tell her that he'd used a good deal of time standing on the balcony captivated by the redhead on the beach.

"Well, go ahead. I'll take in the view while I wait," she said, and kissed him again before walking toward the balcony.

Jeff thought about that view, specifically the view right now, with Babette playing in the waves, as he changed clothes. By the time he returned to his living room to find Kylie back inside and waiting, he'd made up his mind. He wasn't in the mood to go out.

"I'm going to have to cancel our fun night after all."

She sighed, tucked a brown lock of hair behind one ear. "You remembered something you need to take care of? That's the tough part about being the boss, isn't it?"

"Something like that," he said.

"No problem," she said, smiling, but Jeff didn't miss the tinge of disappointment in her tone. "Some other time then." She kissed him, more of an abrupt peck than a kiss, and then headed for the door.

"Some other time," Jeff repeated, as the door closed behind her.

He waited a moment before he stopped fighting the temptation and returned to the balcony.

She was gone.

# Chapter 8

Babette had planned on talking to Jeff tonight, one way or another. However, after her fun in the waves was ruined when she saw the brunette on his balcony *again*, she'd ditched that idea, opting for a night of pizza, searching for Rowdy Slidell, and watching reruns of *Friends*. So much for making progress getting him back with Kitty.

Her cell phone rang. She picked it up, saw Kitty's number and dropped it on the couch. She'd answered all of Kitty's calls and all of her endless questions up until an hour ago, and thanks to Jeff spending yet another night with the Jaguar lady, she had nothing new to report to his ex. So she let the phone ring until her voice mail kicked in, and then she set it to vibrate. It was after 9:00 P.M., and even if Kitty was footing the bill for the trip, she shouldn't have access to Babette 24/7.

The phone immediately started vibrating, and Babette knew before looking that Kitty hadn't given up so easily. Voice mail picked up again, and Kitty predictably left another message.

Then the phone buzzed a third time. "No way." Babette glanced at the caller ID and was pleasantly surprised to see Clarise's number displayed. She turned off the television and answered the phone. "Everything okay?" Clarise rarely called at night. She was usually too busy getting the twins ready for bed and then spending time with Ethan.

"Everything is fine here, but I was wondering how things are going down there, with you and Jeff."

Babette propped her feet on the coffee table, rested her head against the back of the couch and proceeded to tell her sister about why she hadn't even spoken to Jeff yet, much less been around him enough to read his emotions for Kitty and attempt to talk him into giving her another chance. In other words, Babette told her about the rude Jag lady.

Clarise was silent. Too silent.

"Don't worry. I'll talk to him tomorrow, assuming at some point he takes a break from his *activities*."

"I'm not worried about you doing your job," Clarise quickly explained. "I'm just surprised."

"About what?"

"That you haven't spoken to him yet, or that he hasn't found you."

Babette dropped her feet to the floor and sat up. "Why would he be looking for me?" Then she shook her head, knowing the answer. "Ethan told him I was coming, didn't he?"

"Only because I asked him to. I know how important this job is to you, and I didn't want Jeff to give you a hard time."

Babette winced. "How long has he known I was coming?"

"Ethan talked to him yesterday afternoon. I kept waiting for you to call and give us an update, and when I didn't hear from you, I thought maybe you were a bit ticked at us for giving him a heads-up on what you were doing. That's why I kept calling and checking in with you. I was wanting to see if he heeded my warning."

"Your *warning*?"

"To be nice, or I'd kill him."

"Super. Does he know why I'm here too?" Babette groaned.

"I just thought it'd lessen the shock of it for him if he had a chance to prepare. I mean, think about it, Babette. When he saw you down there, he'd probably assume you came to see him for yourself. To hear you explain that you want to get him back with Kitty, when he didn't even know about your new love doctor position, would probably knock him sideways. And with Jeff, well, you never know how he'll react to things. So I thought we'd warn—I mean tell—him." She paused. "Maybe I shouldn't have asked Ethan to call."

Babette tried to put herself in Clarise's place, and she realized that if it'd been her sister walking into this situation, she'd have tried to soften the blow too. "No, it's okay. I'd have probably done the same thing, and I should've realized that you would've asked Ethan to let him know I was coming. But now I'm wondering, if he knows I'm here, why hasn't he made an effort to find me? To tell me to leave, if nothing else?"

"I don't know. That's why I was surprised. I figured even if you hadn't found him, he'd have found you. He is a bull-by-the-horns kind of guy, you know."

"I know." That was one of several qualities the two of

them had in common, along with their stubborn streaks, and their pride.

"Well, after you talk to him, give me a call and let me know how it goes."

"I will."

They said their goodbyes and disconnected, then Babette contemplated the reasons Jeff hadn't found her yet. A couple came to mind. The first was that he wanted to sit back and enjoy watching her attempt the impossible, trying to get him back with his ex-fiancée. He'd let things run their course, see how she worked this new career, and then be a part of her first failure.

But that didn't feel like Jeff. He was hard-headed, like she was, but he wasn't cruel, which made Babette think that perhaps the second reason he might not have looked for her might be the more plausible of the two. And of the two, Babette would rather him be cruel. Because the second reason he wouldn't have looked for her was simple—he didn't care. Didn't care about Kitty, and didn't care about Babette.

She stood, crossed the room and moved onto the balcony, where she gripped the top of the railing and inhaled the warm salty breeze. The wind made her eyes water, or Babette told herself that was why they were watering. She wasn't going to admit that this venture was a failure, not yet. Never in her life had she stuck to a commitment. Never had she made anything work. But the love doctor business was different; it was her means to make a change, to show her family, the business world, and herself, that she had what it took to succeed. But if she failed with Kitty Carelle, then she could kiss her business move into Birmingham's social elite goodbye.

Of all people, why did Kitty's ex have to be Jeff?

Babette suddenly felt the need to get out. To leave the condo and get air. Even though the place was expansive, and even though she could take in the beach from the balcony, that wasn't enough. She felt as though the walls, and the world, was closing in, and was going to snuff her out completely. The reality of her circumstances floored her.

She turned from the balcony, moved mechanically through the condo and exited.

Within minutes, though her mind was still worrying over how she was going to accomplish the impossible, she was breathing a little easier, the warm Gulf breeze enveloping her completely as she walked across the sand toward the water.

Typically, she wouldn't think it all that safe for a woman to walk on her own down the beach after dark, but this portion of Destin was well-lit from the resorts along the shore, and she'd make sure not to go too far, just enough to enjoy the luxury of a beautiful beach on a gorgeous night. She'd been working nonstop over the past few months, and she really hadn't taken time to stop and smell the roses, or in this case, the salty breeze.

She hadn't taken time for men either, or sex, and that fact became blatantly obvious when she caught herself noticing all of the cuddling couples also enjoying the perfect night. It'd been a long time. Way too long. And seeing Jeff's newest lady on the balcony hadn't helped. He apparently hadn't been a long time without sex, at all.

She headed toward the water and walked along its edge, the waves occasionally creeping across the smooth portion of the sand and trickling over her feet.

One of those cuddling couples walked toward her, and she looked out toward a ship in the distance to let them have their privacy. Their bodies were completely in sync, curving naturally against each other with every step. It didn't take much to read them. Babette could define it with one word—love.

"I think I'd like that too," the woman said as they neared Babette. The man stopped walking, leaned toward her and kissed her, and Babette wondered what it was that the woman thought she'd like. Whatever it was, it certainly made him happy. The kiss was still going.

Babette slowed her pace and tried to hide the fact that she very much wanted to know what they were talking about. But they'd deepened the kiss even further, their bodies so close now that there wasn't any light between them, and she simply couldn't walk that slowly without drawing attention to the fact that she was eavesdropping. Apparently Rose's spy fetish was contagious.

Sighing, she ventured a little closer to the waves, which slapped her feet almost nonstop as she walked. Her new path made it easy for her to spot seashells washing along the shore. One glistened in the moonlight, and she bent down and picked it up, then rubbed the excess sand away with her thumb before slipping it in her pocket. Several more shells were scattered around it, but those weren't to her liking, so she kept walking.

After bypassing additional clusters of seashells, she saw another one that stood out, capturing the moon's light and reflecting it, and she made her way toward that one and added it to the other one in her pocket. By the time she made it to the cove, well beyond the end of all the resorts, she had a pocket full of shells, and she'd walked way farther than she'd intended.

Besides the moonlight, there was no illumination on this section of the beach, but Babette liked that about the cove. No, she hadn't intentionally walked here, but she wasn't naïve enough to think that perhaps she hadn't walked directly here subconsciously. She and Jeff had made love here several times, and each time had been incredible. She gazed at the water glistening in the darkened cove and could almost feel the warmth of his body entering hers.

Had he brought Kitty here too? She thought of Kitty's shiny blond hair, and the way every single hair seemed to fall into place, her beyond-expensive clothes and her I-look-good-and-I-know-it attitude.

No, he hadn't brought Kitty here. Kitty wasn't the sex-on-the-sand type. She wouldn't have liked the risk, wouldn't have liked the sand, wouldn't have liked the wildness of exploring each other thoroughly beneath the stars. And Kitty wouldn't have even considered getting naked and hot and writhing with Jeff in this cove the way Babette did. She remembered the way the warm water felt moving against their naked bodies, and the way she'd totally lost herself when he kissed her in the moonlight.

Overcome with the intensity of that particular memory, she didn't realize she was no longer alone. Not until the man who was merely a few feet away cleared his throat.

"It's me. Don't be afraid," he commanded.

Like hell. Babette could run pretty fast, but she had no doubt the tall, muscled creature beside her could run faster. With no other beachcombers in sight, she had no choice but to try to slow him down if she wanted a halfway decent chance of making it back to the resort area of the beach first. With full survival instincts in motion, she brought her leg up and to the side, delivering a sharp, hard heel to the crotch. She was rewarded with a thick, guttural grunt, and the bastard stumbled backward. Then she sucked in a big breath, started to run and prepared to yell . . .

Except the sound of her name, and the familiar voice emitting the sound of her name, stopped her cold.

"Damn it, Babette!"

She whirled around to see Jeff, shaking his head and glaring at her.

"What do you think you're doing?" he growled.

"What am *I* doing? What do you think *you're* doing? Coming out here in the dark and sneaking up on me!" She backed away, lost her footing, and fell butt-first into the cove, then yelped when her seashells cut into her side.

The ass had the nerve to laugh, and she glared. Standing, she slapped at her wet, sandy behind, then fished out the shells that had broken and dropped them in the water. "What are you doing out here?" she demanded. "I thought you had plans."

He'd turned enough that his face was clearly visible in the moonlight, and Babette noticed one sandy brow inch upward. Damn, she'd said too much.

"What made you think I had plans, Babette?"

"You always have plans," she said, and it sounded like a pathetic response even to her, so she promptly reverted to the previous subject. "And why are you out here sneaking up on me?"

"I didn't intend to sneak up on you. I had no idea you were here," he said, then before she could argue, he added,

"I mean in the cove. I knew you were in Destin, but I didn't know you were in the cove." He ran a hand through his hair, and Babette forced her eyes not to venture toward his biceps, flexing with the action. "I went for a walk and ended up here," he explained. "I wasn't looking for you."

Unfortunately, his explanation only reminded Babette that she was quite irritated over his apathy toward her visit and her purpose, to get him back with Kitty. "Why *haven't* you been looking for me, if you knew I was here and needing to talk to you? You had to know I was trying to catch you at the condo!"

"Maybe because I knew what you were going to talk to me about, and I'm not interested. You're wasting your time, Babette, so you might as well go home."

Go home? Go—home? "Not in this life. I have a job to do, and I'm going to do it."

"You can't play Love Doctor for me, so you might as well give Kitty back her money. Go home, Babette."

No way. She was *not* giving Kitty back her money; she needed that money. And she was going to do her job. The Love Doctor was the first thing she'd done right in a very long time. It was the only thing that she'd actually stuck to for more than eight weeks, the only thing she'd *wanted* to stick to for more than eight weeks, and she wasn't ready to throw in the towel because Jeff was telling her to go home. Nothing was going to stop her from making this work. "I'm not going home until you at least talk to me about giving her another chance."

"Not happening."

"Why not?" Babette was frustrated that she hadn't noticed any body language signals when he mentioned Kitty. She should've been concentrating on those, instead of on the man. She'd have to watch that throughout the remainder of her stay.

"Nope. It's my turn for questions now," he said. "Why were you out here walking on this section of the beach at night by yourself? You're smarter than that, and you weren't even paying attention. I walked up, and you didn't even see or hear me, and I'm not exactly on the small side."

Oh no, he wasn't small; in height, at six-foot-two, or in other areas, which she suddenly remembered with extreme clarity. She was glad that they only had moonlight illuminating them now, or else he'd know that she was blushing. She casually moved her hand to her face to disguise the potential change of hue. Then she remembered the body language interpretation of her hand on her face, that she wanted him to touch her there, and she jerked her hand away.

He noticed. "Babette, are you okay?"

"I was fine until you sneaked up on me."

"You're lucky that it was me. What if it hadn't been me that came up on you out here like that?" He was standing rather awkwardly, she noticed, and she rather triumphantly remembered her heel to the crotch.

She looked at him, *there*, and asked, "Did I hit paydirt?"

"Not enough to make my voice higher, but yeah, you were close enough to make me reconsider my approach in the future."

She smirked. "What did you expect?"

"I expected you to recognize my voice. I didn't expect you to attack."

"You should've said my name sooner."

"Like I said, I thought you'd recognize me, and I did say your name."

She shrugged. "Not before I got a heel to your jewels."

"I said you were close. It wasn't a direct hit."

"I'd have gotten it right the second time."

He smiled, white teeth glistening in the moonlight, and her mind tripped over another time when he smiled at her in the moonlight, and in this cove. "There wouldn't have been a second time."

"Says you."

He stepped closer, so close that Babette's chest tightened, and he asked again, "What were you doing out here?"

"I went for a walk to think about how I was going to talk to you about Kitty, and I guess I walked farther than I intended." Not a total lie, but mostly.

He nodded, but his eyes told her he didn't buy it. And the moonlight did magical things to the turquoise in those blue eyes. It was almost tempting. Too tempting.

She swallowed. Hard. Then, because the air around them seemed to thicken, she blurted, "What were *you* doing out here? Something go wrong with the perky brunette?"

Okay. That last part shouldn't have made it from her mind to her lips, but there it was, out there, and she braced for his response.

Both brows lifted this time, and she could tell that she'd surprised him. Well, nothing wrong with that. He'd sure surprised her tonight. "I'm assuming you're referring to Kylie, but exactly when did you see her?"

"She was on your balcony," Babette said, taking an

interest in the sand at her feet, rather than looking at those eyes. She pushed her toes through the wet mush, made a little path and watched the water trickle through, then she patted it back down with her other foot. Anything to keep her busy, and to keep from looking up. Maybe he'd forget what they were talking about.

And maybe she'd grow wings and simply fly away from this uncomfortable situation.

"You just happened to be looking toward my balcony and saw her?"

That sounded good. "Yep."

"The same way you and Rose were looking toward my balcony last night?"

Her head jerked up, and he was standing so close she was lucky her forehead didn't connect with his chin. She took a step back, slipped a bit on the mushy sand, and caught her bearings. Then she looked directly at him, and her throat closed in. He was giving her that you-and-I-both-know-that's-bullshit look. So she simply stated the facts.

"You saw us!"

"Yes and no. I saw Rose spying on me, like she always does, and I noticed she had someone beside her in the shadows. However, I didn't put it together until your balcony comment just now. Do you really think I could have an eighty-five-year-old woman spying on me practically every day of my life and not notice? I let her have her fun, but I don't let her see any more than I want her to see."

"You knew!" Babette accused, her skin growing hot as the implications of what he was saying settled into place. "You knew we were there when that brunette cut-off queen came out there and climbed all over you?"

Way too much came out that time, too.

"Cut-off queen?"

"She cut me off when I was turning into the resort."

That sexy mouth quirked to the side and he said, "So you're actually staying at White Sands."

Didn't take him long to put that one together. "Where did you think I was staying?"

"I didn't know. Ethan didn't say."

"Kitty rented a condo on the second floor for me."

"Man, that new job of yours comes with all sorts of perks, doesn't it? Is that included in your fee, or did she just throw that in?"

"It was an add-on," Babette said, sticking her chin out for emphasis, "since I needed to travel to do the job."

He gave her one condescending nod that made her a little nervous. "And if you don't 'do the job' do you have to give the money back? Or pay her back for the condo rental?"

"Maybe." She wasn't all that certain how the condo rental played into things. It wasn't in the agreement, and she mentally kicked herself for not adding it. But she definitely had to return the triple Love Doctor fee if she didn't get Kitty back with Jeff. "But I won't have to give it back. In case your brother didn't tell you, I have a hundred percent success rate."

"Not this time."

"Well, we'll see, won't we?" she snapped, her temper getting the best of her and his smugness pushing it over the edge. He was so sure of himself, and that really ticked her off, because she was sure of her Love Doctor abilities too. In her mind, he'd issued a direct challenge, and damn it, she was ready to take it. "I'm going to start walking back. It's late, and I'm tired. But before I leave, I need to find out if the two of us can talk sometime tomorrow, sometime when you don't scare me out of my wits at the beginning of the conversation and when I'm not so tired that I can't think straight." *Or read your hidden emotions.*

"Talking won't do you any good. I'm not interested in taking Kitty back."

She cleared her throat. This was not the time to get into the reasons that he should give Kitty another chance, and besides that, her notes on the subject were in her room, and looking at Jeff out here in the moonlight, next to the cove—their cove—wasn't the best situation for sparking her recollection of all the reasons he should be with the poodle. Er, Kitty. "I'm going back to my condo, and I'll talk to you tomorrow." She did her best to stomp away, but her feet had sunk into the sand, so she kind of slogged away.

His hand on her arm caused her feet to slip again, and she nearly fell. She would have if he hadn't caught her, and damn if he didn't catch her well.

"I don't need your help," she managed, but inside she screamed *Help me, I'm melting*, in a tone similar to the Wicked Witch of the West, but cuter. "I'm going back to the hotel. I mean, the condo."

"You do need my help," he said, his face close enough that she could feel his warm breath on her lips. "And if you know me at all, you know that I'd never let a woman, any woman, walk by herself at night."

Babette had turned to mush the minute his words breathed across her face, but the "any woman" comment reminded her of Perky and brought her right slap out of that. She pulled her arm from his grasp. "Well, aren't you the gentleman? Fine, walk with me. Do whatever you please."

"I will."

Again, she tried to stomp away, to at least put some distance between them as they walked, but again, her feet were lodged and made a disgusting sucking noise as she pulled them free.

He laughed at her. Again.

"Stop it," she warned, moving away from the cove and trying to get to the main portion of the beach, where they wouldn't be so alone.

"Or what?" he challenged.

Damn. She didn't know. She shrugged, and kept walking ahead of him. Thankfully she was at the edge of the main beach strip, and she moved toward the water so she could let it rinse the thick sand from her feet. Within a few steps, she was walking fine, and feeling better too. And he'd stopped talking, which was good. She guessed. She knew he was right behind her even though he wasn't saying anything, and she could hear the water splashing with his steps. Occasionally, she felt a tiny spray on her butt.

Then a bigger spray moved a little higher up, and hit her lower back. He was *not* kicking water at her.

The next one met her shoulders.

She kept walking. He was the same childish prankster he'd always been. He knew she was mad at him, and he was picking on her to see if she'd rise to the bait.

Wasn't going to happen.

She took several more steps and thankfully the irritating splashes ceased. Well good, he'd finally decided to act his age. She took a deep breath of salty air, smiled at the

way she was running the show . . . and was completely
drenched by a flume of water that smacked her entire
backside, all the way to her head.

She whirled around, saw the smartass smiling, and
attacked.

"You're such an immature, irritating, bothersome kid!"
she screamed, running full blast and then launching into
him.

They hit the water with a splashing thud, and she silently cheered when a wave washed over his face. He
shook off the excess water and then that damn smile was
right back, claiming his gorgeous face and reminding her
how good-looking he was.

It infuriated her.

"You're a little boy trapped in a thirty-eight-year-old
body, and you really need to grow up!" She opened her
mouth to continue her tirade, and at that precise moment,
a big, salty wave slammed into the shore and covered
them both completely.

She fell off her prey and swallowed enough saltwater
to take care of an entire winter of sore throats. Granny
Gert would be proud; Babette hated gargling with saltwater. Pushing heavy wet curls out of her eyes, she
blinked a few times, and realized that her eyes were filled
with saltwater too. They burned like hell.

As if things couldn't get worse, Jeff, completely wet,
was looking at her, all drop-dead and dripping six-foot-
two inches of him.

Then he laughed, and all desire went out the window,
or out to sea. He really did drive her nuts.

She stood, wrung out the ends of her hair, and then
attempted to wring some of the water out of her T-shirt,

which was futile. The fabric was heavy and pressed against her like a mud wrap. So she turned away from the hunk in the water and started toward the condo, not caring whether he followed her or not. They were in the lighted area now anyway. Safe enough. She didn't need a man, and she sure as hell didn't need a Jeff Eubanks.

Unfortunately, her waterlogged state made her progression down the beach a little slower than she'd have liked. Besides that, her eyes were having a tough time focusing after that saltwater rinse, and he caught up.

He walked directly beside her this time, but she paid him no mind. Instead, she concentrated on acting as though she were on her own, looking at the condos she passed, taking in the way the water danced along the shore, checking out the seashells.

A small batch of seashells caught her eye, and she slowed to look at them. She'd lost quite a few of hers back in the cove, when he'd scared the shit out of her. One of these glistened in the moonlight, and she started toward it, but before she had a chance to pick it up, Jeff stepped ahead of her, bent toward the cluster of shells and picked up the very one that she wanted.

"Here," he said, not a hint of laughter in his voice this time. "This will replace one of the ones you broke when I scared you."

She licked her lips, tasted salt. Then she reached for the shell, and fought the impulse to shiver when her fingertips grazed his palm.

"That's the one you wanted, right?"

She nodded, not knowing what else to do. Had she reached toward the shell? She didn't think so; she was merely thinking about picking it up.

"You only keep the white ones." He made the statement with certainty.

Her eyes burned again, but it wasn't entirely due to the saltwater. She squinted. She wasn't going to cry, not in front of him, anyway. She tried to remember if they'd ever discussed which seashells she preferred, the pearly white ones that appeared iridescent in the moonlight, and she knew that she'd never said anything to him about those being the ones she liked, the ones that made her feel good inside, because they embodied everything she wanted to be. Shiny and bold and beautiful, standing out in the crowd and reflecting light from within. Something that people would remember.

"Yeah, that's the one I wanted."

They walked in silence until they reached White Sands. Babette's mind was reeling. Getting him back with Kitty was going to be extremely difficult if she couldn't get a grip on her own attraction to him. She stepped ahead of him and started toward the rear entrance to the resort, then stopped when he called her name.

She took a deep breath, fought for composure and turned. "Yeah?"

"I realize that we're going to distribute sand along our paths to our rooms anyway, from what's captured on our clothes, but we should probably at least wash the excess from our feet." He grinned. "Wouldn't want to offend the management when you just got here."

She looked down at her feet and ankles, completely covered in sand, and shook her head. "I should have thought of that." She walked back toward where he was standing, beside the outdoor showers on the deck. A large black showerhead hung from a seven foot pole. Beneath it, a water faucet for washing feet protruded.

Babette moved beneath the showerhead and leaned over to turn on the faucet, but then recalled a time a couple of years ago when she'd done the very same thing, and Jeff had turned on the overhead shower, dousing her completely. She jerked her attention from the faucet to him, and made sure his hands were by his sides and nowhere near the shower controls.

He grinned. "I wouldn't."

"But you thought about it."

"I'm breathing, aren't I?" he said, lowering to his knees beside her, then looking up at her. "Here, will this make you trust me? If the shower comes on, I'll get wet too."

"Yeah, but if I wash my feet, you're going to get splattered."

He reached toward the faucet and slowly turned it on, letting the water come out at slightly more than trickle. Then he eased his hand to her calf and gently moved her foot toward the water. "Not if I'm controlling the water, I won't," he said, and his voice was husky and raw and oh, so sexy.

Babette quaked as he held her foot under the water's stream, then rubbed his hands all over her heel, her sole, her toes, slowly washing the sand away. Then he eased both hands up her ankle, then higher, massaging her calf as his thumbs and fingers worked magic, and slowly, very slowly, washed the sand away.

Her knees went weak, completely, totally, and she started to fall forward. Reflexively, she grabbed him, her hands finding his shoulders, strong and muscled and firm. Then he looked up, and she felt her panties dampen, and it had nothing to do with falling in the water earlier. And everything to do with the way those turquoise eyes made her *need*.

"You okay?" he asked, in the same thick, rich, husky voice.

*No. No. No.* "Yes." She forced the word, then worked even harder to force the next ones out. "But I can do it."

He nodded, then backed away, and she tried to catch her breath as she finished rinsing that foot, and then the other.

Then she backed away from the shower while he put one tan foot beneath the water's stream. She watched the way that liquid pooled across his feet, dripped off his heel. And to think, she'd never known how sexy feet could be. She turned abruptly, and hoped he didn't realize why.

In a few seconds, or minutes—she didn't know because her brain was frozen on the image of Jeff washing her feet, and his—the water shut off, and she praised herself for not attacking him on the spot. Quite a feat for a girl who'd been way too long without sex. Real sex, that is. She'd brought herself to orgasm on many an occasion and would do so tonight, as soon as the condo door snapped closed and she knew Jeff was out of earshot. From the way her body was already burning, tonight's would be a screamer. And probably a panter.

Finally, they entered White Sands and walked to the lobby. Again, neither of them spoke. She wasn't sure what to say, and she wasn't sure she could control her surge of emotions if she did. So she got on the elevator with him by her side, and didn't even balk when he stepped off with her at the second floor.

He'd already stated that he wouldn't let a woman walk

on the beach alone at night; he was simply seeing her to her condo for the same reason. Safety. He didn't expect to go inside, didn't expect her to invite him in. And she wouldn't. She couldn't. She was down here to get him back with Kitty, and she needed to remember that, and not remember that he was the kind of guy who walked a girl home at night, remembered which kind of seashells she collected, and tenderly, oh so tenderly, washed the sand from her feet.

Then again, the fact that he walked Babette to her door didn't really mean anything more than walking with any other female. He'd probably walked Perky to her car too.

Babette stopped at her door, turned. "That brunette."

He leaned against the wall by her door, folded his arms at his chest. Babette remembered that chest, and the fact that his nipples were about two shades darker than the remainder of his beautifully tanned body, and she vividly recalled the way she'd flicked her tongue across them, bit them, kissed them.

"The one you called Perky?" he asked, and she blinked back to the here and now.

She nodded. *Did you sleep with her tonight?* "What's her name?"

"Her name is Kylie Banks."

"How did the two of you—" She didn't finish the question, because he moved closer, much, much closer.

"How did the two of us—what, Babette?" He ran a finger across her lower lip, slowly, so that her tongue longed to ease out and lick it, to taste him again, just a little.

She had to focus, to force the right words to come out, instead of the ones that were inching their way forward— *Love me, just once, before you go.* Delicious heated waves rippled through her, pushing downward, to the spot that wanted to feel him most. Then she thought about Kitty, and the fact that he'd asked her to be his wife. She eased away from the tempting finger. "I was curious about how you met, but you can tell me tomorrow, when we talk. Goodnight, Jeff. And I do need to talk to you tomorrow, about Kitty."

He nodded. "Okay, Babette. Fine. We'll talk tomorrow, and you'll see that you're wasting your time on this particular love doctor gig."

"We'll see." She slid her key into the lock and thanked heaven above that she had held it together enough to keep from begging him to stay. A hot shower would be so nice right now. *You wash the sand off me; I'll wash the sand off you . . .*

He took a step away, then turned, holding up that amazing finger as though he'd forgotten something. "One thing that we need to discuss tomorrow, since we're going to be talking and all."

"What's that?"

"Why you were at that cove tonight."

"I told you," she started, but he shook his head.

"No, I don't think you did. But you will."

# Chapter 9

"Can I speak to Rowdy Slidell, please?" Babette asked. She'd made twenty-two calls already this morning and had consequently struck twenty-two more names off her list. She'd been out at the pool for two hours and making calls the entire time, but no one had provided any helpful information regarding locating Rowdy. And Granny was getting impatient. She'd left six messages last night and then woke Babette with another phone call this morning wondering if she'd gotten in touch with him. The only person calling Babette more than her grandmother was Kitty, who'd left nine messages last night and had called twice today.

"Did you say Rowdy?" the voice on the other end asked, and Babette sat up on her lounger.

"Yes. Is he there? Can I speak to him?"

"No, he's not here. You've dialed his grandson, but I can give you his number."

Babette dashed her hand inside her beach bag and scrounged around for her pen. Then she realized she didn't have any paper and stole the napkin from beneath another woman's glass on a nearby table. "Yes, I'd like that please."

The guy recited the phone number, and Babette quickly wrote it down.

"Um, could you give me his address too? An old school friend of his is interested in visiting him." She'd decided not to give too many specifics about her grandmother, in case Granny Gert didn't want him to know she was on her way.

Rowdy's grandson gave her the address, and Babette jotted it down too, then thanked him for his time.

"Hallelujah," she said, closing her phone. She finally had Granny's information. At least she could help one person hook up with someone this week, since Jeff was going to take a little longer.

Rose's white hair shone as she climbed the steps to the White Sands deck and made a beeline toward Babette.

Babette had already flipped her cell phone back open to call Granny, but Rose was walking as though whatever she had to say was important, so Babette snapped it shut. She'd call Granny as soon as she figured out what was going on with Rose.

As usual, Rose had a bejeweled comb holding back her soft hair, though only one side was held back today, and the tiny pink seashells and rhinestones on today's comb matched the pink flowers in her dress. Today's shawl was mint green, rather than the white one she'd worn the past couple of days, and had a fringed edging. The pale green picked up the exact hue of the leaves and vines connecting the flowers on her dress. She was also wearing white shoes that didn't look quite as therapeutic as the black ones she traditionally wore, and her knee highs matched.

"You look very pretty," Babette said, as Rose sat on the lounger next to hers.

"Thanks, and where are your sunglasses? Surely you've got some in that monster bag of yours." She picked up Babette's huge striped beach tote and rummaged through it, then withdrew the new sunglasses Babette had bought at TJ Maxx. "Put these on. You're hurting me with your squint."

"I couldn't see the numbers on my cell phone when I was wearing them," Babette explained, sliding the glasses on.

"How are you, Jonlyn?" Rose asked the woman on the next lounger.

Jonlyn smiled. "I'm fine, Rose. How are you?"

"I'm breathing. For me, that's progress."

Babette laughed, enjoying watching Rose in her element. Elderly or not, she was a breath of fresh air at both Sunny Beaches and White Sands, and she was apparently on a first-name basis with the residents at both.

Jonlyn also laughed at the older lady. "You didn't want to lay out with us today? This is great sun."

"I'm protecting my skin from wrinkles, you know, for when I get old."

Babette and Jonlyn both grinned at that. Then Jonlyn stood, stretched and took the few steps necessary to get to the pool and dive in. Her splash sprayed Rose's back, and Rose promptly turned and snarled at her. "Jonlyn, if I wanted to get wet, I'd have worn a suit," she said.

Babette nodded toward Rose's carefully coordinated ensemble. "You look like you want to get noticed. That's what you look like. And by the way, your nails look very nice too." Her fingernails were painted a pale, shimmering pink. It wasn't anywhere near as flamboyant a color as Granny Gert would wear, but it truly suited Rose.

"Thank you," she said, holding one hand out and letting the soft pink catch the light.

"Any reason you're so dressed up?" Babette asked, assuming that's why Rose had come over for this impromptu visit.

Rose's bottom lip curled in as she bit back a smile.

"Rose?"

"You remember Otis Payne?"

Babette nodded, clearly picturing the elderly gentleman who always wore a smile and who still played in the ocean every now and then, whenever his knees let him, or so he'd say.

"Well, Otis mentioned that maybe the two of us would take in the movie today. They show one in the rec room every Saturday at two, you know."

"So you have a date." Babette nodded her approval.

"I suppose it is a date, and it's kind of funny that he asked me today."

"Why's that?"

"Because after you told me about how people pay you to help fix them up, the way the poodle is doing, I decided to see if I could hire you to, you know, give Otis a nudge." She shrugged, smiled. "But he finally came around on his own."

"I'm glad. Let me know how the movie goes."

"I will. And I also wanted to tell you that I told some of the other girls at Sunny Beaches about you being a love doctor."

"You told the other girls?" Babette asked, thinking

it adorable that Rose called her friends, the youngest of whom was over seventy, "girls."

"Yes, and I think I've stirred you up some clients."

"Clients?"

"Oh, don't worry. They'll pay you. Loads of retirement money over there, you know."

"No, I didn't mean that," Babette said. "But I'm really not looking for more clients down here. After I get Jeff back with Kitty, I'm going home."

Rose's disappointment was more apparent than any she'd ever seen. Her shoulders dropped, mouth eased downward, eyes blinked several times, fighting tears. "I understand."

"But I'd be happy to talk to them and do what I can to mend their fences while I'm here."

Rose's disposition did a one-eighty, and she beamed. "Wonderful! I'll talk to them to see when they want to get started. Now, about your other case," Rose said, "Why aren't you with Jeff? Today's going to be your best day to talk to him, and if you wait until tonight, that'll be too late. He's never alone on a Saturday night."

Rose's statement bothered Babette, but she smiled past it. "Oddly enough, he was gone when I got up. I called his condo, and then I even went up there and knocked on his door. But he'd headed out."

Rose shook her head. "How are you ever going to talk to him about the poodle if you can't catch him at home?"

"Oh, I talked to him last night." Talked . . . and then some.

"About the poodle?"

"A bit." A very little bit. "But he knew I wanted to chat with him more today, and he left."

"Running from you?"

"So it seems."

"Doesn't sound like the Jeff Eubanks I know," Rose said.

"Well, I'll talk to him today, whether he likes it or not. Wait and see." She had to talk to him today, somehow. Kitty was driving her crazy with the nonstop calling, and she needed to give the woman something that she could hold onto, at least enough to keep her from calling every hour on the hour. And this morning, Kitty had even suggested that perhaps she should drive down so Jeff could see her and remember how good they were together.

*Uh, no.* That's all Babette needed, Kitty reminding him what a stalker she could be. How Jeff ever got hooked on a clingy one in the first place still befuddled her mind.

"Well, if he's working, or outright ignoring you, you may be out here a while," Rose said, once again picking up Babette's bag and helping herself to everything inside. This time, she found an apple Jolly Rancher, unwrapped it and popped it in her mouth, then continued searching. Apparently, candy wasn't the main goal. Eventually, she withdrew a blue bottle of sunscreen. "Aha, here it is," she said, reading the SPF number on the side. "Good. Put this on. You'll cook if you don't."

"You're right," Babette said, accepting the bottle, then lathering up with it. Redheads didn't fare well in the sun without sunscreen, and she hadn't put any on this morning before hitting the poolside. Normally, that would've been an automatic occurrence, but she attributed that oversight to her eagerness to start her day by the pool. "Thanks."

"Alrighty, well, it's getting close to movie time," Rose said, standing. "How do I look?"

"It's nearly two already?" She hadn't realized how

long it'd taken to make all of those calls. "I haven't even eaten."

"All day? Have mercy. I'll go get you something," Rose said.

"I'll get her something," a deep, very nice voice said from behind Rose.

Both of them turned toward the voice, and a dark-haired, tanned, buff, beautiful, bold and intoxicating man smiled back.

"Oooh, hello, Chris," Rose gushed.

"Hey."

Babette recognized him. He was the beach lifeguard, or he usually was. Right now, he had on regular swim trunks instead of the usual red ones with the white cross on one leg. She twisted to look at the lifeguard stand on the beach, and found it occupied by a female in a red suit.

"Today's my day off," he acknowledged, apparently impressed that she recognized him.

Well of course she recognized him, what woman wouldn't remember *him*? He was right pleasing on the eyes, as Granny Gert would say. And speaking of Granny . . .

"I need to call my grandmother," Babette said, and the hottie lifeguard grinned.

"I'm assuming that calling her doesn't preclude you from requiring food?"

"Oh, no," Babette said, while Rose laughed softly.

"They make a mean turkey and bacon sandwich." He indicated the pool snack bar, and Babette nodded.

"That does sound good."

"Nice to see you, Rose," he said, then moved toward the snack bar, while Babette widened her eyes at Rose.

"You know him? I mean, more than merely gawking at him when he's on his lifeguard stand?"

"Everyone knows Chris. Chris Langley is the best-looking lifeguard on the entire beach, and he's ours," she said with pride. "I'd go after that one, if I were you, if you aren't going to get back with Jeff."

"I'm not," Babette said, and thought she sounded convincing. She watched as a group of teens sauntered up the steps from the beach and washed the sand from their feet to prepare for heading indoors. Memories of her own sandy feet, and Jeff's hands rubbing all over them, sent a swift flutter of desire through her. Then there was the way he'd picked the seashell that she'd wanted, and the way he'd pressed his finger to her mouth. . . .

She shook off the memory. Letting anything physical happen with him would jeopardize her chance of getting him back with Kitty and sending her business soaring. And for what? To be yet another notch on his current over-notched bedpost?

No. Sure, she had a lot of sexual tension and blatant sexual needs that had been brought to the surface by their little interaction last night, but she didn't have to fill that need with Jeff.

"You going to call your Granny?" Rose asked.

"Yes," Babette said, realizing she still held the phone in her hand.

"Well, I'll leave and let you call her before Chris comes back. Let me know what happens with him, and whether you get to talk to Jeff before the day's over. I'll keep you posted on how the movie goes." She waved at the lifeguard as she left the lounger and headed back toward Sunny Beaches.

Babette quickly dialed Granny Gert and gave her Rowdy's information. Apparently Granny was excited, because she hurriedly repeated it, then told Babette she was "on it" and hung up. Knowing her grandmother, she might pull up the directions to Rowdy's house on Mapquest and head on down there. Babette definitely got her feisty spirit honestly.

Speaking of feisty, Chris Langley was apparently attracted to feist. He continued glancing at Babette throughout placing the order, and each time he gave her a smile that'd melt butter.

She watched his biceps flex as he reached for two sandwich plates. Yeah, she did need a sexual release, or two, or twenty, something beyond her own personal adventures in the shower, and she didn't need Jeff to provide it. Judging from the way Chris was looking at her, and the way Chris looked period, she could probably get her fill, and then some, from the good-looking lifeguard headed her way.

"I've been wanting to meet you," he said, sitting on the lounger Rose had vacated. He extended one of the sandwich plates toward Babette. "Turkey and bacon. I had them add Swiss cheese."

"Perfect," she said, accepting the plate. He had big hands, long fingers, and smoky eyes that said he aimed to please.

She took a bite of the sandwich and enjoyed turkey and lettuce and cheese and tomatoes and pickles . . . and a drop dead gorgeous hunk watching her mouth as she chewed. He was hungry.

She was hungry too.

# Chapter 10

Gert parked her Camry in a VISITOR spot at Mirror Lakes, cut off the ignition and stared at the rolling terrain, the elevated tees and the massive clubhouse that she'd frequented quite often many years ago. She glanced at her bag in the passenger's seat, the bag that contained her new golf shoes, soft-spiked to follow proper course attire. Her collared shirt also followed course attire, even if it wasn't nearly as ladylike as her usual clothing style. At least it was a pretty color, a bright pink, and it matched her skirt, navy with a pink hem. No, she wasn't as feminine as usual, but to get on the course she had to dress the part.

Then again, to get on the course, she'd have to figure out what to do once she was on it. And she also had to determine how she could get the answers that she so desperately needed. She had an idea, a fairly novel idea if she did say so herself. However, in order for it to work she had to find a way to golf, and she really didn't want to waste time about it. She wasn't getting any younger.

She opened her bag and fingered the tiny notepad

where she'd written the information Babette had provided. Rowdy Slidell's phone number and address. She could call him, see if they could reconnect over the phone, and then perhaps arrange to get together for a cup of coffee, or maybe a Starbuck's Caramel Macchiato with whipped cream.

Then she'd see what happened.

A fairly normal chain of events, she assumed, as long as it was okay with Henry. And the only way to know was to get out of the car.

Swallowing thickly, she dropped the visor and checked her face in the mirror. She didn't look nervous, or not too nervous, she supposed. Her cheeks were a little more pink than normal, but that might be because she got a little carried away with the blush—probably because she *was* nervous.

She snapped the visor back in place and reached for her bag.

No time like the present.

Inhaling the mingled scents of cut grass and warm asphalt, she walked toward the rock-built clubhouse, only slowing her pace momentarily when the large water fountain outside misted her with its spray. The touch was gentle, tender.

"Henry?" she whispered, looking toward the water as though something magical would happen. Would she see his face? Hear his voice? She stood there, staring and wondering if something would happen to let her know what to do about finding Rowdy, seeing Rowdy.

Nothing did. She saw a hint of a rainbow forming in the path of the spray, but a rainbow wasn't what she was looking for, even if she didn't know what she was actually trying to find.

She continued walking toward the heavy wooden doors leading to the clubhouse. Before she had a chance to reach for them, a man exited, held one of the doors open, and smiled to her as she passed.

"Beautiful day, isn't it?" he said cheerfully, and Gert nodded. It was a beautiful day, and it reminded her of many other beautiful days that she'd spent at this course, riding in the cart and enjoying being a part of Henry's world.

She entered the clubhouse and immediately noticed two things: first, that she was the only female here, which wasn't all that unusual. She'd often been the only female around when she came with Henry, but it hadn't felt quite so awkward then with her husband by her side. She tried to control her racing pulse and silently faced the fact that she would be subjected to an abundance of testosterone, mostly retired testosterone, but testosterone nonetheless.

The second thing she noticed was that she didn't feel as comfortable here as she'd thought she would. It wasn't like she remembered. Like many other moments when she'd visited a place that held a special memory in her heart, many things had changed. There was nothing sadder than realizing that you were out of place now, when once upon a time, you'd belonged here.

Her throat pinched tight, and she swallowed past it. There wasn't really anything that should make her this uneasy; they'd simply remodeled. That was all.

The entire interior had been renovated, with cherry wood paneling, vaulted ceilings, and exposed beams. Or maybe those beams had been here before; she wasn't certain. But the limestone fireplace taking up the entire right side of the building was definitely new, and the French doors offering sweeping views of the golf course along the back of the building were also new.

It was incredible, and it was a place Henry would have loved, a place Gert felt certain he still loved. Gert's chest constricted and it became more difficult to swallow. What was she doing here? She didn't need anyone else. She had her memories of Henry, and they were undeniably still very strong, very real.

What made her think she should even consider asking Henry whether she should see Rowdy Slidell?

*Because you thought he might say yes, and you thought he might be tired of you sitting home alone, all the time, and wishing you were still a part of the world, instead of merely an observer,* her mind whispered.

Without really meaning to, she ventured toward the French doors, opened them and stepped out the back of the clubhouse. Then she walked a bit more until she stood on the edge of the course. Memories of the last time she had stepped on this grass flooded her very being, and she fought to overcome the onslaught of pain, and of loss. She hadn't worried about wearing proper golf attire then, hadn't questioned what kind of shoes were appropriate or whether what she was doing was right or wrong. None of that mattered, since she had been the only one here. She'd simply been asked to keep a promise, and she had.

The scent of grass was stronger here, giving her a heady feeling that made her momentarily lightheaded. She took a deep breath, let it out slowly.

"Gertrude? Gert? Is that you?"

The sound of her name surprised her; this course

wasn't near her new residence, and she hadn't been to Mirror Lakes in so long, who would remember . . .

"Paul?" she questioned, viewing the familiar yet more tanned and more wrinkled, face of Paul Stovall.

His smile slid the wrinkles in different directions, but even so, it was a nice smile, and a nice face. "I thought that was you," he said, walking toward her. He was dressed for a day of golf, in a pale yellow collared shirt, tan pants and a pair of golf shoes that she was fairly certain she'd seen in the store the other day when she'd bought her own.

The wrinkles and the tan weren't the only difference since the last time she'd seen Paul, when she'd said good-bye to Henry at the funeral. His hair was a lighter gray now, even more silver, and it suited him well. "It's been a long time," she said.

"Too long," he agreed, then he surprised her by step-ping forward and giving her a friendly hug. His scent, that musky masculine scent that said he was comfortable outdoors, enveloped her, and she caught herself trying to inhale a bit deeper. It'd been a long time since she'd been held, even in friendly fashion, by a man.

"I'm really glad to see you, Gert. How've you been? You look terrific, as always. I heard you were living next door to one of your granddaughters."

She smiled. Leave it to Paul to keep up with her, even if she hadn't even thought to call him after she lost Henry. He'd been Henry's best friend and golf partner, and Paul's wife, Emily, had been a dear friend of Gert's. She'd passed on nearly fifteen years ago, well before Gert lost Henry. Paul looked as if he were doing okay now. Gert hoped she looked the same. She was doing okay, after all. She was simply a little lonely at times.

"Was it Clarise? I believe that's what I heard, that you were living next to her," he continued.

Gertrude nodded. "I was, but then she married a nice young man and they live in a neighborhood not too far away from my apartment. But I was fortunate that my other granddaughter, Babette, moved into that apartment."

"Babette, the one you said was so much like you it scared you?"

What a memory he had. She laughed. "That's the one."

"Well good. I'm glad that they've been taking care of you," he said, then grimaced. "That isn't what I meant. I know you can take care of yourself. I'm just glad that you have them here, in town and nearby, for companionship."

"I knew what you meant," she said softly. He'd been in the same position, losing Emily, so he understood.

"What brings you back to Mirror Lakes? You haven't been here since, well, everything."

"I was thinking of taking lessons."

Unfortunately, he was a bit slow on the uptake of disguising his shock. His eyes practically bulged with surprise. "Lessons?"

"Golf lessons," she said, as though there were any other kind of lessons taught here.

"No, I know that," he said, then made a little half-smile, half-frown thing with his mouth that didn't really let Gert in on what he thought about it. But then he told her. "It's just that you never really cared all that much about the game itself. Unless I totally misunderstood, I thought the reason you came was to be with Henry and to ride in the cart."

Paul never held his punches; that's what Henry had liked about him. Good thing Gert liked it too. "That is why I came, but I need to—want to—take lessons now and learn to golf," she said, then added, "I think." Looking out at the span of rolling hills, lakes, trees, sandy dunes—was that the right word, or was it sandy pits? sand pits?—anyway, she began to have second thoughts. She was supposed to hit a tiny little ball in all of that? And she'd planned on talking to Henry and having him give her answers throughout the journey. How would that happen if she couldn't even find her way through the course, much less knock a tiny ball through it?

"Gertrude, if you aren't careful, your face will stick that way, or that's what Emily used to always say."

She realized that her face was, indeed, squished up like she'd eaten a persimmon as she pondered whether she'd made a colossal mistake coming out here and expecting to start golfing in a day. *A day!*

Henry was probably laughing at her right now, and she didn't blame him.

She relaxed her face, forced a smile.

"Gert, why are you thinking it necessary to take golf lessons? You don't look all that excited about it."

"I need answers," she whispered.

He took an audible breath and then indicated a black wrought iron table nearby. A large green canvas umbrella shaded the table and also gave it an air of privacy, even though it was in the middle of the traffic from men going to and from the course. "Why don't you sit with me and tell me what's going on?"

She nodded, followed him and sat down, placing her bag on top of the table. *Dear God, don't let me cry.* "I bought golf shoes." There was no doubt that wasn't what he planned to talk about, but that's what she wanted to say. Anything else would make her whimper, and she was pushing her gumption to the limit by even coming here; she didn't want to ruin it now by losing it in front of Paul.

He remained silent for a second, and then he nodded and peeked into the bag. "Want to show them to me?"

Her gratitude was instant. He knew that wasn't what she was thinking about, but he didn't question her, and he really did look interested in seeing her new shoes. She smiled, reached into her bag and withdrew the rectangular box. "I wasn't certain what kind was best, so I trusted the salesperson at the sports store at the Galleria."

He lifted the top from the box, pushed the white paper aside. "They're pink."

Gert nodded proudly. "I like pink."

He smiled, and Gert, once again, admired the effortless way he smiled. Paul was an easy guy to talk to, and to sit with; no wonder he and Henry had been so close. "They suit you, Gert."

"Chintz rose," she said, looking at the beautiful shoes again. "And that trim is full grain leather."

"I can tell."

"And the kilties aren't attached, so I can remove them to have a totally different look. Oh, and they're water resistant, and very flexible."

"I guess all you need now is to wear them," he said teasingly, and unfortunately, Gert knew he was right.

"Yeah, and that's my problem." Putting the shoes on meant she was ready to hit the course, and even if she were merely going out there for lessons, she wasn't so certain she was ready. Paul was right; she'd never really paid that much attention to the game. She'd liked being outside, being with Henry and riding in the cart. The actual game of golf had never overly excited her, and now she was wondering whether her sole means for communicating with Henry—or at least the main means she'd come up with for communicating with him—might not be all that great of a method after all. She swallowed, frowned, watched a man tee off and send his little golf ball soaring. Would she even be able to hit the thing? How did they make it go up in the air? Would she have to keep pecking hers all through the course on the ground? And wouldn't that be a tad embarrassing?

"Gertrude."

Paul's voice snapped her back to the table, away from the image of her ripping the greens to shreds trying to figure out how to hit the ball in the air. The groundskeepers probably wouldn't appreciate her for that.

"Yes?" she asked.

"Have you eaten? Because the Grille has an amazing Reuben on rye, and if memory serves, that's your favorite. Still like extra kraut?"

Her stomach chose that precise moment to growl. Loudly.

He laughed. "Take that as a yes." Then he strode toward the clubhouse café known as The Grille, while Gert sat dumbfounded. She'd forgotten how close the four of them had been, she, Henry, Emily and Paul, and she'd forgotten what a good friend Paul had been. He even knew her favorite sandwich. Incredible. She tried to recall his favorite, or Emily's favorite. She couldn't.

What did that say about her? Maybe she hadn't been

all that great of a friend, but she'd always thought she was. However, a friend should remember those kinds of details. Perhaps her memory was going. Maybe she should make an appointment with her doctor and get that checked out. She might have forgotten all sorts of things, and didn't even know it. Maybe she'd even known Rowdy's real name and had forgotten that too.

"Oh," she said, then opened her bag and looked inside to spot the tiny notebook where she'd written his information. She pulled it out, read what she'd written, and frowned. Babette hadn't told her his real name. She'd only provided the address and phone number. She'd need to call Babette later and ask, not that she'd actually address him by his real name, since everyone knew him as Rowdy, but if she were going to make a go at connecting with him again, she should probably know his name.

Other things were important too, but she'd figure those out when they finally got together for coffee or whatever. She'd need to ask what he'd been doing all these years, how many kids he'd had, whether he had grandchildren, how he was enjoying retirement. She assumed he was retired. From Sally Mae Lovett, she'd learned that he was a widower, that he was bald, and that he had his own teeth. But that was about it.

Seemed she should know more. But first, she'd need to make sure Henry was okay with her trying to learn more.

Paul returned to the table with their sandwiches. "Sorry. It took a little while, but I think it'll be worth it."

Gert thanked him and began eating the sandwich. Amazing how certain foods spark certain memories. This Reuben, toasted lightly and seasoned with just the right amount of Thousand Island dressing and with way more kraut than anyone else would want, but the perfect amount for her, sparked a vivid collage of days sitting on this deck with Henry and Paul and Emily, all of them laughing and chatting and getting to know each other. Paul and Emily had a daughter . . .

"Kate," Gert said, remembering their pride and joy. "How is she?"

"Fine. She and Ike, her husband, are living in Vermont now. They have three kids, all of them coming up on those fun teenage years."

Gert thought about that. Kate was his only daughter, and she was living in Vermont. "You didn't want to move closer to them?" she asked.

He shrugged. "This is home. And I don't much care for cold weather. Besides, they come down at least three times a year and let me properly spoil the kids."

She continued eating, and was inwardly grateful that she had family nearby. Three times a year didn't seem quite enough, though Paul seemed okay with it. What did he do the rest of the year? He'd been a doctor, but had retired. Did he golf a lot? Did he stay home? He still had the athletic appearance he'd always had, so he must be active doing something fairly regularly. Gert wondered if all widows and widowers were as content in their single-again status as Paul appeared to be.

"How is it?" he asked between bites. "As good as you remember?"

She nodded. "Yes. In fact, it's perfect."

"Wait until you try the lemonade."

Oh, she remembered that too. Mirror Lakes had the best fresh-squeezed lemonade, the club's gentle reminder that this was a Southern golf course, and that the owners were known for traditional Southern charm. She wrapped one palm around the glass and brought it to her lips. The tart-yet-sweet combination that hit her palate was a welcome reminder that this really was a place where she was comfortable, a place that'd been something special to her way back then, and Henry's very favorite place in the world. She smiled.

"Feeling better?" he asked, and she realized that whether he'd mentioned it or not, he'd understood the difficulty she had at even setting foot on the grounds at Mirror Lakes.

"Yes, thanks." She knew a simple "thanks" wasn't enough to express her gratitude to him for helping her accomplish the task at hand, readjusting to this part of her past, but she didn't have the right words to convey the depth of her appreciation. However, Paul's nod and gentle smile told her he understood that as well.

He finished his sandwich first, then leaned back and surveyed his surroundings, including Gert, while she continued on hers. The Reuben was too good to leave on the plate, and she'd always been a healthy eater, so she ate every bite, then every chip, and finished off with the pickle spear. When she was done, she drank the rest of the lemonade, and then looked at Paul, simply sitting in the chair and relaxing, and still looking at her.

"Something wrong?" she asked.

"You have a little Thousand Island," he said, the hint of a smirk playing with one corner of his mouth, "right there." He pointed just above the curve of that smirk, and Gert dashed her tongue out to lick the extra dressing away.

"Did I get it?" she asked.

His eyes widened a bit, but then he nodded. "Gert, I want to ask you something."

Heavens, that sounded ominous, but she merely said, "Okay."

"Do you really want to learn how to play golf?" He pushed his plate aside, then leaned forward, his elbows on the table and his fingers clasped in front of them. "Because if you do, I'll do my best to teach you. But something tells me that playing golf isn't what you really want to do."

"But I need to."

His head bobbed slowly, giving her one of those nods that said he realized she'd made up her mind, and that there wasn't anything he could do to change it.

And that about summed it up, even if the thought of actually taking a golf club on that course terrified her. Speaking of that . . .

"I need to see about renting clubs, I suppose."

"Yeah," he said, pulling the word out with his natural drawl, "Or . . ."

"Or?"

"You're finished, right?" He grabbed his plate, then reached for hers.

She laughed. "I'd better be. There's nothing left."

His laughter joined hers. "I'm glad you enjoyed your lunch. Okay, then, let me get rid of these, and then I want to show you something."

She grabbed her bag and was standing beside the table by the time he returned from tossing their trash. "Show me what?" she asked, like a child waiting for a present.

"Come with me." He moved toward her, as though he

might take her hand and lead the way, then he seemed to catch himself, and he paused. "If you want to, I mean."

"Of course."

They walked around the side of the clubhouse, down a rock pathway sprinkled with bold red tulips, and then toward a thick hedge of hot pink azaleas. Gert didn't remember the hedge and was fairly certain that the pretty rock pathway hadn't been here the last time she was here either. "Where are we going?"

"Around here. You'll see." He moved to one end of the hedge, than flipped his palm and waved her ahead. "See what you think of this."

Gert stepped through and saw a miniature golf course, set up much like Twin Mirrors, with tiny little pools on each side of the course, small bushes instead of trees, and cute little sand-colored dunes—pits, whatever—composing a course that had obviously been built for kids. "It's adorable!"

He nodded. "Yeah, the owners wanted to provide something for children, or for teens on dates. I see a lot of them out here at night, putting around the course and having a good time."

"It does look like a lot of fun," she said, noticing two teenage girls at the far end of the course trying their luck at pecking—putting?—a ball over one of the sand areas.

"Yeah, and the best part is that it's actually a part of the original course. This area, I mean. It used to be part of the main golf course." He waited a beat, then two. "Isn't that something?" he asked, and his voice had softened, or maybe it seemed that way to Gert because of where her thoughts had headed.

This was a part of Henry's course, and this was a course she could handle.

"How much does it cost?" she asked, her hand already reaching inside her bag to withdraw her wallet.

"Wait here, and I'll find out."

Within a few minutes, he returned holding two putters. "Here you go." He extended one toward her, and she took it. "I rented you a locker for your things," he said, indicating her bag. It's over there." He pointed to a row of taupe covered lockers by the building where he'd gotten the putters. "Locker twelve. You want me to put your things in there for you?"

"You paid for me to play?" she asked, handing him her bag.

"I got you a ten game card." He pulled the rectangular box out of the bag and handed it to her. "You'll want to wear these, won't you?"

She couldn't keep her smile from spreading to her cheeks. "They're not really required for this course, are they?"

"No, but you're a woman with new shoes. I've never known a lady with new shoes who didn't want to wear them."

"You're a very perceptive man, Paul Stovall," she said, moving to a nearby bench, then sitting down and sliding her walking shoes from her feet and slipping on the dreamily soft golf shoes. "Oh, these do feel good."

"I thought that's what you'd say."

"Did you say you bought ten games?"

He laughed. "I don't expect you to use the whole card today, and I was kind of thinking that I might take advantage of five of them, if you want a partner, that is."

She couldn't deny that she'd enjoy this more with company. "That'd be nice."

He turned and headed toward the lockers while Gertrude thought about all of the ways that Paul had helped her break through her barriers today. Whether he knew it or not, Paul was helping her determine her future, today, on a miniature golf course. Because before the day ended, she intended to get an answer from Henry.

# Chapter 11

Jeff spent the entire day at the Seaside store, since it was his new store manager's first Saturday on the job. He had promoted the woman from within the compay, so he'd known that she was prepared, but he still didn't want to leave her completely on her own today, so he'd been at the store at the crack of dawn going over everything that traditionally occurred on a Saturday. Everyone in Florida knew that was when the tourists came out in full force, and when the locals finally got that long-awaited day off from work and went shopping. Forty percent of the store's weekly sales occurred on Saturday, and although Jeff didn't anticipate his new manager doing anything that would change that on her first day, he also didn't want to throw that much responsibility at her too quickly.

He'd planned to stay at the store until noon, make certain that everything was running smoothly and then head home for the day. However, the store had been even busier than usual, and he'd ended up staying the whole afternoon. That wouldn't have been a hardship if he hadn't stayed up so late talking with Babette, walking on the beach with Babette, taking Babette back to her condo, merely two floors down, and then—and this was the biggee— fantasizing about her all damn night.

Jeff assumed that he'd probably spend every night the same way, as long as Red was in town. He wondered how many times she'd beaten on the door to his condo trying to see if he was home, or how many times she'd called. It was four o'clock in the afternoon, so she'd had plenty of time to try to talk to him and plenty of time to get pissed when she didn't find him. Knowing Babette, she probably thought he'd left the resort to keep from talking to her.

While he really had needed to help his newest man- ager today, pissing Babette off had plenty of appeal. She was so damn cute when she was mad, like she had been last night when he splashed her during their walk back. It was a childish gesture, as she'd said—or screamed—but it also got the response he wanted. He could still feel her body launching into his, the power of the two of them hit- ting the water and the way she felt on top of him.

He stepped off the elevator and walked toward his condo, half expecting to see her standing outside his door and fuming. She wasn't there. Nor was the phone ringing when he went inside or the message light blinking on his machine. Obviously, she'd developed patience during the past year.

As was his usual custom, he dropped his keys on the table and walked toward the balcony. It didn't matter that he'd been outside only a few short minutes ago. It didn't matter that he'd seen the beach throughout his drive home from Seaside. What mattered was that now he could go to his balcony, with his personal view of the beach, his bliss. *This* was his favorite feature of the condo and the primary reason he'd selected White Sands. It centered the most captivating area of the beach, and with its ceiling-to-floor windows, his condo had an outstanding view from any angle. More than that, he'd picked the fourth floor because it wasn't too low to get a full view of the spectacular beach, nor too high to appreciate being a part of the scene.

He moved toward the railing and peered toward the Gulf, where a mass of seagulls, their silver-tipped wings a stunning contrast to their white pelts, dived to catch fish just beyond where the waves were breaking. Then he watched as wave after wave pitched a whitecap to its peak before slamming into the shore. He listened to the beach-goers enjoying the sun, the sand, and each other. Then he scanned those on the beach, teens and adults and little kids . . . and didn't see what he was looking for, or rather, *who* he was looking for.

He was surprised she wasn't out there; it wasn't like Babette to miss out on such a gorgeous day. Maybe she'd been out earlier and had headed inside, and Jeff had missed the chance to see her play again, or sunbathe the way she always did whenever she came down to see him.

A horde of sunbathers were taking advantage of the hotel pool, he noticed, and he glanced in that direction, not really looking for her, since he knew she preferred the beach, but on the off chance that . . .

Her bikini was emerald and shiny, a beautiful contrast to that long, red, curly hair. Her lips glistened, either from some kind of sunscreen lip balm or from the drink currently gracing the table beside her, a piña colada, her favorite poolside beverage of choice, and one that used to leave her slightly tipsy and undeniably horny.

From the way she was eyeing Chris Langley, resident lifeguard and resident "stud" according to the females at White Sands, the horny part was already in motion.

"Hell," Jeff muttered, leaving the balcony. No way was she going to tease him the way she'd done last night and then sleep with someone else today.

Wasn't happening.

Babette had run her own show for way too long, and he wasn't going to be yet another male puppet on her eternal set of strings. It was time she learned that someone else could call the shots, and whether she liked it or not, that someone was going to be him.

Babette closed her eyes and stretched on the lounger. What an amazing day. Sure, she still hadn't talked to Jeff about Kitty, and that marred the perfection somewhat, but hey, she was in Destin, staying at an elaborate condo resort, enjoying a relaxing day by the pool with a piña colada at hand and a hunky lifeguard by her side.

The only thing missing was sex, and she was planning to take care of that detail ASAP. She was already mentally considering this day with Chris by the pool as their first date. Even though it was kind of cheating, she'd probably consider whatever they did together tonight—and she just knew he was going to ask her to do something, dinner, dancing, whatever—as date number two. By tomorrow, she could technically say that they were on their third date, and she could move on to all things that third dates involved.

She sure wished they'd already achieved third date

status, because she seriously needed a hard and heavy romp in the sheets, or on the floor, perhaps a table. She thought about Kitty's two-month rule. Maybe if she'd played harder to get then she'd have been the one that had Jeff's ring on her finger.

Her eyes popped open. She hadn't wanted a ring from Jeff back then.

Back then? She didn't want a ring from Jeff now.

"You okay?" Chris asked, leaning toward her from the lounger that he'd moved within centimeters of hers. They might as well be on the same one, he was so close, but she didn't mind. It felt very good to have a big brawny male by her side.

She inhaled, let it out slowly, and remembered the business goal of her trip. And that her own new personal goal for the trip was to remember how amazing sex could be. It was not to find out why Jeff had picked Kitty over her. Though it sure would be helpful if she could get it off her mind. And she'd bet Chris could totally help her, and probably wouldn't mind doing whatever it took to make that happen.

Babette resolved to let him do just that, as soon as they hit date three, which she also resolved would happen no later than tomorrow. She. Needed. Sex.

"Hey," Chris said, and she realized she hadn't answered his question.

"Yeah, I'm okay." She smiled, and he lifted his sunglasses and winked at her. It was undoubtedly a move he'd practiced, because it was sexy as all get-out and very lifeguard-like. She could almost see him doing the same thing to bikini babes walking along the beach when he was in his lifeguard stand. And then came that curiosity.

How *many* bikini babes did he do on a regular basis? And how careful was he when he did?

Rose's case of condoms came to mind. Jeff was experienced too, probably the most experienced guy she'd ever met, if he was actually sleeping with every female that Rose had spied on his balcony. Babette seriously hoped Jeff was taking advantage of Rose's "gift." Then again, he'd always been careful with Babette, so she was sure he took the same care with other women. But she had no idea whether Chris did.

She made a mental note to pick up condoms tonight. If Chris didn't offer to wear one, she'd make the request—demand—whatever. Of course, the whole idea of his potential other women made her start to second-guess whether she really wanted a date three with him. She frowned. She did want sex, and sadly, he wasn't looking like the right guy to fit the bill anymore.

"You need another drink?" he asked, lifting her empty glass.

"That'd be great."

He smiled again, and once more, it looked very practiced, and she shook her head. The lust was gone, just like that. She still wanted sex, but she didn't want it with the hottie lifeguard, and that simply sucked. When had she become so picky?

Quite a while back, she realized, since she hadn't had sex in months. She blinked. Thought about how long it had *really* been.

"Oh, my," she whispered. She hadn't had sex since Jeff. And that wasn't merely a few months; it was an entire year!

A year without sex? Was that even normal? No, no it

wasn't; she had no doubt that a healthy thirty-four year old (knocking on thirty-five's door, but she wouldn't go there now) did not go a year without. But she had. She pondered what it meant that she hadn't allowed herself to get to date three, that she'd found some fault with every single guy she'd dated, since Jeff.

Every woman around the pool shifted in her seat, all heads turning toward the doors leading to the lobby at White Sands. Naturally, Babette looked to see what had gotten their attention.

"Oh, my," she repeated, watching Jeff stride toward the pool, his sandy hair tousled, his tall frame looking all mighty and powerful in his white pullover and khaki pants. His chest pressed against the soft fabric of the sweater and flexed slightly with every move, as did his thighs against his pants, his quads making a subtle appearance with each step forward. His jaw was firmly set, as though he were on a mission, and those turquoise eyes were focused and determined.

"Good Lord, I hope he's coming to me," the woman a few chairs down from Babette said, but Babette knew better. He was looking straight at her, and he had that I-won't-take-no-for-an-answer glare.

She swallowed, and wondered what the question was, because saying no wasn't anywhere in her current equation. God help her, she hoped he didn't ask for more than she needed to give. Because right now, turned on and needy and having just realized that he was the last guy she'd had sex with—she wouldn't say no.

As well as he knew her, he probably could tell all that by merely looking at her. She diverted her attention to the pool, sunlight reflecting off the water, a lady swimming, a beach raft floating near the . . .

"I'll take that." Jeff's voice was gruff, and she simply couldn't keep looking at the pool. She turned and saw him grab her drink from Chris's hand.

"I was getting her a . . ." Chris started, attempting to sound rough, but nowhere near the level that Jeff had already accomplished, and Jeff knew it.

"Well, I'm getting it for her now." Jeff stopped walking and simply stood there, daring Chris to even attempt to take the drink from his hand, or to keep breathing.

Chris shot a look at Babette, probably to gauge her expression. She was dumbfounded and had no earthly idea what to say, since she had no earthly idea what was happening.

"Hey, man, we were just talking. I had no idea you two were a thing," Chris said defensively, and with that, all at once, he didn't look hot anymore. He looked *young*. Good God, she'd never even asked his age. What was he? Thirty? Twenty-eight? Twenty-*five*?

"We're not a thing," Jeff quickly corrected, which was good, since Babette had temporarily lost the ability to form words.

"O-kay," Chris said, perplexed.

Babette, Chris, and everyone at the pool waited for Jeff to provide some sliver of an explanation. Didn't happen. He merely stood his ground and waited for Chris to retreat. Chris took another longing look at Babette, shook his head, shrugged a little, then turned and headed toward the beach.

"Get your things." It wasn't a request.

Get her things? Babette glared at him. "You've already

caused a scene. Now stop snapping at me as though I've done something wrong here." Her temper was coming back into play, and she welcomed it. Being mad was better than being turned on, sort of. Or at least when Jeff was standing there looking all rugged and broody and right.

He stepped closer, and his broad shadow covered her completely. "You said you wanted to talk," he said, his voice still gravelly, but not quite as demanding. "So get your things."

If he hadn't added that last mandate, she'd have answered him civilly. But he had, so there. "I did want to talk, but you weren't home, and I decided to enjoy the pool—and everything it has to offer," she added, to remind him that the lifeguard he'd shooed away had been here because she'd wanted him here. And she had, until right before Jeff arrived, when she'd started pondering how to get rid of him. Thanks to Jeff, she didn't have to worry about *that* anymore.

And that pissed her off. Who was he to force Chris to leave? She should have been able to do that on her own, in her own way, when she was good and ready.

"Babette. I'm ready to talk. Now. You're getting paid to talk to me, so unless you want me to call Kitty and tell her that—one, you aren't doing your job, and two, I wouldn't get back with her if she was the last woman on the planet, then I suggest you get—your—things."

She got her things. But she huffed and puffed while she was doing it. "And bring my drink. I have a feeling I'm gonna need it," she hissed, then stamped toward the lobby. "Are we going inside, or what? Because I really don't understand why we can't simply talk out here." She kept walking, never breaking stride as she fussed about having to leave the poolside in the first place.

"You're burnt," he said, right before she stepped into the lobby.

She took a couple more steps to get out of the sun so she could see better, whipped off her sunglasses and glanced down. Not good. She was pink, very pink, and if she was that pink already, then later she'd be lobster-esque.

"Oh, no."

"That's the reason I told you to get your things, because you needed to get inside," he explained, and his voice was back to semi-normal, still a little raw at the edges, but better than before.

"You could have explained that out there," she snapped, then lifted one leg to see that the burn factor wasn't merely on her arms and belly. Oh no, every part of her was pink. That shower was going to sting, big time. "How did this happen?"

"You didn't wear sunscreen," he said, scanning the lobby. "We need to find somewhere to sit and talk."

"Why don't we just go to my room?" she asked, then realized what a mistake that'd be. A gruff and rough and gorgeous Jeff in her room, with her needing sex the way she knew she did, wouldn't be so great. "Or not."

"Not," he agreed, without further explanation.

She shivered. The air conditioning system in the lobby was certainly in full working order, but then again, her sunburn probably made it seem even more frigid.

"You have a T-shirt in there?" he asked, indicating her bag.

She shook her head.

"A cover-up?"

Another shake.

"Towel?"

"I used one that the pool guy provided, and then I left it out there."

He frowned. "Come on." Then he took her hand and led her toward the elevator.

"Where are we going?"

"Your room. You're freezing, and you need to put something on. I may be pissed at you, but I'm not about to make you stay down here and freeze to death."

She followed him into the elevator and then stood on the opposite side, shifting from one foot to the other as she tried to find a comfortable stance in her bikini. Talk about awkward. Jeff, in his dress clothes and looking impeccable, and her, in a teeny-tiny bikini and looking burnt. At least red and green went well together; she was definitely red.

"I don't get it," she said. "Chris put sunscreen on me." He had, and he'd certainly enjoyed doing it, being extremely thorough in making certain all parts were covered.

"Where is the sunscreen?" he asked, his voice all gravelly again.

"What?"

"The sunscreen that *Chris* put on you." He said Chris's name as though it scorched his tongue.

She opened her beach bag, withdrew the bottle and handed it to him.

The elevator doors opened, and she led the way to her room while he examined the bottle.

"It's SPF thirty," she said. "There's no reason for it not to have worked."

"Except that the date on this bottle is a year ago," he said, stopping beside her at her door while she opened it.

She had no idea sunscreen even had an expiration date. "Expired?"

"Yeah. Where did you get this, Babette? Because it shouldn't have been on the shelf. It's long since lost its ability to protect anyone from sunburn, especially a redhead with a tendency to burn anyway."

She stepped into her condo and shivered again. It was even colder than the lobby. She always turned the thermostat down at night, because she liked it cold when she slept so she could snuggle into the sheets. But now it felt absolutely icy. "You mean where did I buy it?" she asked, trying to remember, as she hustled toward the thermostat and started punching the arrow to make it go up, up, up. "I've got to get a T-shirt," she said, hurrying into her bedroom. "And I don't remember where I bought it." She grabbed her sleepshirt off the bed and threw it on over her swimsuit.

Returning to the living room, she found he'd made himself at home on the white sofa, propping his feet on the coffee table while he continued frowning at the sunscreen bottle. "Well, whoever still had this on the shelf should be shot. It won't protect anyone, certainly not you." He looked up at her, and the turquoise pillows on the couch seemed to cause his eyes to look even more striking, and Babette momentarily forgot what they were talking about.

"Huh?"

"You need to try to remember the name of the store, Babette. I'll call them and let them know that this stuff has expired, or other people are going to get burned as well. Literally."

Then her memory kicked in, and she said, "But I bought it the last time I went to the beach."

"Last year?" he asked, raising his brows enough that they disappeared beneath his sandy waves.

"Oh," she said, understanding. "Guess I should have bought a new stash for this trip. I had that in my bathroom cabinet at home and figured I would use what I already had."

"Tell me you at least throw away expired medicine."

"I think Granny Gert cleans it out every now and then."

"It's amazing you're still alive," he muttered, but at least he was smiling now. Then he looked up and his eyes seemed to fixate on her, all of her, since they moved down the length of her and then back up again.

Babette glanced down, and realized that the sleepshirt she'd donned gave the impression that she wasn't wearing anything underneath. She lifted it to prove she was. "I still have on my bikini."

He swallowed. "Yeah."

Suddenly uncomfortable, she started to sit on the loveseat across from the couch, then remembered that she still had the sunscreen on, even if it hadn't been strong enough to do its job. "I need to get a towel," she said, leaving momentarily to grab one, then returning to find him waiting, and still holding her piña colada.

She spread the towel on the loveseat, sat on it, then curled her legs beneath her. "Can I have my drink please?"

He looked at the glass as though he'd forgotten he was

holding it, then leaned forward and handed it to her. "It might not be the best thing for you to have at the moment," he said, but she was already sucking on the straw.

The delicious concoction of rum, coconut milk and pineapple juice was heavenly on her tongue, and when she swallowed it, it warmed her up . . . everywhere. "Mmm, I'm not driving anytime soon, or anything. Why wouldn't this be the best thing for me to have right now?"

"Because it makes you horny."

She sputtered on the straw, swallowed way too much and started to cough. And, of course, hearing him say the word had the effect of making it real. "What?" she asked, and did her damnedest to appear as though she didn't suddenly picture herself standing, dropping her bikini bottoms to the floor and taking advantage of him on that couch.

"Piña coladas make you horny," he repeated smoothly, and she literally felt her center pulse when she heard the word. Or maybe it was the way he said the word. Or something. "Could be that it's only when you have them on the beach. I don't know, but I do know that they make you want sex. Badly. Things like that, a guy remembers. And that may not be the best thing for you right now, given my proposition."

*Proposition?*

"Your proposition?" she managed, pretty impressed that she was able to say it, given her current horny state of mind, and get all of the syllables right to boot. She sipped more piña colada. It was good, after all.

"Yeah, my proposition," he repeated, nodding slightly as he said it as though he were still formulating the idea.

She drank more. Swallowed. "What proposition?"

"You want me to give Kitty another chance, right?"

She nodded, though it wasn't exactly that she wanted him to; she needed him to.

"You do know that she left merely a month before the wedding."

Ouch. It sounded much worse when he said it than when Clarise had relayed Kitty's stupid move. Babette nodded. "Clarise told me."

"And her leaving proved a theory that I'd had a while back, and now totally believe."

Okay, now they were getting somewhere. "Theory?"

"That it isn't men who can't commit; it's women."

"Women—can't commit," she said, and suddenly recalled all the times when they were dating that he'd proclaimed emphatically that he wasn't interested in commitment. Clearly, his feelings about it had changed when he met Kitty, for some strange reason, since he had attempted to commit with her.

"Right." He shifted on the couch to face her more directly, leaned forward a bit, then asked, "You've never had a serious commitment with any man, have you?"

"No." Easy question, easy answer.

"In fact, have you ever really been committed to anything, Babette? Not merely men, but anything in general?" He held up a finger as though just realizing something. "You know, you're the perfect example to prove my point. You didn't commit to one degree, or one job, or one man."

Unfortunately, she had the straw in her mouth when he threw that thorny statement out there, and she sucked in way too much piña colada. The brain freeze that followed smarted. She put one hand to her temple. "Ow."

"Sorry, that was cruel."

She shook her head. "That wasn't it. I drank too fast." She attempted to make it sound flippant, as though his words hadn't hurt more than the brain freeze. "And what you said is true, except for the job part. For the past six months, I have been committed to one job, and I still am, which is why I want to make things work with you and Kitty."

He nodded again, and she got the sneaking suspicion that he'd expected her answer. "That's right, you have."

"You said you had a proposition," she reminded, because she was dying to hear what it was, and because she didn't really want to talk about her commitment, or lack thereof, anymore. Unfortunately, his proposition brought that subject right back to the forefront.

"I do. You're committed to your job as Love Doctor, right?"

"Yes."

"And right now, in order to do your job, you need me to give Kitty another chance."

"Yes." So far, this was simple.

"Okay. I'll talk to Kitty and see what she has to say . . ."

"Great!" Wow, that had been way easier than she'd thought. So she could get Jeff with Kitty, then she could get away from him, and away from all of the serious temptation that surrounded her every time he was around. She might even be able to keep from fantasizing about him with her, if she concentrated on the fact that he was back with Kitty.

"I wasn't finished."

Damn. "You weren't?"

"Not hardly," he said. "I'll talk to her, *if* you prove that women can commit to something."

"If *I* prove it?"

He nodded and smiled.

Babette suddenly felt very uneasy with where this "proposition" was headed. "How would I do that?" She took another sip of piña colada to prepare for his answer. And she was beginning to think he was right; piña coladas did make her horny. She kept picturing him on that couch, naked.

She looked away from him as he answered.

"How long are you down here, in Destin, for Kitty?"

"Two weeks total, but I've already been here for three days, and if you and Kitty got back together before my time ends, then I guess I'd go home early."

"We won't."

She was secretly glad for that; she really liked the beach. "Okay."

"Here's my proposition: for the remainder of your time here, you remain committed to your job and nothing else. If you can prove to me that you can stay focused on that, then I'll talk to Kitty."

"Get back with her, you mean?"

"I'm not promising that, at all. I'll listen to what she has to say, and then I'll decide what will happen afterward."

"And all I have to do is my job, which means talking to you about her, determining what feelings are still there, answering any questions you have about her and what happened back then, and conveying her thoughts, feelings and such to you. Right? Is that what you mean by committing fully to my job?" She could so do that, piece of cake.

"Not quite."

As that slow smile spread back across Jeff's lips, Babette felt the need for more piña colada. Holding her breath, she placed her empty glass on the end table and waited for the other shoe to drop.

"It's not just commitment that concerns me," he said. "It's the fact that women simply can't be satisfied. They're constantly flirting, constantly on the hunt. I've heard that it's believed that males think about sex three times as much as females. Bullshit. You think about it all the time, and you act on those thoughts, ever so subtly, all the time."

"Are you talking about women in general, or me specifically?" she asked, irritation skimming to the surface again. He did know how to push her buttons.

"Both."

"That's not true."

"Okay, *that's* what I want to see. You prove it, and if you do, then I'll talk to Kitty."

"Prove it—how?"

"For the remainder of the time you're here, you remain focused on the job and you forgo the temptation to flirt with every guy on the beach."

"I don't flirt with every—"

"Babette," he said sternly, and she snapped her mouth shut and glared at him. What was he trying to do to her?

"I'm supposed to be at the beach for two weeks and not even flirt? In order to prove to you that women can commit?" she asked, appalled at his audacity to ask her to do something so ridiculous. It wasn't as though she was some teenager, flirting with everything that moved, or every male that moved. She could control the natural impulse. "That makes no sense." Although in the back of her mind, she wondered if drive-by flirting counted. Because it came so naturally.

He stood. "Fine. That was my offer. Just tell Kitty that we're finished. Case closed." He started walking toward the door, and Babette gawked at his ass in those pants. Damn piña colada. Definitely would have to lay off them over the next two weeks, because she was accepting his ridiculous challenge.

"You're on."

He stopped with his hand on the door, waited a beat, then turned. "Not so much as an eye flirt, and definitely no returned whistles."

He did know her. And there went drive-by flirting.

"Fine. And you'll give Kitty another chance when I've done my part."

"I'll talk to her, *if* you do your part," he said, then he left, and Babette wondered how she'd survive two weeks on the beach without whistling back.

# Chapter 12

There were eighteen holes on the miniature course, and Gertrude and Paul were on number seventeen, one that had a small pond as its main feature. So far, she'd asked Henry sixteen questions, and so far, he either hadn't answered, or he'd said no. She assumed anytime she didn't meet the requirement for a yes, that meant no, but since she really hadn't decided that was the way it'd work before she started, she wasn't totally certain.

She probably should have written down some rules.

Paul went first, putting his ball perfectly up a little rise along one side of the green and then nodding when it hopped over that mini pond as though it were a stone skipping across the top of a lake. The ball ended up near the hole, and he merely tapped it in.

"Okay, your turn, Gert."

She forced a smile, put her ball in the same little notch Paul had used on the square rubber pad at the beginning; she guessed in miniature golf that the little square pads were kind of like the tees. Anyway, she put the ball there, then held her putter, and thought about what to ask Henry this time.

*If I make it in two, I should call Rowdy.*

Okay, so she'd asked Henry the same thing three times already, and varied it somewhat on other holes by asking if she should drive to Tuscaloosa, or if she should get Babette to call on her behalf. But every time, the ball, or Henry, or both, didn't cooperate.

She putted toward that same riser that Paul had used to bank the ball over that pond, and to her surprise, her shot did exactly the same thing as his, popped right over the pond then landed even closer to the hole than his had.

Henry was about to say yes, and her pulse skittered at the reality. When she left the golf course, she'd call Rowdy and see about getting together for coffee. All she had to do was tap the little ball in the hole.

"Good shot," Paul said.

Pleased with herself, and with Paul's praise, she nodded, then stepped close to her ball and prepared to finally get a yes from Henry.

She tapped the ball, and it scampered toward the hole, then rolled all the way around the edge before flittering off to the other side.

"Man, that was close," Paul said.

Gert bit back her disappointment and nodded. "Yes, it was," she said, tapping the ball again and watching it drop in the hole. "Very close."

They moved to the last hole, the most difficult one on the course, according to the information on the scorecard, and Paul, once again, made it with two putts. "Your turn."

Gertrude decided that this time she'd ask Henry something totally different from all of the seventeen questions before.

*Henry, if you think I'm being ridiculous and should forget this whole communicating with you thing, let me know. I'll make it easy for you. I haven't gotten a hole in one yet, and this is the hardest one. If I get one this time, then I'll assume you're talking to me and want me to come back here again and use the other games Paul bought. If I get anything other than a hole in one, then I'm going back home and will be content to live my life as I have. I really don't need anyone else anyway. I have your memories, and I treasure those.* She put her ball on one of the notches in the rubber pad and didn't worry that it wasn't the same notch Paul had used. What were the chances of her getting a hole in one?

*A hole in one, I'll continue talking to you and trying to find out what you want me to do. Anything else, then I'll stop being such a ninny.*

She eased the putter back, then tapped it fairly hard against the side of the ball.

Hole eighteen had a big hill at the beginning (or big for this course), so she couldn't determine where the ball went on the other side. But Paul could.

"Come here, Gert. You've got to see this. Hurry."

She quickly moved around the side to peer toward the end of the tiny lane, where the hole was on the backside of yet another hill.

"Hurry, Gert, I think you did it," Paul encouraged and she continued her trek toward the hole and got there just in time to see her ball bounce off the back edge, then veer back toward the center . . . and drop in.

Paul cheered, and she gasped. He moved toward her and wrapped an arm around her. "You did it!"

"Oh, my, I did, didn't I?" *Okay, Henry. I guess I'll talk to you again tomorrow.*

It was ten o'clock when Jeff pulled back into the White Sands parking lot after his date with Rita Kay Payne. Rita Kay had invited him to attend the Seaside Festival of the Arts with her two weeks ago, and he hadn't wanted to break the date at the last minute, even though he hadn't been all that into the idea of going out tonight after pulling his caveman bit with Babette this afternoon. He'd much rather have continued playing caveman, or at least spent a little time determining why he had. But instead of continuing his role as resident Neanderthal at White Sands, he'd kept his commitment and went out with Rita Kay.

Rita Kay was a former Miss Florida with an eye to make herself a Mrs., and soon. She was tall, black-haired and big-boobed, extremely obvious tonight with the way her black dress was open all the way down to her navel, with merely a few lines of rhinestones barely holding the fabric over the swells of her breasts. She definitely hadn't purchased the dress at one of Jeff's stores; it moved beyond elegant and straight into trashy, in his opinion.

However, every guy in the place stared at Jeff with envy. Little did they know, he didn't want to see how easily that fabric would fall to the floor; his mind was on an oversized pale pink T-shirt with a disgruntled cat and a caption that read "Need Coffee" on the front, and the gorgeous sunburned redhead that had been wearing it a few hours ago.

He thought about this afternoon, how he'd dragged her

away from Chris Langley and then gave her that ridiculous task of going two weeks without flirting.

Where had he come up with that, anyway?

Hell, he knew where he came up with it. He didn't want to have to watch her flirting for two weeks, so he'd found a way to keep it from happening. As much. He seriously didn't think Babette would be able to pull it off, so he ran no risk of having to talk to Kitty when this was over. But at least his challenge might keep Babette from flaunting her sexual escapades in front of his face. He didn't like thinking about them, and he sure as hell didn't want to see them.

And *he* should be having a sexual escapade of his own tonight, courtesy of Rita Kay, who would have probably done him in his car while driving down the highway, if he'd let her. He couldn't count the number of times her hand had ventured near or across his crotch during the night. But if she did feel something substantial on those occasional brushes against his pants, it hadn't been caused by her. He'd been semi-hard ever since seeing Babette in that itty bitty bikini, and then when she'd put on that ugly T-shirt and he'd momentarily thought she was naked underneath, he hadn't thought of anything but getting her that way.

So he'd dropped Rita Kay off at her beach house and declined her offer to come in for a drink, then he'd driven back to White Sands with Babette, not Rita Kay, on his mind.

He entered the lobby and immediately spotted Rose standing impatiently by the elevator with a small, spiky plant cradled in her hands.

"Rose, it's after ten. Aren't you normally asleep by now?"

"Yes, I am, and I was, until about five minutes ago, when Babette called. She needs me." She stared at the elevator doors as though watching them would make them open sooner. "I should've taken the stairs. Where's the stairwell?"

"What does she need, Rose?"

"Well, this," Rose said, as though he should have known that by the fact that she was holding it.

He took another look at the odd-shaped plant and recognized it. "Aloe?" Then realization dawned. "She's that sunburned?"

"She can't move. Can't even get in the bed, poor dear. And she didn't know who to call, so she called me." She nodded toward the plant. "I can break off the stems and put the aloe directly on her. I'm hoping that will help. She already tried a cool bath, but that wasn't good enough. What is taking this elevator so long?"

"Rose, take your plant back to your place. You may need it yourself someday. I have aloe in my condo, the kind that's in lotion form and not so sticky." He'd tried using pure aloe before, and his body had felt like it'd been coated with super glue. Not what Babette needed if she planned to get any sleep tonight. "I'll go get the lotion and some additional treatments for sunburn that I have and take them to her. You head on back to Sunny Beaches. You look exhausted, and I promise I'm fine to take care of Babette tonight."

"You sure?" she asked, squinting one eye at him as though trying to decide whether he was capable of handling the task.

"I'm positive," he said, then held up a hand. "Wait here." He quickly crossed the lobby to find the off-duty policeman White Sands employed to patrol the resort at night, then he brought him back to Rose and asked him to escort her home.

Rose smiled thankfully. "You really are a good boy, aren't you?" she asked Jeff.

He grinned. "I try."

"Take care of her, and tell her that I can bring that plant back over if she needs it. I'll come check on her in the morning too. Tell her," she instructed.

"I will," Jeff said, then watched the guard and Rose leave, as the elevator doors finally opened.

He went to his condo, grabbed a bag and filled it with everything he thought she needed. Then, silently cursing himself for not even considering the fact that her sunburn might be worse than he'd realized, he took the stairs to the second floor. He wasn't in the mood to wait on temperamental elevators. Plus, there was no telling how long she waited before calling Rose for help. Babette, queen of stubborn, probably held out until she was absolutely miserable before accepting defeat and calling in the troops.

He knocked on her door and wondered just how bad a sunburn it was. After a few seconds, the lock clicked, the door eased open and he didn't have to wonder.

"Hell." He didn't know what else to say, and the tears that slipped from her eyes at his exclamation didn't make him feel any better about saying the only word that came to mind.

"Why are *you* here?" Her face was nearly as red as her hair, her eyes bloodshot from crying—or was that from the sun?—and her lips were swollen so much that she looked like Angelina Jolie with a collagen job. "I thought you were Rose," she said, turning and walking, very carefully, back toward the couch, where she sat down, slowly, cringing as her skin touched the fabric. And it was her skin touching, because all she was wearing was a silky button-up shirt, like a man's dress shirt, but cranberry in color and very shiny and very short. She looked sexy. Sunburned, but still sexy.

She whimpered as she tried to situate herself more comfortably on the couch, and Jeff felt like an ass for having sexual thoughts while she was obviously in pain.

"I saw Rose on her way up and told her I'd take care of you. She was bringing an aloe plant and planned to put the stuff all over you."

She frowned. "Sticky."

"My thoughts, too. I brought you something that I think you can handle a little better without gluing yourself to your sheets."

She blinked a couple of times, nodded, then tilted her head. "Where've you been?"

He hadn't changed, and still had on the black dress shirt and pants that he'd worn to the art festival. "The Seaside Art Festival," he said, opting for the occasion, rather than the company.

She wasn't fooled. "With the brunette?"

"No."

"This one blond?"

"She has black hair," he said, knowing Babette wouldn't stop asking until she got an answer.

"Figures."

"Listen, I brought you some stuff for your sunburn. Where do you want me to leave it?"

"You're just leaving it?" she asked, then another tear fell, and she sniffed noisily. "Why do you insist on making my life so miserable? First you take me away from the lifeguard, who I didn't really like all that much anyway, but that shouldn't matter to you in the first place, and then you tell me that I can't date, or flirt, or whatever, for two weeks so you can see if women can commit, then you come in here looking all hot and all that in black, and now you're going to leave the sunburn stuff and not even help me use it?" Another loud sniff. "Rose would've helped me use it."

More tears fell, and Jeff suddenly realized that this wasn't the Babette he knew talking. Something wasn't right.

"Babette, have you been drinking?"

"No, my head hurts too much already. Why would I want to drink and make it worse?" As if to emphasize the hurting head part, she leaned her head back and let it drop on the back of the couch. "Ouch."

Jeff crossed the room in less than a second and placed his hand against her forehead. "Babette, you're burning up."

"No, I'm not. I'm cold. Freezing. But I can't stand the sheets on me, because my legs hurt."

He looked at her legs, completely bare and totally red. All of her was red, in fact, and all of her was cooking with fever. "Come on," he said, reaching for her.

"No." She shook her head. "Don't touch me. I'm hurting too much, and you look too good, but I don't think I could take it tonight. Maybe tomorrow."

He smiled at that. "Babette," he said, easing his hand to hers, "Come on. We need to get you in a cool bath, and I'm going to find something to help bring your fever down."

"I already did the bath thing. It didn't work."

"We're going to try again."

She let him help her up and, barely touching her, he guided her through her bedroom to her bath, where water was still in the tub.

"Did I forget to get in?" she asked, and her words were slurred.

"Looks that way," he said, glancing around the bathroom to see if he could figure out where things were kept. "Do you know if there's a thermometer in here?" He wasn't certain whether a cool bath would work, or whether he needed to do something different, like take her to a doctor.

"No thermometer," she said, bumbling the last two syllables. "I looked."

He decided to try the tub first. "Listen, Babette, I'm going to unbutton your shirt and help you to the tub. Then I'm going to see if you've got any Advil or something to bring that fever down." He began unbuttoning the silky shirt, and she put her hands on his.

"You just want to see me naked, don't you?"

"As much as I have to say yes to that, because I'd be lying if I said no, I also don't see any way around it, unless you're going to undress yourself and get in the tub. And from the look of your first attempt, you didn't do that so well."

"Point taken," she said, and moved her hands from his.

"I'm not wearing underwear," she said as he pushed the buttons through the holes in the shirt, then let the fabric fall to the floor.

"I see that." In fact, he saw everything, and she was as incredible as he remembered, even if she was completely red, save the oh-so-important portions that had been covered by her bikini, and thank God they were, or she'd really be in a world of hurt now.

She looked down at her chest. "Pathetic, don't you think?"

"Here," he said, helping her step into the cool water. She shivered instantly and looked pleadingly at him.

"It's too cold."

"You need it, honey."

She bit her inner mouth—he could tell by the way her cheeks suddenly dipped in—and sat in the water. Then she let her breath out in a hiss and sank further in, until it came up to her shoulders and her long curls sank beneath the surface. "I never could resist you when you called me honey."

When he was certain she was cooling down, he sat beside the tub for a moment, just to make sure she didn't close her eyes and fall asleep, then slip completely in. Her shape was subtle, but superb, with lithe muscles beneath the surface and tiny curves that were extremely sensitive. He remembered.

"I see you looking," she said. Unfortunately, at that moment, his attention had been focused on the strawberry curls between her legs, and that part of her that had always been so hot, so wet, so ready, every time he touched her there.

He looked at her face. "Sorry." And then he smiled guiltily, "And for the record, there's nothing 'pathetic' about any part of you, Babette. These,"—he eased his hand into the water and held it near but not touching her pink-tipped breasts, "are just right."

"Yeah, I guess they'll do," she said, and surprisingly, she moved her hands to her breasts, cupped them lightly, and said, "For the record, they like you too."

Okay. She was still out of it from the fever, or the sunburn, or something, because that was not at all a very Babette thing to do. And then, as if emphasizing that she was still not herself, a couple of tears slipped from her eyes again. "How did she do it?"

"How did who do what?"

"Kitty," she whispered, then softly added, "How did she stick to her rule with you?" She frowned. "I couldn't."

"What rule?"

"Eight weeks. Two months. However she figured it," Babette mumbled, her swollen mouth muffling her words.

"Eight weeks?" He'd help her out, but he was clueless.

"She doesn't sleep with guys until they've hit eight weeks," Babette said, and every "s" lasted a little too long.

Jeff blinked. So *that* was why Kitty kept putting him off in the beginning, and then suddenly couldn't get him naked fast enough? She'd been . . . counting days.

The second part of Babette's statement snapped into place, and he asked, "What do you mean, you couldn't?"

"My rule. I broke my rule with you." This time, each "r" took a while to roll out, but Jeff wasn't about to let it go now.

"What was your rule, Babette?"

"Third date."

"Third date?"

"I've never slept with anyone until the third date."

He opened his mouth, ready to remind her about their first date, but then she continued.

"Except for you. I was so lost, the minute you touched me. One minute we were talking, and I was thinking about how much I wanted you, and the next I was naked and begging for it." She paused a beat. "Wasn't I?"

That was pretty much the way he remembered it. She'd shocked the hell out of him, and turned him on more than any other woman ever had. "Yeah, you were, but I didn't complain."

"No more third dates. I can't even get past date two anymore," she mumbled, then moaned. "I feel terrible."

"Hold on, I'll get something." He got up, opened the bathroom cabinet and spied a bottle of Ibuprofen. He grabbed it and, after their talk this afternoon about expired dates, turned it to check that it was, in fact, okay through next year. "Good." Then he grabbed a glass from beside the sink, filled it with water and moved back to the tub. "Here."

She didn't move her hands toward the pills, though they had left her boobs, which was good, due to what that image had done to his manhood. But instead, she leaned forward and licked the two pills from his palm, then she moved her mouth toward the glass, and Jeff realized that what relief his dick had received from her putting her hands back in the water was lost with the sensation of her tongue against his palm.

"Thanks," she said, resting her head against the back of the tub again and closing her eyes.

He swallowed. It took a damn decent man not to take advantage of this situation. Then again, the fact that he was sitting beside the tub and taking in Babette in all her wet glory was probably taking advantage enough, but he couldn't very well leave her soaking in the tub in the state she was in. She might drown. Or he'd tell himself that, because he really did like sitting here, not necessarily because Babette was nude in the tub, but because he really liked helping Babette, period.

"I think I'm done." She pushed on the sides of the tub and stood up.

He pressed a hand to her forehead, and it didn't feel as hot. Not exactly cool, but not as hot either.

She stepped out of the tub and stood there dripping on the floor.

"Hang on, I'll get a towel." He grabbed one off a rack nearby and handed it to her.

She took it, moved it to her face and yelped. Then she dropped it to the floor. "Hurts."

He hadn't thought of that. He scanned the room for something to use and spotted the silky shirt she'd been wearing. "How about this?"

She took it, dabbed at her face, and then started patting the remainder of her body dry. "Thanks."

"You're okay?" he asked.

"Still stinging, but not as much."

"I'll go get the stuff I brought to help." He left the bathroom and then returned with the bag of medicine and the sheets he'd brought from his condo. She was standing near the tub with the silky shirt held in front of her and covering everything important.

"I've got an aloe lotion with Lidocaine to help numb the pain." He lifted the bottle from the bag and placed it on the counter. "Can you put it on?"

She smiled, but it was kind of lopsided with her mouth so swollen. "I think I can."

"Good. Use that lotion, while I put these on your bed."

"What are those?" she looked toward the folded sheets he held.

"Satin sheets. They'll be softer than the cotton ones you have on there now, and hopefully, they won't bother your burn so you can sleep."

Another lopsided smile. "Thanks."

While she used the aloe lotion, he put the navy satin sheets on her bed and turned back the coverlet. "Where are your sleep shirts?"

"Top drawer on the right," she called from the bathroom.

Jeff opened the drawer, found the one he thought was the softest, the least likely to hurt her skin, and then turned.

She stood near the bathroom door still holding the damp satin shirt in front of her.

"I really do feel better now. I can already tell the Lidocaine is working."

"Good," he said, placing the night shirt on the bed. "Here, I think this one will feel the best." He cleared his throat. "If you need anything during the night, just call. I'll be right down."

"Thanks."

He left the bedroom, made it through the living room and to the door, then he paused, wondering if she'd want him to stay, not in her bed, but on the couch, just in case she needed him during the night.

"Jeff?"

He turned and saw she'd already put on the pale blue nightshirt and had followed him into the living room. "Yeah?"

"I shouldn't have any trouble for the next day or so. Keeping the rule, I mean."

He'd expected her to ask him to stay, so her statement didn't make sense, until she continued.

"About no flirting. Kind of tough to flirt, or even look all that appealing, when you're sunburned."

He could tell her it'd take more than a sunburn to squelch her appeal to any male, but he didn't. Instead he said, "That's okay. You'll still have another week to go."

"I *can* do it. And you will talk to Kitty."

"No, you can't. And I won't."

"We'll see." She smiled, then moved a hand to those swollen lips.

"I put some petroleum jelly in that bag. You should put it on your mouth."

"Hey, maybe the big lips will make it impossible for me to whistle-flirt. I might just keep them."

"Use the jelly, Babette. You don't want your lips to peel."

Her nose wrinkled at that. "Right. Thanks." She gently tapped her forefinger across her lower lip to apparently test just how swollen it was. "Do I look like Mick Jagger?"

"I was thinking Angelina Jolie."

She nodded. "That'll work. Good night, Jeff."

"Night, Babette."

# Chapter 13

The phone in Babette's condo rang promptly at 4:30 Tuesday afternoon, exactly when Jeff had told Rose that he'd get off work. He'd been calling periodically ever since he left Babette Saturday night, and each time, she made sure her personal guardian took the call. However, this time, Rose had her hands covered in flour and was busy rolling out biscuit dough. She shot a look over her shoulder at Babette, gently stirring the gravy on the stove while Rose's friend Tillie watched approvingly.

"Babette, you're going to have to get it this time," Rose said. "I'm busy."

"Now Rose, you know she can't leave the gravy now. It'll get lumpy. She has to keep stirring."

"And I can't get it anyway," Babette said. "Or he'll know I can talk."

"Oh, Good Lord, you can't keep hiding from him, Babette," Rose said, yelling over the shrill ring of the phone. The three of them stared at it, but no one left their current post in the kitchen, and it blessedly stopped ringing.

"I know I can't hide from him forever, but the longer Jeff thinks I'm too sunburned to get out of the condo, the more days I'm not out there tempted to flirt. And if I make it without flirting, then he has to talk to Kitty, and I get to keep my hundred percent rating, and Kitty's money."

"What I don't understand is why you don't just meet with him, do your people reading thing, like you're going to do for us, and then tell him why he and Kitty should be together," Tillie said, making it all sound so easy. And it would be, if Jeff was like any normal Love Doctor assignment. But he wasn't. And that was the problem.

"She can't," Rose said flatly, running a hand over the rolled biscuit dough and patting the yeast bubbles as she did. "Did you see how I did this, Babette? You roll gently. If you bear down too hard, you'll make the dough too flat, and the biscuits will be harder than rocks."

"I saw," Babette said. "But I probably still need to do some myself, don't you think?"

"Oh, definitely. I just knew you were busy with the gravy this time. We'll do biscuits again another day."

"What do you mean she can't?" Tillie asked, unswayed by the cooking instruction in the middle of their conversation. "Why can't you just get them together the way you do everyone else?" She turned an accusing eye toward Rose. "You told all of us that she never misses, that she could help us with the guys at Sunny Beaches, and all we had to do was teach her how to cook."

Rose pursed her lips. "She doesn't miss." Then she opened Babette's cabinets until she found the glasses, got one and turned it upside down, then pressed it in the rolled dough to cut the first biscuit. Babette watched with awe, and promptly got a hand slap from Tillie.

"You can't stop stirring the gravy."

"Right. Sorry," Babette said, then turned her attention back to her own project.

"And why *can't* you do the normal Love Doctor thing with Jeff?" Tillie pressed.

"I can't read him," Babette said honestly. "Or I forget to, or something. But I've been with him a few times since I got here, and not once have I even thought to check for body language, or signals when he says Kitty's name, or anything. It's like I totally blank out when I'm around him. He's not like anyone else I've ever talked to."

"Wonder why that is," Rose muttered from the other side of the kitchen.

"So, are you just going to ignore him the rest of the time you're here?" Tillie asked. "And what good will that do?"

"I know I can't ignore him the whole time, but I'm going to keep it up as long as I can. If he doesn't see me, he can't see me flirting. And if I can pull off not flirting until next week, then he'll have to see her, talk to Kitty, and I'll keep my business thriving. Better than thriving, with Kitty Carelle on my list of satisfied clients."

"And you won't even have to read him," Tillie surmised.

"That's the plan, though there is the problem of Kitty wanting to know something now. She wants me to tell her *something* about Jeff's comments regarding her."

"And if you don't talk to him about her, you've got nil, right?" Tillie asked.

Babette nodded.

Rose mumbled something else, but Babette didn't catch it.

"What are you saying over there?" Babette asked, while Tillie popped her wrist, and then she promptly picked back up with her stirring in progress.

"I'm saying that he's not the one who needs reading around here. You are."

"What?" Babette asked, while the phone rang again. "Rose, can you get it this time?"

"I'm not lying to him," she said, the same way she had every other time he'd called.

Babette looked at Tillie. "Will you finish stirring it for me? I get the gist of it now. Keep it on low heat, and stir it forever."

Tillie smirked, took over control of the wooden spoon. "Yeah, that's pretty much it. Okay, go get in the bed," she said, shooing Babette out of the kitchen.

Babette dashed through the condo and dived into the bed at the very moment that Rose picked up the phone.

"Hello," Rose said sweetly. "Oh, hi, Jeff. Yeah, I couldn't get to the phone a little bit ago, busy cooking some dinner for Babette. We're having breakfast for supper. I always like having breakfast for supper. Kind of changes things up, you know." She was rambling, and Babette listened appreciatively. Thanks to the Lidocaine, aloe and Ibuprofen, she'd felt relatively normal by Sunday afternoon. Monday was even better, and today even more. So she'd taken advantage of being holed up in her condo by letting Rose's sidekicks teach her how to cook and tell her about the guys they wanted to meet over at Sunny Beaches. It'd been a lot of fun, kind of like an elderly summer camp, and the best part was she hadn't been tempted whatsoever to flirt and had consequently crossed three days off her time that she had to go without doing so. From the look of things, next week Jeff would meet with Kitty and Babette would be a successful business-woman once more. Committed to her job, and proving to Jeff that women—more specifically, she—could commit.

Life was good.

"No, I don't think she's up for company," Rose said, like she'd told him every other time he'd called. "Her lips?" She peeked in at Babette, who smiled broadly. "Well, I think they're going to be just fine. Her arms started peel-ing a bit today, but we put some lotion on them and they're going to be okay." Rose paused, frowned, and Babette got a tad worried. He'd evidently asked a tougher question. "I guess she's just being safe, you know, staying out of the sun while her skin is healing and all. And she's taking it easy at night, hasn't really felt up to going out after the sunburn ordeal. She says it even hurts her to talk." Rose nodded, and Babette breathed a sigh of relief. It looked like she'd made it another day, and she was thrilled.

Finally, Rose hung up the phone.

"What did he ask, that last time?"

"He wanted to know why you weren't at least getting out of the condo at night, since he knows how much you enjoy the beach in the evening. Then he asked again to come see you, and I told him you didn't want to see any-one until you felt better."

"Did he believe you?" Tillie asked, while Babette left the bedroom and went back to the kitchen to check on the gravy.

"I think he did." Rose's eyes followed Babette as she moved across the room. "But I'm not going to mislead him again, Babette. And I honestly think you need to face whatever is really going on here. There's a reason you can't read him, and I think you know what it is."

Babette started to argue, but before she could get the first word out, someone knocked at the door.

"That's probably Hannah," Tillie said. "She was waiting until after Bingo to come over and help with the cooking."

"I'll get it." Babette smiled at the two women taking over her kitchen, then moved to the door to let the third one in. But upon opening the door, she didn't find the four-foot-nothing eighty-two-year-old who'd proclaimed her cinnamon roll recipe the best ever. On the contrary, she found a six-foot-two thirty-eight-year-old who hadn't been calling from his office. Jeff held a cell phone to his ear and looked at her as though she'd been . . . caught.

"I thought you were in bed," he said. "Too sore from your sunburn to get up." He stepped inside, sniffed, and said toward the kitchen, "At least the part about cooking breakfast for dinner was true, huh, Rose?"

Rose slammed the oven door closed—she'd been checking on the biscuits—and scurried toward Jeff, her black granny shoes working double-time in the effort. "I promise you, she was in the bed when I said she was," Rose said matter-of-factly. "I told her I wasn't going to lie. I may spy, but I don't lie," she said, nodding for emphasis. "So she got in the bed, and then I said she was there."

He grinned, and Babette gawked. "Rose!"

"That's what happened. I told you we wouldn't be able to fool him that much longer." Rose shrugged. "Her sunburn isn't that bad at all anymore, so I guess you did a pretty good job doctoring her on Saturday."

"Not that I'd have known that from my phone calls," he said.

Rose muttered something about needing to check the biscuits, looked at Babette in an I-told-you-so manner, then went back to the kitchen.

"You did do a good job doctoring the sunburn," Babette said. "I'm not even peeling all that much." She'd hoped that the compliment would take his mind off her deception. But this was Jeff, and he knew her. Well.

"Yeah, I got to thinking about that today at the office," he said, standing way too near, all tall and gorgeous and intimidating. "And I thought that if the Lidocaine and aloe hadn't worked, and if you still were in such bad shape, then you should go see a doctor. I was even going to offer to drive you."

"But?" she prompted, knowing more was coming.

"But then I realized that Rose wouldn't let you suffer for three days straight. She'd have already gotten you to a doctor, one way or another, if you weren't getting better. And then I started wondering why you would lie about how bad your sunburn was, for three days straight."

"I am peeling a bit," she reminded, and turned so he could see the small area on her biceps where she'd started peeling.

"But you're also talking, and quite well," he pointed out.

She snapped her mouth shut, not knowing how to argue with that, since she hadn't stopped attempting to explain herself since he got here.

"And then it hit me, the reason you'd want me to think you can't leave this condo."

"Because I'm trying to learn to cook," she said quickly, rather proud of herself for responding so fast.

It didn't fool him. "Because you're afraid you'll flirt, and that I'll catch you flirting, and then you won't succeed in getting me to talk with Kitty."

She gasped, but it sounded bogus even to her own ears.

He grinned. "Be ready in an hour, Babette. We're going dancing."

"Dancing?"

"Yeah. Dancing. You know, couples, music, a band. Dancing."

She swallowed hard, felt a twinge of panic. Dancing was a prelude to sex, and dancing was such an easy means for flirting. He was trying to trap her, and she wasn't sure how to get out of it.

"But we're cooking dinner," Tillie called from the kitchen. "And Hannah is coming over to teach her how to make cinnamon rolls. Then we're going to talk about the guys at Sunny Beaches and then spend the night here with Babette. It's our girls night out. You wouldn't ruin that for us, would you?"

Tillie was telling the truth, exactly what Babette had promised they'd do tonight, and she was beyond thankful that they'd planned their special girls night out. Surely he wouldn't disappoint three women in their eighties simply because he wanted to prove a point to one in her thirties.

"That's right. I can't go dancing tonight," she said. "Sorry." She tried to look apologetic, but a smile of pure triumph was itching to be set free. It was itching so much, in fact, that she had to squish her mouth up like a persimmon to keep from smiling, and then cheering. Tillie had just become her new BFF.

Jeff's turquoise eyes narrowed suspiciously, but then he seemed to regroup, and smiled.

That smile made her nervous. She really needed him to go. Because suddenly, and quite out of the blue, she recalled him helping her on Saturday night, drying her off with her shirt, putting those spectacular sheets on her bed, getting her a night shirt, taking care of her, being more than a friend . . . and she wanted to kiss that smile.

"Tomorrow then. That's even better, in fact. There's a benefit dance at a nightclub in Panama City. We're going. Be ready at 6:00."

"But we're cooking at 6:00," Tillie said. "I've already bought the stuff to teach her how to make beef stew. We're cooking it here, then taking it over to Sunny Beaches to feed the guys. Pick her up at 8:00."

Babette didn't know whether to laugh at Tillie ordering Jeff, or cry because she could almost feel her impending failure. Dancing without flirting. She wasn't even sure that was possible. "We are cooking again tomorrow night," she said. "And truthfully, it could take longer than we'd thought. Probably another night would be better for you and I to . . ."

"Be ready at 8:00. We'll be a little late arriving, but that's okay." He nodded goodbye to the two women leaning out of the kitchen and hanging on every word, then he grinned at Babette. "Be ready." And then he was gone.

"I'm so screwed," she said, at the precise moment that her cell phone started ringing. She picked it up, checked the caller ID, and prepared to talk to Kitty for the tenth time today. Once again, Babette would have to dodge her questions about specifics that Jeff had said about their relationship. Then she'd tell her the same thing she had all day, that she'd been making progress, and that Kitty could count on Jeff talking to her by next week. That would be true, if Babette could make it without flirting. "I'm *so* screwed," she repeated, and answered the phone.

Jeff felt like he was picking up a date for the prom when he arrived at Babette's condo Wednesday night. Except instead of having to face the parents, he had to face an excited group of senior citizens. Rose and Tillie had apparently told all of the women at Sunny Beaches about Babette's cooking lessons, or maybe about Jeff's demand that she go dancing, but in any case, Babette's apartment was overflowing with silver-haired women, all of them fussing over Babette.

"Don't drink too much," one warned, fastening a beaded black choker around Babette's neck as she spoke.

"Watch the guys with cowboy hats. I never trusted a guy wearing a cowboy hat," came from another. "And I certainly wouldn't trust them if I looked that good in a dress."

Babette grinned. "Thanks, Tillie."

"There shouldn't be any cowboy hats where we're going," Jeff affirmed, and he silently agreed with Tillie. Babette looked very tempting in the black cocktail dress.

"Just use that stuff I gave you, and you won't have any troubles," Tillie continued.

Jeff ushered Babette out of the condo and to the elevator, but resolved to ask her about "that stuff" later. Because he knew her so well, he could see the nerves bristling beneath the surface, the way she fidgeted with the straps on the black halter dress and the way she wasn't looking at him any more than absolutely necessary. She was either very nervous, or very mad. He decided to find out which.

"You look very nice."

"Thanks." No eye contact.

"That dress came from one of our stores, didn't it?"

He noticed her cheek inch up slightly, as though she were fighting a grin, and then she checked it, and said, "It did. When I shot the last Eubanks catalog, Preston gave me a discount card that's good at all of your stores. I don't use it too often, but I didn't have a dress for the benefit, so I took advantage of it today."

"You bought that today?" he asked, thinking he now knew why she'd almost smiled.

She nodded.

"At which store?"

"Panama City."

"You drove right past the Seaside store to get to that one. Could've just bought the dress there and saved some gas."

This time, she looked at him directly, and Jeff knew she was secretly pleased that he'd caught on. "Yeah, I could have, but you were at that store. I saw your car. So I kept driving."

"You're that pissed at me for taking you dancing?" he asked, as they stepped off the elevator and started across the lobby.

"I'm that pissed at you for trying to make me lose your challenge," she clarified. "I'm not going to flirt." She lifted a brow as though expecting him to dispute her. He wasn't going to. He was simply going to prove her wrong, when he caught her flirting on the dance floor.

Then he realized that he didn't even have to take Babette to a night club to have her face a flirting challenge. All she had to do was walk through the White Sands lobby. Several men nodded at her on their way into the building. She smiled politely, but then averted her eyes, completely turning away from their interested gazes. Then the valet attendant brought his car, and that guy also smiled a little too broadly at her.

"If you'd have been that nice when I first came in with Sylvia, you'd have gotten a decent tip," she mumbled when she got in the car.

Jeff chuckled. He wouldn't catch her flirting with the valet guy; that's for sure. "He didn't appreciate Sylvia's charm?"

"He was too busy appreciating your brunette's Jag," she said, and Jeff grinned. At least she was talking to him, even if it was merely because she wanted to fuss.

They pulled away, but not before she snarled at the valet attendant.

"I take it you told Rose and her friends about my proposition," he said.

"Yeah, last night. I think it was after my third rum toddy."

"Your girls night out was a drinking party?" he asked, slightly surprised. It was Babette, and if anyone could get the seniors to loosen up, it'd be her.

"Believe it or not, the drinks were Tillie's idea."

"Tillie's the one who said for you to use her 'stuff' tonight."

Babette smirked. "Yeah, she said she had the perfect thing for me to use to keep guys from flirting with me, and therefore keep me from flirting back."

"Should I try to guess?"

"You could try, but it'd be useless. Unless you were going to guess skunk oil."

He glanced at her, and then at her tiny black purse. "In there?"

She opened the purse, fished out a tiny bottle.

"Let me see that."

"Okay, but don't tell Tillie," she said, putting the bottle of oil in his palm.

Jeff rolled down the window and tossed it out.

"That was mine!" she yelled, turning to see where it hit in the opposite ditch. "And you just littered."

"First of all, there's no way I want to risk you spilling skunk oil in my car, or on me, or on yourself, for that matter. And second of all, I'm fairly certain that bottle was biodegradable."

"Sure it was."

He grinned. "That's my story, and I'm sticking to it. And you're not dousing anyone with skunk oil tonight."

"Aren't you the bossy one? You *will* go dancing. You *will* flirt. You *will not* use skunk oil."

He waited. Surely she couldn't spout all of that without laughing.

She didn't disappoint, her throaty laughter filling the car and making him smile. "You're terrible," she said.

"Hey, I might have asked you to do the impossible . . ."

"It isn't impossible, and I'm going to prove it tonight."

"Anyway, I might have asked you to do something difficult, but I didn't lie to you."

"I didn't lie to you."

"You said you couldn't get out of bed and couldn't talk."

"I was in the bed every time Rose told you I was."

"What about the talking?"

She started fiddling with her seatbelt. "How much farther is it?"

"Avoiding the question?"

"Nope, I'm just asking another."

"Fine. It's not too far, ten more minutes."

"Okay, then while we're driving, let's talk about you and Kitty."

That threw him. "You never asked me anything about her Saturday, when that's what you'd said you wanted to do, so I assumed you changed your mind about us talking about her. Remember, if you don't flirt, I'll talk to her. There's no reason for us to discuss her now."

"That's what I thought too," she admitted. "And trust me, I'm much more comfortable with simply winning this challenge and having you do what I need you to in order for me to keep my percentage at a hundred percent. But your ex is growing impatient and wants details."

"Kitty's calling you?"

"I do have to keep my clients informed of my progress. That's part of my job."

"I bet she's your most relentless customer."

"She's very eager for results," Babette said, as though Kitty hadn't probably been calling her every hour on the hour for days. If anyone knew how persistent Kitty could be when she wanted something, he did.

"So you need me to tell you something, so you can relay it to her and get her off your back," he said, pulling into the club's parking lot.

"I just need to report something," Babette said. "I'm not bad-mouthing the woman you'll be seeing again come next week."

That made him laugh. "Don't count on it."

"I am counting on it. A lot. Now, I just need to ask you some questions about Kitty . . ."

"Later. We're here," he said, pulling up to the entrance and turning the car over to the valet.

Babette grumbled as she exited the car. "We're going to talk about her before the night's over," she said, then looked up at the sign for the benefit. "Closed party? Partner swap?"

"Oh, I guess I forgot to mention that. Tonight is a partner swap."

"Which means?"

"It's pretty simple. You can't dance with the same partner twice."

Her brown eyes grew even darker, and her brows dipped severely. "We're not dancing with each other?"

"Sure we will. Once." He grinned, then escorted her inside. "But for the rest of the dances, you'll have other partners. Oh, and if you're going to win your part of this deal, you won't flirt."

Jeff was very pleased with himself. He'd bought tickets to the partner swap night, an elite event planned with all proceeds going toward a new community center, several weeks ago with no intention whatsoever of attending. He'd simply planned to donate the money and let that be it. But now, with his proposition to Babette, this occasion was the perfect opportunity to win this challenge.

He watched the host for the evening, the president of a local bank, greet Babette and saw the way the older gentleman smiled appreciatively at her. He was evidently captivated by the long red hair, the lithe physique, the genuine smile. But he'd really be impressed if he knew the feisty woman within the pretty package.

Jeff neared the two of them and heard the man say, "Yes, we thought this would be a unique way to raise money for the new center. It was my wife's idea, if I must be honest, though. I'd love for you to meet her, Ms. Robinson. There she is, the one in the green dress. She's on her second dance. See, you'll sign up here and get a number, then begin your dance rotation, with your date being your last dance for the evening." He smiled adoringly at his wife as she spun around the dance floor with another older gentleman.

"I'd love to meet her," Babette said, beaming as she turned and looked at Jeff. "In fact, I can't wait to meet everyone here this evening. And the dancing will be so much fun, what a great idea!"

Jeff scanned the room and immediately saw why she was suddenly so happy, and why he had messed up completely. He always bought tickets to the benefits around town, but didn't attend that many. They were usually coordinated by the older crowd and typically, the activities weren't his thing. So he wrote a check to help the cause and that was that. Now he realized that apparently the only business owners who actually attended the events were the seniors. There wasn't a person on that dance floor under sixty, and Babette looked mighty damn pleased about it.

"So, who do I dance with first?" she asked, and was steered toward a stately elderly gentleman on the other side of the room.

"Your first dance belongs to Mrs. Rytower," the man said, and Jeff turned to see a chubby woman with red cheeks fanning herself behind him. She was in her late sixties or early seventies, and her dark gray curls were held in place with bejeweled pins, like something a teen would wear, but admittedly, they suited her "look." She had on a pale turquoise mother-of-the-bride dress, but the color matched her eyes, and the cut was simple but elegant. Jeff grinned to himself. He could leave the Eubanks store, but he couldn't turn off the analysis of clothing.

"Mrs. Rytower," he said, extending a hand and deciding that if he were here, he might as well enjoy himself. "I'm Jeff Eubanks, and I believe this dance is mine."

Her hand flew to her chest and she gushed. "Why, Mr. Eubanks, I know who you are. I love your stores. So nice of you to join us tonight. I saw your name on the list, but I didn't think you usually came to the events. Most of the younger folks don't."

"And just look what they're missing," he said, leading her out on the dance floor.

She laughed, then giggled again when he spun her around. "Do try to get more of them to attend. I head several of the committees, you know. And your date. She's absolutely breathtaking. Be sure to bring her back, and that'll make sure to get all of these men to return." She glanced toward Babette, laughing at something her newest senior partner said.

Jeff grinned. Babette was having a ball, and he was too, not only dancing, but also watching her have so much fun. She moved from a white-haired man to a silver-haired to a bald one, and with each of them, she danced like she was the queen of the ball, but always remembered to wave to their wives. The women looked at her like they would a daughter, not as a threat, because that was the way Babette obviously viewed this interaction, as something akin to when a woman dances with her father or grandfather at her wedding.

By the time they'd both danced with all of their partners and prepared for the last dance, Babette was practically panting.

"That Mr. Moffett says he's seventy-six, but he's got more energy than I had at twenty," she said, grinning at Jeff as she approached him. "And by the way, I believe it's my turn to have a turn with the young fellow."

"You're a riot," he said, silently applauding when the band moved into a slow song and he had a justifiable reason for pulling her close.

"What? Are you disappointed that I haven't flirted tonight? Trust me, I was tempted, especially when Mr. Zimmerman showed me how he could still balance on one foot."

"He didn't."

"He did." She laughed, looked up at him, and then ran her fingertips along his temple. "Why, Mr. Eubanks, you're hot."

"You're not the first woman to think so," he said, and couldn't hold back a smirk. "But if you must know, you're rather glowing yourself, Ms. Robinson."

"Maybe we should go out with the seniors more often, to keep us in shape."

He laughed at that. "Maybe if I actually attended some of the events I bought tickets for every now and then, I'd have realized we were going out with the seniors."

"Well, for the record, I can't think of anything I'd have enjoyed more. I met some terrific people here tonight, and I want to thank you for bringing me."

The music wound down, and Jeff realized that he had

never even listened to see what song they were playing. He'd been too into holding Babette, moving her around the floor and enjoying her excitement. True, he'd wanted to tempt her into flirting tonight, but if he had it to do over again and knew that this event was for the seniors, he'd still have brought her here, just to see her this happy.

"Looks like the night is over," she said.

"Looks like." The music had stopped, but he continued holding her, not ready to let go.

For a moment, her eyes found his, and they simply stayed there, looking at each other. Then his hands moved lower on her back, and he felt her curve slightly, moving toward him. "Jeff," she whispered.

"Yeah?"

"Oh, there's nothing like young love," Mrs. Rytower exclaimed, her voice pitched toward them as she spoke. "I'm betting there's a wedding in their future."

Babette blinked, backed away slightly. Then she cleared her throat. "I almost forgot. We still need to talk about Kitty."

Jeff frowned. She'd been close to saying something, and it had nothing to do with Kitty. "We're not talking about Kitty tonight."

"Then tomorrow. Promise me that you'll talk with me about her tomorrow. It doesn't have to be all that much, just enough to let her know that I'm doing my job. She won't have to know about our little deal."

He didn't want to talk to Babette about Kitty. He didn't want to have anything to do with Kitty again, and if Babette would simply flirt, he could stop listening to her talk about Kitty too.

An idea suddenly sprang to mind, one he liked very much, and he grinned. "Tomorrow. We'll talk about Kitty tomorrow, after you spend a little time with me on the beach."

# Chapter 14

Whats the score, Babette?" Jeff called out, as he'd done continually throughout the past hour.

"You're evil. Absolutely, positively evil," she hissed, but because of all the screams and cheers around her, no one heard.

"Babette? The score?" he asked again, smiling like the devil he was, and sweating and looking like a guy who could do her, and do her well.

"Fourteen serving eighteen," she snapped.

"Come on, guys, we've got some catch-up to do," Jeff rallied his team. He looked at Babette, winked, and she promptly straightened the towel on her lounger. Talk about torture. He'd called all his buddies—all his brawny, gorgeous-as-all-get-out buddies—for a friendly afternoon of beach volleyball, and then asked Babette to keep score. In other words, she was sitting on the beach in the middle of her favorite scene from *Top Gun*, and she couldn't even whistle. It was maddening. And she would make him pay. Somehow, someday, when he least expected it.

"You okay, Babette?" Jeff asked, holding the ball in one palm as he prepared to serve.

She realized she'd been glaring at him as though she were holding a pistol, and his head was the target. "I'm fine." But she wasn't. If she could keep her attention on solely his head, everything would be just smashing. But he happened to be on the "skins" team, so he was out there using each and every one of those perfect, tanned muscles to hit that ball over the net, and all of those muscles working together so well in have-mercy harmony sent an arrow of have-mercy need to her deprived libido.

Jeff tossed the ball in the air, jumped up and slammed it to the other side, reminding Babette of how powerful he really was, and that reminded her of all the other ways he could be powerful and sweaty and delicious.

Delicious? She needed help.

"Yoohoo!" Rose's shrill voice caught her attention, and Babette turned toward the pool deck, where Rose and friends had gathered and were taking in the view.

"Hey, Rose," Babette called. "I can't practice cooking right now."

"Shoot, I'd say you've found what's really cooking around here," Tillie said, lifting her brows as she took in the multitude of testosterone slamming the volleyball.

"Babette? The score?" Jeff asked.

"You know the score," she said.

"I guess we won't be talking about anything after the game," he said smugly.

"Fifteen serving eighteen."

Rose's giggle trailed over the beach, and Babette turned in time to see her snap her palm over her mouth. Then she shrugged.

"We're going up to your place to work on some of the stuff for tomorrow's party," Tillie called. "Okay if we let ourselves in?"

"Sure. Rose has a key."

Babette's attention was drawn from the women when something popped against the side of her leg. She turned to see the volleyball on the sand next to her, and one of the guys from the opposing team heading her way. He was tall, dark and deadly, smiling at Babette as though he'd like nothing better than to make her every wish come true.

She picked up the volleyball, held it toward him.

He grinned, and he had beautiful teeth too. "Hey, thanks."

"No problem," she said, as blandly as she could.

"I'm Kurt, by the way."

"Nice to meet you," she said, handing him the ball, then promptly turning her attention back to the other side of the court, and the guy watching her every move. "Looking for something, Jeff?"

He laughed. "Just the score."

"Sixteen serving eighteen."

She watched him successfully serve again, then subsequently join his team for a round of high fives that was mighty impressive. There wasn't anything quite like a bunch of excited men celebrating each battle along the way to victory. And typically, Babette would be drawn to the entire show, but today, oddly enough, her eyes seemed to be focused on the one attempting to inflict the most torture. Little did he know, he was torturing her, all right, but in a different way. She wasn't all that tempted to flirt with the other guys, though she would whistle if she could;

hey, she was breathing. But the only one she was tempted to flirt with, and do more with, was the one that she was supposed to bring back to Kitty. Her business was a success, and she was finally committed to something. She didn't want to throw that away for a relationship that had always been solely about sex.

However, this time with Jeff, things felt different, and that was throwing her for a loop. She'd sensed it when he took care of her the other night, and then again last night when they'd had so much fun together at the benefit dance. Even now, when he looked at her, she felt something stronger than mere desire for the guy looking so hot, but a pull toward him, because it was him, and because of how he made her feel.

She called out the score three more times, and then the game was done, with the sand-coated guys delivering congratulations and promises of retribution to come. Then Jeff headed her way and extended a hand. "Come on."

"Where are we going now? Is there a competition somewhere nearby for Playgirl models?"

He laughed, and the action made his abs dance. Babette looked toward the waves, splashing against the shore. That was a much easier image to handle at the moment.

"No, I won't try to tempt you again, not now anyway. And for the record, I was shocked, and somewhat impressed, that you didn't find anything to your liking in my group of friends."

"I wouldn't say that." Though she also wouldn't tell him that the only one she'd found to her liking was standing in front of her. "I'm just determined to win. I've worked hard at making this business work, Jeff, and I can't let you ruin that for me."

He opened his mouth, but then shut it, and Babette was left wondering what he'd been about to say.

"In any case, it appears I now owe you a conversation about my ex, as much as I'm not looking forward to it. But first, I want to wash off this sand." He continued extending his hand in front of Babette, and she reached for it, then let him pull her to her feet and lead her toward those waves. He stepped ahead of her and released her hand.

Babette was a bit surprised at how she suddenly missed that hand.

She followed him into the water and laughed when a big wave soaked her completely. Rubbing her eyes, she felt another spray hit her, but this wasn't a wave. This was a man acting like a kid. Opening her eyes, she saw Jeff, a bit farther out and crouched in the water, only his head visible above the surface.

"That one came out of nowhere," he said, and she launched, putting every bit of her weight toward pushing him under, and succeeding. She wasn't fooled, of course. He'd let her, but still, it felt rather rewarding when he came up coughing.

They played for a while, splashing and laughing and sputtering, until she'd drank way more saltwater than she wanted and surrendered.

"Okay, you win. I'm waterlogged," she said, her breath coming out in gasps.

He followed her out of the waves. "A victory on the volleyball court and a victory in the water. Not a bad day."

"Last time I checked, I won too."

"What was that?"

"The no flirting challenge."

"The day isn't over yet, and last time I checked, you've got six more days to go."

"But now you have to talk to me about Kitty. You promised, and I'm going to hold you to it."

"Because she's calling you nonstop?"

"Because I'm supposed to keep my clients aware of my progress," she corrected, starting across the sand toward the condo.

"You're going in already?"

"I thought we were going to talk."

"Hey, I took off half a day to play in that volleyball game and enjoy the beach. So far, I've only done half of that. You do have sunscreen on, don't you?"

"Rose bought me a new bottle, and it's nowhere near the expiration date."

"Good. Then let's go for a walk down the beach while we talk."

"Okay." She wasn't ready to go in either, even if walking on the beach with him triggered memories of other beach walks that had typically ended with them finding somewhere secluded, losing their swimsuits and exploring each other.

Babette gradually tamped down on her current round of Jeff-induced lust, and they walked away from the White Sands area, past Sunny Beaches, and continued beyond several more resorts before either of them spoke. Although she probably should have decided what she wanted to ask him regarding his relationship with Kitty, she hadn't. Or maybe she hadn't come up with any questions because she didn't want to listen to Jeff providing details. It'd been difficult enough hearing them from Kitty.

But Kitty was paying for this trip, and she was expecting Babette to deliver on her promise to get the two of them back together at the end of the two weeks, which, coincidentally, was merely six days away.

She really couldn't afford to keep dodging this conversation. Kitty was getting tired of waiting. This morning she'd told Babette that if she didn't let her know something soon about how things were going, then she'd drive down here so she could see for herself.

"So can I take your silence to mean you've changed your mind about discussing Kitty?" Jeff asked, at the very same moment that Babette blurted, "Tell me what you liked about her."

He visibly swallowed. "Guess you were just getting ready to start." He glanced at her, his blue eyes even brighter in the direct sun, in spite of the fact that he was squinting. "What I liked about Kitty?"

"In the beginning, when the two of you met at the charity golf thing," she said, recalling Kitty's description of how he'd stood out from the crowd. "What did you like about her? What was the first thing that caught your attention?"

He continued walking, but turned his head toward the waves so Babette couldn't see his expression. "You realize that this is rather awkward, given the time frame of when I met Kitty. I'm assuming you know when we got together."

"I didn't until she told me, but it wasn't all that hard to figure out. You met her right after we stopped talking." Babette was rather impressed that she said it so easily, as though it didn't sting. "How does that affect what you first noticed about her?"

He looked back at Babette, and he was smiling, but it wasn't his usual smile. It was rather pensive, as though he wasn't sure what to say, or how to say it. "The truth is, I didn't notice anything about her. I didn't notice her at all."

Not what she had been expecting. "You didn't notice Kitty Carelle?" Babette couldn't control her shocked tone and couldn't fathom how any man, let alone Jeff, wouldn't notice someone who looked like Kitty.

"No, I didn't. And as bizarre as it may sound, I think that's what got her attention."

"I'm certain that isn't something she's used to." A major understatement.

He shrugged. "I wasn't looking for anyone then. Didn't want another relationship."

Babette was thrown by that. The whole time they were together, he hadn't wanted a relationship period. Nothing beyond burning up the sheets, anyway. Or that's what he'd implied. Yet he now said he didn't want *another* relationship. In order for it to be *another*, there had to have been a first. Was the one he was counting theirs? "You didn't want another relationship," she repeated, mainly to make sure she heard him right.

"No, I didn't."

"Why not?" Okay, that wasn't the exact question that she wanted to ask, but it could still give her the answer she wanted.

"Because I'd recently learned I wasn't commitment material, and I wasn't in the mood to start yet another no-strings deal with no potential to go anywhere." He looked at her pointedly, and in that instant, Babette recalled that last phone conversation, the one that ended . . . whatever it was they'd had.

"You were talking about Lindy and Little Ethan, and you said that you wondered whether your kids would be anything like them." Then she'd told him he didn't have to worry about it, because having kids involved commitment, and he wasn't the commitment type.

"I was trying to get your take on having kids," he said. "Or, more accurately, your thoughts on the possibility of having mine."

Babette stumbled over a tiny ledge in the sand, or maybe she just stumbled over the jolt of what she was hearing. "My thoughts on having kids—with you? But you'd always said you didn't want any part of long-term, that what you liked about us was that there were no strings, no commitments."

"So I'd started wanting string. We began seeing each other when I was thirty-four, and I was suddenly thirty-seven, ready to grow up and move our relationship to the next level, but you didn't see things the same way I did." He continued walking, but more slowly, and he kept his attention on her face, watching her response to his statement. There was no way she could control her body language now. Her pulse thundered, her skin bristled, and her breath caught in her throat. She was surprised—no, shocked—at his sudden proclamation. She shook her head. This was so not what she'd planned to hear. "You ended things with me because I said you weren't commitment material."

"We weren't going anywhere but to bed, Babette. I wanted more." Then he paused, grinned. "Not that I minded going to bed, but there comes a time when a relationship gets more serious. I was ready for that, and you didn't see me, didn't see us, that way."

Her head was throbbing. Pounding. He'd wanted more, with her, and she'd blown him off, thinking they were just picking at each other the way they always did. In other words, she'd hurt him, terribly. And then, he'd met Kitty.

Kitty. That's what she was supposed to be talking about, his relationship with Kitty, not his relationship with Babette. She had to stay focused, or she could kiss her career—and her proof that she could commit to something—goodbye.

"If you didn't notice Kitty, then what happened?" she asked, not knowing how to make sense of it all, and not all that certain what to do about it either.

"She apparently took my lack of interest as a challenge and set about meeting me, and I know it's pretty shallow, but hell, at that time, I wanted the ego stroke. And then, as I got to know her, I really did come to care about her."

"You fell in love with her," Babette said. "After I'd turned your love away and bruised your ego doing it."

"Yeah. And then, I asked her to marry me, started foreseeing myself with Kitty for life, and she left with Sam Farraday." He smiled, but this wasn't his usual smile. This one was *bitter*.

They continued walking, both of them apparently reflecting on everything that went wrong back then, and everything that had gone still wrong now.

"I really only said that back then because I thought that's how you felt," Babette whispered.

"And because it was how you felt," he said. "You didn't see me as the kind of guy who'd be a good father."

"We'd never even talked that way, so I hadn't even

thought about it." They'd agreed that they weren't interested in long-term. She had no way of knowing that he'd changed his thoughts on the matter, or maybe she would have considered settling down before now.

Before now. Funny, now she was thinking she liked the whole commitment thing, and now Jeff wanted no part of settling down, with her or with Kitty or with anyone, from the looks of things.

"That's why you came up with this commitment proposition," she said, putting it all together. "You don't think any female can commit to anything."

"Hell, I wouldn't say it about all females. But . . ."

"But you'd say it about me."

He started to answer, but then a crowd gathering ahead of them caught his eye, as did the surfer running directly toward them.

"Hey, are you here to enter?" he asked Babette.

Babette blinked, looked past him and saw a large stage in front of the crowd, and the sign above that stage.

BIKINI CONTEST. $1000 TOP PRIZE.

"I don't think so," she said.

"Oh, come on. There's no preparation involved. You're already dressed for it. First prize is a thousand bucks, but second gets five hundred and third gets two-fifty," the guy urged. "And I bet you could work those judges too. That's more of what it takes, you know, than other stuff."

Whether he intended to or not, his attention skittered past her breasts, and Babette felt her cheeks redden. This was turning out to be a splendid day. First she'd found out that Jeff had wanted her for more than just sex last year, and that because she'd turned him down, he'd been vulnerable to a Kitty on the prowl. And now this surfer dude insulted her boobs, and she didn't need anyone reminding her that they were virtually nonexistent; and more than that, he did it in front of Jeff.

Yep, a splendid day.

"I'm not interested," she repeated, but Jeff was withdrawing a rolled up wad of cash from the waist pocket of his swimsuit.

"How much is the entry fee?"

Surfer guy's grin broadened as he checked out the cash, still damp from their romp in the waves, in Jeff's palm. "Fifty bucks."

"What are you doing?" Babette asked, watching in disbelief as Jeff forked over the money. "I'm not entering. I don't stand a chance, and I'm not in the mood to embarrass myself royally in front of a crowd."

She wasn't in the mood for much of anything at the moment. She was frustrated. Frustrated with the fact that she'd let him go last year, frustrated that she had to get him back with Kitty this year—and she did have to get him back, or she'd prove she couldn't commit, wouldn't she?—and frustrated that this surfer guy insulted her tits.

She. Was. Frustrated.

And Jeff was smiling.

"What is that look for?" she asked.

"Thanks, dude. Hey, what's your name? I'll go sign you up," the guy asked Babette.

"I'm not entering," she repeated, sternly.

"Babette Robinson," Jeff said, and continued grinning as he watched the guy jog back through the sand to the small sign-in table near the stage.

"What do you think you're doing?" she asked, glaring.

"He said he thought you looked like you could work the judges."

"He said that because he didn't think I had the 'other stuff' it took to place. And like I told him, I'm not interested."

"No, but I am. I'm interested in seeing if you can place in this contest *without* working the judges."

Realization dawned. "I'd have to flirt to place," she hissed, mad now. He was also insinuating that she couldn't win this thing without flirting, because she didn't have the "other stuff" required. "And if I flirted, I'd lose your challenge, and you wouldn't talk to Kitty." And he'd believe, once again, that she couldn't commit.

He didn't answer, but simply stood there, turquoise eyes examining her every move, every breath. And damn it, she felt desire stir even now, when she wanted to pummel him.

"You said you wanted to see if I can place," she said, anger driving her forward as she formulated her own plan. "What if I do better?"

One corner of his mouth crooked up. "Do better?"

"What do I get if I win, without flirting?"

His eyes sparkled. "As long as it has nothing to do with Kitty, you can have whatever you want."

Whatever she wanted. That caused her to pause for a moment, made her almost blurt out the first thing she thought, which was that she wanted him, now. But that was ridiculous. He was trying to bait her, make her lose his challenge and prove that she couldn't commit. Wasn't going to happen.

"Do you have plans tomorrow night?"

He blinked, and she knew she'd caught him off guard. Good. "Tomorrow night?"

"Yes. Do you have plans?"

He tilted his head as though thinking, then answered, "Actually, I do, but—"

"Cancel them."

Those blue eyes widened. "Why would I want to do that?"

"Because if I win—no, *when* I win—I want a full day's reprieve from your little flirt challenges. And then tomorrow night, I want you to come to my condo."

"Come to your condo and what?"

"You'll see. So cancel your plans."

"You haven't won yet, Babette."

"No," she said, turning and slinging her hair as she strode toward the stage. "But I will."

# Chapter 15

Jeff watched Babette near the stage and then saw them pin the number 34 to the tiny bikini string at her right hip. While she wasn't paying attention to him, he shot a look at the bleach-blond surfer guy who'd had the nerve to insult her boobs. Jeff had wanted to deck the guy, but when he'd seen how frazzled Babette was by his remark, he'd thought of a better way to handle the situation. Let Babette show the guy that she had plenty of "other stuff."

Jeff grinned. Hell, he'd been so pleased with his idea, and even more with the way Babette bought into it, determined to show both him and the blond fool that she could win this thing. And Jeff had no doubt she would.

He worked his way through the crowd until he stood behind the three men judging the event, and he was using the term "men" loosely. All three were college-age, twenty-two tops.

He scanned the women in line for the competition. Babette was probably the oldest female in the lot, a fact that he assumed she recognized, given the way she'd leaned out a bit to scan the other women.

The surfer guy jogged to the center of the stage to pump up the crowd and announce how the contest would work. Basically, the girls would make two passes, a first pass, and then another one set to music. The audience could convey their opinion by applause, and the three guys sitting at the table would decide the winner.

Jeff had two reasons for issuing this challenge to Babette. One, he knew she could win, and two, he knew that she'd always thought her body a bit inferior due to her small breasts. But he also knew that she was beautiful, and perfect, and that these three guys, and the crowd for that matter, would see that, and maybe finally show Babette that she had nothing, nothing at all, to feel inferior about.

Surfer guy called out number one, and the first contestant, a teen who looked like she'd already had a couple of "selective surgeries," pranced across the stage like a prize show horse. She wore a white one-piece that was little more than strategically placed dental floss and red stilettos. The crowd went wild, and so did the three judges.

Jeff leaned forward, trying to glimpse what they'd written on their judging pads, but he couldn't see a thing for all the other people crowded around them.

The remaining women followed suit after the first one, strutting their stuff across the stage, blowing kisses to the crowd and doing shimmy moves that were quite impressive toward the judges. Of course, the impressive part was that they could keep their massive boobs within flimsy material when they were shaking them to high heaven.

Then number 30 came out. She was older than the college kids but younger than Babette, and she wore one of those Texas flag bikinis that always got Jeff's attention on the beach, and the attention of every other red-blooded male, judging by the way the shouts of the crowd suddenly escalated, and every judge leaned forward.

"Damn," Jeff muttered, glancing toward the side stage and toward Babette, who was suddenly looking a bit worried.

Texas Flag didn't exactly strut; she sauntered. And she wasn't blond, as most of the other contestants were, but she had long, straight brunette hair that reminded Jeff of Demi Moore's. As a matter of fact, she had that Demi Moore look. Or maybe it was more Penelope Cruz. Or Eva Mendes. Jeff didn't know, but the woman had that something that stood out, and obviously, everyone noticed.

Jeff swallowed hard, and suddenly regretted the fact that he wasn't allowing Babette to flirt. Flirting, she'd beat Miss Texas hands down. But without flirting, he wasn't so sure. And damn it, he didn't want her embarrassed. He didn't want her to lose.

The next three contestants passed without much fanfare, and then the only redhead in the bunch, consequently the last contestant, stepped onto the stage.

Unlike the majority of the other contestants, Babette wasn't wearing stilettos, or anything else on her feet, which made her suddenly seem smaller, or younger, or something. Her hair had that beach-mussed look, all wild and red, curls that toppled down her back like a fountain of fire.

Her tiny green bikini caught the sunlight and shimmered as she moved toward the center of the stage and stopped in front of the judges. Every other contestant had smiled, winked, blown kisses or shimmied to gain their attention.

Babette didn't. In fact, she looked at them as though she didn't want anything to do with them, as though they weren't worthy of her smile, or of her touch. It was a brooding, sultry look that was only heightened when she put one hand to the strap at her shoulder, fiddled with it as though she were attempting to flash a breast, then shook her head, turned, and stalked off stage.

Jeff's cock twitched. He wanted her. Now. And from the screams and caveman grunts of every male in the audience, so did every other guy.

Surfer guy reappeared on the stage, and he released a low whistle into the microphone toward Babette. "Have mercy, have we got a competition or what?" he asked. "Now tell me if you like what you see!"

The crowd went ballistic, and more people from the beach ran toward the commotion to get in on the fun. Jeff turned, saw that he couldn't even see where the crowd ended anymore, since the back rows were now composed of people sitting on other's shoulders to catch the show.

To catch Babette's show.

Surfer guy announced that the contestants would cross once more, this time to music, and then the judges would make their decision. He also encouraged the girls to "Work it, and work it good!"

Jeff watched as contestant after contestant danced her way across the stage, with three of them displaying their boobs as a part of their act. But he already suspected that the judges had seen the same thing he had in round one. There was Miss Texas and there was Red. No one else even hit the radar, whether they displayed their breasts or not. So Jeff waited, and then held his breath when number 30 was called.

The brunette's song was, predictably, "God Bless Texas." Evidently, she'd taken note of the response Babette got on the first pass, because she didn't flirt with the judges; she tempted them. She pranced toward them, leaned over as though preparing to offer them their own peek show into her top, and then turned, slinging silky brown hair behind her as she danced. She waited for the song to hit those last three beats, to which she pumped her hips from side to side and then let the crowd sing the last three words.

*Boom, boom, boom . . .* God Bless Texas!

This was it. Miss Texas had given it her best shot, and it was a pretty good one, but Jeff had no doubt it wasn't good enough. He watched Babette exit the line, go over to the surfer dude and ask him a question. He smiled broadly, nodded, and then started swapping the CDs in the lineup. Then she moved back to the line and turned her head away from the crowd while the next three contestants did their dances.

Jeff didn't watch any of them; his attention was on Babette, her body slightly swaying as she apparently got ready for her turn. He couldn't wait to see what song she'd selected, and how she planned to work the crowd this time.

Finally, surfer dude announced number 34, and "Cyclone" by Baby Bash boomed from the speakers on the stage. Jeff, of course, had seen the sizzling strip club video that went along with the song.

Evidently, so had Babette.

In striptease fashion, she moved seductively across the stage, stopped in the center, and proceeded to dance to the steamy lyrics. But this was no ordinary dance. She paid no attention to the crowd, obvious by her closed eyes and the way her body moved, swaying similarly to those lap dancers in the video, as though she weren't moving, but flowing. Her hands moved up her side, skimmed over her breasts and then continued along her jaw, her mouth slightly open as she tunneled her fingers through her hair and lifted the heavy mass from her tiny frame.

Her hips undulated in complete harmony to the melody, which steadily built and escalated in the same rhythm as sex. Or that's the way it seemed to Jeff. And to every other guy panting in the audience. Jeff had no doubt that they were all wishing they could "do it all night long" with Babette, just like the lyrics stated. But when the song ended, she exited the stage, and they were all left wanting her.

The same way Jeff wanted her.

"Damn, anybody got her number?" some guy asked beside Jeff.

Jeff didn't bother turning to see who'd asked; there were too many guys asking, anyway. They were all talking and gawking and leering, and Jeff was suddenly fuming. He'd thought this was a great idea, but standing here with a mob of men who'd like nothing better than to get their hands on Babette wasn't the way he pictured this little challenge ending.

Thankfully, surfer guy finally made his way back up on stage and announced the judges had selected the winners. He started with third place, the blond with the one-piece dental floss number. Then he announced second place.

Jeff, and everyone else, from the sound of things, wasn't surprised when he announced Miss Texas.

"And our winner is," he said loudly, his voice bellowing through the speakers now, "Contestant thirty-four!"

Babette smiled broadly, and blushed slightly, as she took the stage and accepted her check. The crowd yelled and cheered, and she graciously nodded her appreciation.

After everything finally died down, the event ended, and Jeff moved to the side of the stage, where she was completely surrounded by adoring, and apparently horny, males.

"Thank you," she repeated again and again, while Jeff worked his way through the pack, took her hand, and stated, "We're leaving now."

Babette was still smiling when they neared White Sands, and Jeff was merely enjoying listening to her chat about her victory.

"I told you I'd win," she said again, for about the tenth time, as they made their way toward the back of their resort.

"Yes, you did, and you were right."

She stopped walking.

"What?" he asked.

"You knew I would, didn't you? And without flirting."

He grinned. "Yeah, I did, though I'll admit that Miss Lone Star gave you a decent run for the money."

She smirked at that. "Why? Why did you think I'd win, especially when I'm not built like the typical bikini contest winner?"

He'd had enough. He'd thought winning that contest would show her she had everything every other woman had and then some, but she was still dwelling on what she considered her main negative aspect. And he wasn't listening to it anymore. It was time she understood, and he was going to set the record straight.

"Babette, I've told you before, and I'm telling you again, your body is perfect."

Her head had already started shaking to disagree, and she opened her mouth to argue, but then she looked at him, and apparently she saw that this wasn't the time to disagree. He wasn't backing down.

"There's nothing—nothing—wrong with you. I wouldn't change a thing. You're natural, and you're exceptional. And it goes way beyond how well you fill out your top. You mesmerized every guy there the minute you walked on that stage, and I can guarantee you that if they weren't all at least marginally hard just looking at you, then they don't belong in the male gender."

She gaped at that, but he was on a roll, and he wasn't ready to stop.

"I won't listen to you put yourself down again. You're what every guy there wants, and while they only wanted in your pants, or your bikini, as the case may be, if they had a chance to get to know that the fire extends beyond the surface, then they'd want even more than a romp in the sack. That's what happens when I—when guys—get to know you. They want more." He could tell he'd said too much, because her head tilted slightly, and her eyes glistened, just a bit, but he noticed. He swallowed. "Just don't let me ever hear you put yourself down again. Understood?"

She nodded.

"Babette! Yoohoo! Are you ready for your cooking lesson now?" Rose's shrill squeal stood out among the other sounds on the beach, and they both turned toward Rose and her friends, perched on the Sunny Beaches deck. "Are you ready?" she repeated.

"Yes," Babette answered, her voice a little shaky. Then she turned to Jeff and said, "Don't forget to cancel your plans for tomorrow night. That was the deal. And come to my condo, around seven. I have something to show you."

He really didn't want to wait until tomorrow night to continue whatever they'd touched on now, whatever had transpired between them this afternoon with the walk on the beach and the contest and his sudden blurt of honesty now, but Rose and her crew were already climbing down the deck stairs and heading toward White Sands.

"Deal?" Babette repeated.

"Wouldn't want to miss anything you have to show me, Babette. Deal."

# Chapter 16

Gertrude Robinson was frustrated beyond measure. She and Paul had been through this course four days in a row, and her patience was running thin. The only answer Henry seemed to give her was the one telling her to keep asking questions.

It simply made no sense.

She glanced down at her pink shoes, and then at the pink golf ball that Paul had bought her, for good luck. He'd also bought her some pink golf gloves, which she was very thankful for; she'd started to get a couple of blisters after the second day. Today, she'd decided that perhaps Paul was right; maybe she needed more pink. Pink did make her feel better, after all, so she'd bought a new collared shirt, pink, of course, and a new pink and white skirt. Even so, it wasn't lucky enough, because Henry was being particularly stubborn, which simply wasn't like the Henry she knew.

"You okay, Gertrude? It's your turn," Paul said, as they neared hole sixteen.

"Yes, I'm fine," she said, putting her ball on one of the notches and hitting it without any real care where it went. The little pink thing popped completely out of the lane and ended up on the green for hole fifteen.

Chuckling, Paul retrieved it, came back to Gertrude, and held it out for her. "Wanna talk about it?"

She felt her lower lip quiver. "I'm so dispirited that I forgot to ask a question."

His chest rose steadily as he took a deep breath, quirked his mouth to the side, and then let it out. "Gert."

"What?"

"I think it's time you tell me what we're doing here, don't you?"

She blinked. "What we're doing?"

"Come over here." He took the pink ball from her left hand, the putter from her right, then he indicated a wooden bench off to the side of hole sixteen.

Too spent to argue, she walked beside him and sat down.

"You're asking questions?"

She nodded, suddenly realizing the error of her statement only moments before. Paul hadn't known she was trying to talk to Henry; he was simply being the good friend that he was and playing golf with her, every day, at any time she wanted. She shouldn't be upset when she had someone so nice who was willing to do all of that and without even questioning why. "I'm sorry," she said, but she didn't know what to say she was sorry for.

"So, what's he saying?" Paul asked.

Gert's eyes widened to the point of pain. "What?"

"Come on, Gertrude. We've been friends way too long for you to be able to pull one over on me, even if I haven't

seen you in a few years. You're talking to Henry, aren't
you?"

She fought for composure. "What makes you say that?
How on earth would I talk to Henry? We both know he's
gone."

"We both know he's here," Paul stated flatly.

There went her eyes again. "What—what are you saying, Paul?"

"During the times when Henry and I came to golf on
our own, without you and Emily with us, we talked about
*things*."

"What sorts of things?" she asked, keeping her voice
as steady as possible, given the subject matter.

"He'd talk about how lucky he was to have you, and
I'd talk about how lucky I was to have Emily, of course.
We were both very fortunate to find a lasting love, the
way we both did, and we knew the value of it. You completed Henry the way Emily completed me." His blue-
gray eyes focused on her as he spoke. "It's not common
to find someone you're so close to, the way we were each
so close to our wives, the way that Henry and I were as
close as brothers, and the way the four of us bonded the
way we did."

Gertrude nodded. They *had* all been very close, which
was why she and Paul had reconnected so easily. Some
bonds were like that, you left off at a spot in the past, but
then later on, you picked right back up where you'd left
off. Those were the best kinds of relationships, in Gert's
book. The ones that stood the test of time.

"So one day back then, he and I were on the course,
and it was an incredible day. The sun was shining, but
it wasn't too hot to stay out for a round of eighteen, and

there was a nice breeze, that time of year, you know, when Spring is in the air."

"My favorite time of year," she whispered.

"Henry said that he knew this golf course was the closest to Heaven on earth that he could get."

"That's what he said," she agreed, remembering how much Henry loved it here.

"And then he told me about a promise."

Gert's chest tightened. "Promise?"

"One that he asked you to keep, if he should go on before you."

She blinked, looked at the ground, at her pink shoes, at anything but Paul. He'd know. If she looked at him, he'd simply know.

If he didn't know already.

"Henry's here, isn't he, Gert?"

She remembered the very day, sitting in the golf cart beside Henry, when he parked beneath some of the trees on the course and looked at her, then told her what he wanted. She'd not wanted to talk about it, didn't want to think of being without him, and certainly didn't want to discuss what he wanted to happen after he was gone.

But Henry wasn't budging. He was stubborn, but in a good way, always resolute when it came to getting what he wanted. Looking back, she wasn't the only one in the marriage with gumption.

On that day, he'd asked her to promise him that if he died before her, that she would bring him here, to the golf course, and let his body remain where he was happiest on earth, while his spirit soared above it. She'd known the owners of the course would never have agreed. Or they might have, but if she'd asked, and then they'd said no, what would she do?

It'd been late, late at night when she'd come to the course with the ornate urn that held her beloved Henry. She'd cried like a baby, weeping madly, as she edged her way through the darkness and fulfilled her promise.

"You're asking Henry questions?" Paul asked again.

"I am."

He put an arm around her. "Has he answered you?"

She worked her mouth into a smile and looked into those caring blue-gray eyes. Paul had been her rock over the past few days, and he hadn't even realized it.

Or had he?

He was looking at her now as though he knew every emotion tearing her apart.

"He just keeps telling me to ask more questions," Gertrude said. "Keeps telling me to come back, but he doesn't answer the real questions I'm asking."

"What is it you're wanting him to tell you?" Paul asked, every ounce of sincerity in his tone. He believed her, and he didn't think she was ridiculous for trying to get approval from Henry.

"I had heard about an old friend from high school, now living in Tuscaloosa."

"A man?" Paul's voice changed slightly, but Gert couldn't define the difference.

"Yes. I asked Babette to help me find his information, his phone number, address, and all, and then I thought about trying to see him again. We'd talked at the reunions, a bit, and I thought—well, I thought it might be nice to try to reconnect."

Paul nodded, but didn't say anything.

"But I wanted to make sure that Henry was okay with it, you know." She sounded so pitiful. This wasn't her usual, confident self, the image she portrayed for the world. But this was Paul, and she could let her guard down with him. He knew her, and he cared. She could tell that now, as his arm tenderly squeezed her as she spoke. And it was so nice to share this with someone who believed her, and who understood.

"But Henry hasn't said it's okay?" Paul asked.

"No."

They sat there silent for a moment, then Paul cleared his throat and sat forward a bit, making Gert turn her head to look at his face.

"What?" she asked.

"You're thinking about seeing someone again, right, Gert? Wondering if it'd be okay with Henry if you did?"

She nodded, feeling rather miserable that she'd allowed her loneliness to bring her to this state, but very glad that Paul was with her through the endeavor.

He cleared his throat again, swallowed. "Gert."

"Yes?"

"I'm going to say something that may make you uncomfortable, but if I don't say it now, I may not ever find the right time, or the nerve, to say it again."

"What is it?"

"Maybe Henry hasn't said yes because you're asking him about the wrong guy."

Those blue-gray eyes were intense now, and she suddenly realized that they were looking at her, not just as a friendly kind of *I understand* look, but really looking at her.

"Paul." She didn't know what else to say. Paul? Paul

thought of her that way? And then again, why wouldn't he? They already knew each other; there wasn't that need to reconnect between the two of them. They knew each other, knew their histories, knew their pasts. And they both understood that each of them had been blessed to have had love, a strong and lasting love, once in their lives already.

Could they find it a second time? Together? And would Henry want her to give that possibility a try?

"Gert."

"Yes?"

"Ask Henry."

She blinked, swallowed, looked back at hole sixteen, merely a few feet away. "What if he says no?"

"What do you want him to say?" Paul asked, and suddenly, his arm around her felt more warm, more intense, more right.

"I want him to say yes," she said, and at once, the pieces fell into place. Paul. She'd come to the course to have Henry help her find someone that she could share her life with, and he'd shown her Paul.

Could it be that she'd had the man she truly needed right here, all along?

"Ask him," Paul repeated.

She stood and took the putter from where he'd propped it against the side of the bench. Then he held out the pink ball and she took it.

Three steps and she was at the rubber square at the beginning of the lane. She bent, put the ball on the middle notch, then stood and looked at Paul. Paul, who had been here all along, and who knew her better than any man in the world, except Henry.

*Henry, this is it. Let me know. A hole in one says that Paul and I should . . . see where this goes.*

She brought the putter back, then forward, and hit the pretty pink ball. Maybe because of nerves, or maybe because of adrenaline, she hit it harder than she intended. And toward the wrong side. She shook her head as it banked off the left. She wasn't meant to be with Paul either. She wasn't meant to be with anyone. And she was okay with that, she supposed, although now she had to admit that she'd really enjoyed the last few days, on the golf course, visiting, chatting and golfing with Paul.

But the ball was moving every which way but toward the hole.

"Gert," he said, and she turned her attention from the maddening, non-stopping ball to see Paul, standing near her. "I want more, if you do."

She blinked. What if Henry didn't want her to have more, with anyone? Even Paul?

"Do you?" he repeated, and she fought the urge to turn around and see where the ball had finally landed.

"Do you?" he asked again, and heaven help her, she knew the answer.

"I do." She dropped the putter and stepped toward him, then melted into arms that had held her before in friendship, but now that held her with something more. And it felt . . . right.

"Gertrude," he said, and he leaned back to look at her.

"Yes, Paul?"

"I'd like to kiss you now."

Her heart thundered so loudly she could hear it in her ears, and the exhilaration of his statement made her a tad lightheaded, but not too lightheaded to answer. "I'd like that too."

His kiss was soft, tender, experimental, testing the waters of moving past friendship. And it was a very sweet, amazing, wonderfully satisfying kiss.

He looked at her. "Okay?"

She nodded, tears in her eyes. "Yes, definitely okay."

"Gert," he said softly.

"Yes?"

"The ball went in."

# Chapter 17

Jeff sat on his balcony, laptop open and hands resting on the keyboard. He'd spent another day unable to concentrate on work because he kept seeing Babette, dancing like a high-dollar stripper on that stage. And then, the image that had his emotions in an even bigger uproar: Babette, her eyes glistening when he told her the truth, that any man lucky enough to really get to know her . . . only wanted more.

He'd had plans tonight, another attempt at a date with Kylie, but he'd already planned to break that engagement even before Babette demanded that he cancel tonight's plans and come to her condo. He watched another crowd of women heading over from Sunny Beaches with all their cooking wares. He'd called Babette earlier and asked what time he should arrive, and she'd said that "everything would begin around seven." Then, for some bizarre reason, she'd asked him to wait until eight. Now he realized that whatever "everything" was, it involved the seniors.

He grinned. How stupid had he been to think that she was inviting him down for a little one-on-one time? She'd pledged her duty to her job, and therefore to Kitty, and she wasn't budging. Jeff couldn't decide if he was glad that she had found the ability to commit, or if he wanted to toss it out the window and let them explore what would happen if they got that one-on-one time. No, he didn't want time to talk about Kitty, but he did want to spend more time with Babette.

The seniors were heading over in droves now, with seven o'clock nearing. He was amazed; it was Friday night and she was spending it with the seniors. She was certainly not the Babette he knew from way back when. But there were a lot of things about Babette now that were different from when they'd been together before. She was right about her new commitment ethic; she had been successful at keeping one job for a while. She'd also survived his volleyball flirt challenge yesterday without so much as a whistle. Definitely not something the Babette of the past could've done. And he couldn't forget that she'd been successful in that bikini contest, even bringing home the thousand-dollar prize.

Another group of seniors in a small huddle crossed the pathway from Sunny Beaches to White Sands, and Jeff noticed that this group was primarily male. His curiosity piqued, he powered down the computer and shut the laptop.

Then he left the balcony, put the laptop back in his computer case, and went to take a shower and change clothes. He'd noticed all the seniors were dressed up, and he didn't want to stand out too much in his T-shirt and shorts.

An hour later, he was knocking on Babette's door and dressed for whatever function was loud enough to resonate down the hall.

He knocked again, but knew with all that noise, music, laughing, and talking, no one would hear him. So he grabbed the knob and turned. The door opened, and he entered.

The walls practically vibrated with swing music, and Babette had pushed all of her furniture to one side to expose a makeshift dance floor. Two silver-crowned couples were using it, and they were damn good.

Jeff attempted to control his jaw, but the lone redhead in the group had already seen him. Babette waved, then crossed the room, distributing polite "excuse me's" and "pardon me's" as she passed through the exuberant crowd.

"Hey," she said, breathless, and Jeff saw that she was carrying a white tray filled with hors d'oeuvres.

"Look," she said. "I made them myself. Well, Rose, Tillie and Hannah helped. They haven't given me free rein in the kitchen yet, but I'm getting closer." She smiled as Jeff took one of the tiny tarts and popped it into his mouth. "Mini quiches," she said, her dark eyes watching as he chewed.

"It's very good," he said, shocked.

She used her free hand to poke him in the chest. "Don't be so surprised." Then she laughed. "But to tell the truth, this was the fourth batch. I had way too much salt in the first one, and the next two burned to a crisp, because we got to chatting." She was nearly screaming, since the music and chatter were so loud. "You better shut the door, so I don't get in trouble with the neighbors," she instructed, and he did.

"What is this?" Jeff asked, and realized that the female portions of the two couples dancing were two of the ladies he'd met the other day.

"They're good, aren't they?" Babette said, noticing where his attention had landed. "I had no idea Tillie and Hannah could dance like that, and I don't think the guys knew either. You should've seen how excited they were when I told them we were having a mixer."

"A mixer," he repeated and couldn't hold back his smile. Leave it to Babette to convert the resort into a fraternity house for seniors.

"They talked to the owners at Sunny Beaches about having them weekly, at the toddy bar."

"The toddy bar."

"Their pool bar," Babette corrected loudly, since the music had kicked up a notch, or twenty.

"Jeff!" Rose scooted through the crowd dragging a tall man who appeared a little younger than she, but not by much. He had charcoal hair and a weathered face, and he appeared to be having a really good time, smiling from ear to ear as he stuck out his hand toward Jeff.

Jeff accepted the hand and shook it, while Rose scurried through introductions. "Jeff, this is Otis; Otis, this is Jeff."

"Nice to meet you," Otis said, and Jeff reciprocated, while Rose beamed at her new man. "You're the one she spies on," Otis started, and Rose promptly pinched his arm.

"Otis!"

"I just wanted to let him know that I'm going to try to

keep your attention enough that you won't have to pass your time in the spy cubby."

Her scowl turned into an embarrassed flush. "Oh," she said, so lightly that Jeff couldn't hear her over the music, but her lips and her expression gave it away. She was surprised, and captivated.

"Care to dance?" Otis asked his lady.

"I don't, I can't . . ." Rose stammered.

"No problem. I'll teach." Otis nodded his goodbye to Babette and Jeff, then ushered Rose through the crowd and toward the makeshift dance floor, where Tillie and her fellow were doing some sort of twirling thing that seemed a little out of control, judging from the way the elderly spectators surrounding them started backing up.

"Oh, I hope they don't fall." Babette watched until the two slowed down and apparently got their bearings. "I guess I should've probably at least learned where the nearest hospital was before I decided to have this thing."

Jeff laughed. "A mixer for seniors. Who'd have thought?"

"Well, the Love Doctor, of course."

"Still getting paid with cooking lessons?"

She held up the tray filled with quiches again, and he took another. "What do you think?"

He grinned. "You're really good at this Love Doctor thing, aren't you?"

She opened her mouth, then closed it.

"What?" he asked.

"I suppose if I'm really good, then you'll be talking to Kitty in a few days." She waited, as though wanting him to say something, then she frowned.

"Babette!" one of the seniors called, and she turned.

"Wait." His word was more of a command than that of the other person merely screaming her name, and she pivoted, her eyes focused on him.

"What?"

The words, the possibilities of what was the right thing to say, what was the wrong thing to say, tripped across his brain with the rapid beats of the music. And none of them came out.

"What is it?" she repeated, then she jumped slightly and glanced at her hip. "Oh, hold this." She handed him the tray and fished her cell phone out of her pocket. "Hello?"

She gave Jeff a knowing nod, and something about it told him he knew exactly who was on the other end of that phone.

"Yes, Kitty, everything is going great. Yeah, I'm at a party." She covered her other ear when the music picked back up so she could hear what Kitty was saying, and then she said, "Actually, that's why I'm at the party; he is here. And yes, we *were* just talking about you."

Jeff wanted to hit something. He put the tray on a table nearby. No way was he going to stand here and listen to the woman he wanted tell the one he didn't that she was totally willing to deliver him to her on a silver platter. Wasn't going to happen anyway. If Babette managed to keep from flirting for the remainder of the time, which he had to admit now she might, then he'd talk to Kitty. He'd keep his word. But talking was it. And then he'd send her on her way, just like Babette would head on her way in five days, without looking back. She may be committed, but to her job, not him, which meant she was also committed to getting him back with Kitty.

"You want to talk to him?" Babette said into the phone.

"Sorry, I'm leaving." He turned, exited, and didn't worry when the sound of the slamming door overpowered the music. He had to do something about this Kitty situation, and he was going to put that in motion right now. And he wouldn't converse via a Dear John, the way she had. He'd do it in person, face to face. So yes, he would talk to Kitty when he had to, but it certainly wouldn't be the conversation she wanted.

Babette should've been on cloud nine as she cleaned up after the party. There were five new elderly couples at Sunny Beaches, and they'd all gotten together courtesy of the Love Doctor. Meanwhile, she now knew how to make four different meals, spaghetti with meatballs, chicken fettuccine, beef stew and seven-layer casserole. Granted, they were all kind of old-fashioned meals and nothing that would give her Rachael Ray status, but they were edible. She hadn't made any of them on her own yet, but she truly thought she could. Granny Gert had sounded so excited when Babette told her how much she'd learned already, and how much she was looking forward to Granny Gert helping her learn to cook even more meals when she returned home. When Babette asked about Rowdy, Granny had said that things hadn't worked out as planned, and that she would explain later. That would've concerned Babette, but Granny had sounded so happy, ecstatic even, that she didn't question it. If things hadn't worked out, it sure hadn't seemed to bother her, and as she said, she'd explain everything to Babette when she returned home to Birmingham.

She swallowed. Returning home meant leaving all of her friends at Sunny Beaches, and it meant leaving Jeff. Fortunately, all of her time spent with the seniors today had kept her mind off him and off all the feelings he'd brought to the surface during their walk on the beach yesterday. But then he'd shown up at the party, and they'd all come crashing back over her, a tidal wave of emotion. She thought she'd held it all together pretty well, even keeping an upbeat tone when she talked to Kitty. But then Jeff had stormed out, and she'd known that she'd evidently messed up, again.

Her cell phone rang, and she glanced at the caller ID. Amazingly, it wasn't Kitty. She grinned at the name on display and answered. "Hey, Granny. You're up late, aren't you?"

"Ten o'clock," Granny said. "And I couldn't sleep. I had you on my mind, so I decided to call."

"I'm fine," Babette lied.

"No, you're not. I heard it this afternoon when I called, and I hear it even more now. And I'm afraid I was so wrapped up in everything here that I didn't pick up on it until I wound down for the night and started pondering my day. Honey, what happened?"

Babette should've known Granny would be able to tell she was upset. And unfortunately, hearing Granny Gert ask brought it to the surface. Tears leaked free, and all the thoughts and feelings she'd been fighting all day pushed forward. "Oh, Granny, I finally found out why Jeff never called me back last year, and why he got so hooked on Kitty so fast, and why he doesn't trust any women to commit now," she blurted. "He wanted more from me back then, and I was too stupid to realize it. And then he wanted more with Kitty, and she was even more stupid, knowing he wanted her and leaving him. Now he's not willing to give anyone another chance."

Granny was quiet for a moment, then she said, "You're not talking about him giving Kitty another chance, are you? You want him for yourself."

Babette swiped at her tears. "I don't know. I mean, yes, I do know. I want him, but not the way we were back then. I want more, I want what he wanted when we ended things. But he doesn't think I can commit to anything, and he doesn't want a woman who can't commit."

"Oh, honey, then you just need to prove to him that you can," Granny soothed.

"But that's just it. The one thing he says that he can tell I'm committed to is my job. He's been impressed with that," she said, sniffing through her words. "But if I'm truly committed to my job, then I have to try and get him and Kitty back together. And if I tell him I still want him, then he'll have proof that I can't commit."

"Babette, a job isn't anywhere near the same as love," Granny said, as a loud knock echoed on Babette's door.

"I've got to let you go," Babette said, quickly drying her tears. That knock sounded very masculine, very Jeff.

She said goodbye to Granny Gert, snapped the phone closed and dropped it on the table. Then she wiped her face again and checked it in the mirror before finally heading toward the door. She opened it, but unfortunately couldn't control the disappointment when she found Otis and Rose on the other side. More tears dripped free.

"Have mercy, what happened after we left?" Rose asked, peering past her as though she'd find the source of Babette's splotchy, wet face.

"Rose forgot her shawl, and I didn't want her to walk back this late by herself," Otis said, moving past the two women to search for the shawl, and probably just wanting to put some distance between himself and the weepy female.

"I don't know what's wrong with me," Babette said. "The party went great, and I should be very happy."

"Your man left in the middle of it," Rose said. "Why should you be happy about that?"

"He's not my man."

"And there's your problem. Honey, you're so good at fixing everybody else up, mending old fences, and all of that, but you're damn clueless about fixing your own."

Otis's head jerked toward them at Rose's colorful language.

"Well, it's true," she said toward him, then she turned back to Babette. "Okay, let's pretend I'm the Love Doctor and you're the client, just for fun."

Babette gave her a watery smile. Rose really was trying to help.

"Now, I get what you're saying about showing him you can commit to something, in your case, your job."

"It's the first thing I've ever been committed to, and if I blow it, then to him, I haven't changed."

"And you want him to see that you've changed."

Babette nodded. "Which means I've got to go through with getting him back with Kitty."

"You do realize, child, that even if he talks to Kitty, which he probably will, since you're batting a thousand on that no-flirting thing, that doesn't mean he'll take her back."

Babette knew that, but she was trying to take this pro-

cess one step at a time, and she'd never had a Love Doctor
assignment when the two parties didn't mend fences once
they got together and talked things out. Of course, she'd
never had one where she couldn't read the guy's body
language either.

"So, let's say you go through with your no-flirting thing,
and he talks to her, but there's no connection anymore.
There's no love left, and he tells the poodle to vamoose.
Then, in my book, you've done your part, attempting to
get them together. He chose not to get together with her,
which means he's still available for you. And you never
lost the commitment battle, because you remained committed to the job until they talked."

Babette was drawn to the intensity of Rose's pale blue
eyes, and then Rose lowered her voice and leaned closer,
as though she was back in the world of elderly espionage
and delivering her young protégé's first assignment.

"And then, here's what you'll do. You'll tell him that
you've proven that you've been committed to the job,
and now, you're going to prove you can be committed
to him, if he'll give you another chance. Then you beg
him for that chance, if necessary, but you get it. And you
get—your—man."

"I don't know everything she's telling you, but from
the sound of her voice, I'd say you should listen to her,"
Otis said, grinning as he moved toward Rose with her pale
pink shawl in his hand.

"She should listen to me," Rose said, turning while he
draped her with the shawl. "You will, won't you?"

Babette couldn't deny that it sounded like a decent
plan. True, her record wouldn't be a hundred percent

anymore, but she'd have done her part toward getting them back together.

The thought of that last student loan niggled her brain, but Babette no longer cared. It'd take a while longer to pay the thing off, but if that's what it took, that's what it took. If Jeff would give their relationship another chance, give Babette another chance to show him she could stick to something long-term, then it'd be worth it.

*Kitty will ruin you in Birmingham if you don't pull this off*, her mind whispered.

Babette thought of Jeff, thought of how much she wanted to be the woman in his world, for life. And then she realized, if Kitty halted her progress in Birmingham, well, there were other cities that could use Love Doctors too. Destin, for one. She glanced at Otis and Rose, not the typical Love Doctor clients, since they hadn't needed a fence mended; they'd merely needed a nudge in the right direction. But she had helped them tonight, and she'd helped several other elderly couples too.

"Babette?" Rose questioned.

"Yeah?"

"What do you think of that? My idea?"

Babette grinned. "I'm thinking you're a perfect candidate for a love doctor, Rose."

Rose beamed. "Perfect. Then everything's settled here." She looked at Otis. "My work is done. Ready to go back?"

"Sure," Otis said, then he inhaled thickly and glanced toward the kitchen. "You still cooking something?"

Babette had nearly forgotten. "I'm giving Hannah's cinnamon roll recipe a shot. That's the dough in the bread maker."

Rose's eyes went wide. "You're trying them on your own? Want me to stay?"

"No, I wrote everything down and watched her do it, so I'm good to go. Besides, you can't stand over my shoulder every time I'm in the kitchen. The whole point is for me to learn how to do it on my own."

"Okay, but if you need me, call me, even if it's late. Cinnamon rolls can be kind of tricky."

Babette couldn't fathom how, since she'd watched Hannah simply follow the recipe and then they'd turned out great, but she agreed.

Rose hugged her. "We'll check on you in the morning and see how your cinnamon rolls turn out."

A solid, rapping knock echoed from Babette's door. "You expecting company?" Rose asked.

"No," Babette whispered, but she had a strong suspicion that she knew who was on the other side of the door this time.

The knock continued.

Rose smiled. "Maybe you should go let him in." Then she and Otis walked behind her to the door, and Babette opened it to find that this time, it was exactly who she'd hoped it'd be.

"Hello, Jeff," Rose said, easing past him with Otis at her heels.

"We came back for Rose's shawl," Otis explained to Jeff as they left.

Then they were gone, and she was left standing there alone with the guy who had dominated her thoughts all day. No, he'd dominated them for a large portion of the last four years, the three they were together and the one that they were apart. Why she ever thought she could

convince him to be with someone else was beyond
her. She didn't want him with Kitty; she wanted him
with her.

But first, she had to prove to him that she had changed,
that she could commit. Just a few more days. Then she'd
follow Rose's advice, and go for the man she wanted.
She moistened her lips, and took him all in, the guy who
understood her better than anyone, who had the ability
to make her laugh and to make her dream. Dream about
being with him for something long-term, more than what
they'd had before, much more. A guy who'd, at one point,
considered her as the woman to be with him forever.

If he'd consider that again, she wouldn't bat an eye.
She was ready.

"Babette, can I come in? I need to talk to you."

"Oh," she gasped, realizing that he was still in the
doorway, and that she was gawking. "Sorry, yes. Come
on in."

He stepped inside, and Babette caught herself leaning
toward him, breathing in the scent of him, all male and
perfect. And she recognized that, thanks to Rose, she now
had a new dilemma. Now that she'd made the decision to
let him know how she felt and to attempt to get him back,
she was yearning to get started on the process. Right here,
right now. But proving herself to him, proving her ability to commit to him, meant maintaining her distance, for
five more days.

Unaware of her inner struggle, Jeff crossed the room
and sat on one end of the couch. Babette followed, sitting
on the other end and trying to act casual, as though she
wasn't on the brink of losing control of the temptation of
having him here, with her, alone in her condo.

"First, I want to apologize for leaving like I did earlier." He put one arm on the back of the couch, and her attention was drawn to the long, tan fingers resting so near her head, and her mouth. A powerful urge to kiss each finger, and then his palm, and then . . .

"I shouldn't have lost my temper. But I didn't want to talk to Kitty, and I really didn't want to hear you ask me to."

Babette stopped thinking about kissing him all over, which typically would've been difficult to stop, and thought about how she should respond. If she said she didn't want him talking to Kitty either, then she was showing him she wasn't committed to her job, and she was, except for when she was supposed to get him back with his ex. And if she said that she really wanted him to talk to Kitty, then she'd be lying, and she wasn't going to lie to Jeff again. Ever.

So she remained silent, which proved okay, because he kept talking.

"Since it looks like you're going to make it without flirting," he said, a slight grin playing on his lips, "I'll talk to her then, but not before. And I'll tell you right now, that there's no way the two of us are getting back together, so don't go spending all her money yet."

Babette cheered inwardly, but said nothing outwardly. She really was in a fix with her portion of this conversation, which was, so far, nonexistent.

Thankfully, he didn't seem to notice, and continued again.

"But that's not all I wanted to talk to you about, and the other thing is what's most important to me anyway."

"What's most important?" she repeated, thankful

that he might have moved on to a topic that allowed her participation.

"Yeah. You said something the other night that I didn't really analyze at the time. I guess because you were so sick from the sunburn, and I was so focused on trying to help that I didn't think about it. But tonight, I remembered it, and I guess I just want to know the answer."

She had no earthly idea what he was talking about. "The answer to what?"

"Your third-date rule."

Uh-oh. "Third-date rule?" she asked, turning away from him and repositioning the magazines on the end table so she could gather her composure. Heaven help her, in her fever-induced state, she'd told him about her third-date rule! Which made her wonder what else she'd said.

"The rule that you don't sleep with guys until the third date," he said. "The rule you broke once, with me."

"Right, that third-date rule," she said, swallowing hard as she continued arranging the magazines. They could stay fanned on the table, or maybe stacked in a pile would be better. How many ways could she rearrange magazines? "You wanted to talk about my third-date rule?" She couldn't imagine what else there was to say, since he seemed to know all about it.

"Kind of. Actually, I was wondering when the last time was that you actually had a third date."

Her head jerked around so fast, her hair kept going and hit her in the face.

"You talk a lot when you have a fever. You said something about no more third dates, and that got me to wondering how long it'd been."

She literally felt her cheeks sting with embarrassment.

"How long, Babette? Since you had a third date?"

Those had to be the most incredible eyes she'd ever seen. She'd forgotten how much she missed them, or how blue they were, with that brilliant turquoise, and then the tiniest ring of navy around the edge. And the mouth, the mouth that had done so many wickedly wonderful things to her, to every part of her, when they'd been together. The same mouth that had laughed with her so freely this week, when they danced with the seniors at the benefit and when they played on the beach. He'd ruined her for anyone else, because after him, no one else would do.

"How long?" he repeated.

There was no use lying. He'd be able to tell; he could always tell when she lied. "The last time was with you."

"Why." The way he said it, it didn't sound like a question. "Or why not?" The last part, however, did.

She shrugged. She'd told him enough already, and she still wasn't all that certain why not. She'd only recently started to put it together; before, she'd thought that no one had "done it" for her in a while. She simply hadn't realized how long a while that had been.

He looked up at the ceiling and didn't say anything.

Feeling extremely uncomfortable with his silence, she attempted to fill the lull in conversation. "I guess I just haven't wanted that in a while."

"Bullshit."

She didn't know what to say to that, so she turned away from him and the way-too-uncomfortable conversation, and refocused on the magazines. Maybe they'd look better on the corner of the table instead of in the center. She'd move them and see.

The cushions on the couch shifted, and her back was

suddenly very warm. He'd moved closer. She wasn't going to turn around and verify it, or they might end up way too close for comfort. Five more days. If she could wait five days, long enough for her to remain committed in her current assignment and get him to at least talk to Kitty, then they could see where things went. Caving before that would only prove to him that she still couldn't handle commitment, and she wasn't going to cave. "Are you trying to make me flirt? Because I've made it this long, and I can make it longer, even if you were the last one to have a third date with me."

He said nothing. But she could feel him breathing in the scent of her hair, and she now felt more than merely his heat. His body was definitely brushing against hers now, and unless she was really off the mark, one part of him was more prominent than the rest. He was breaking her resistance, determined to prove she couldn't win the challenge. And if he tempted her with himself, she wouldn't. But she wasn't trying to win for herself anymore, and she wasn't trying to win for Kitty; she was trying to win . . . for him.

"I mean it, Jeff. Leave me alone. I want to make this work, to prove I can be committed to something—my career—and I've been doing a damn good job."

"You're right," he said, and have mercy, she felt the warmth of his breath against her left ear. And he might as well have breathed directly between her legs, because she felt the heat there too.

"Then go, please."

"No. In fact, I have an idea that will require me to stay."

She should not look at him. She shouldn't. But she

shifted slightly, so that she was looking over her shoulder at him. So much for what she shouldn't do. "What idea?"

"You're right. You've remained committed to your job this week, even when I tried tempting you with that beach volleyball game and the bikini contest."

"And don't forget the partner swap dance," she said, then smiled.

"That one kind of backfired."

"I don't know. Mr. Moffett was pretty sexy."

"Babette," he said, his voice lowering again and losing all pretense of joking around.

"Yeah?"

"I've been fighting something here, not just fighting talking to Kitty again, but something bigger." He paused. "I want you, Babette."

"But what about—"

"I don't want to hear anything about her, not tonight. We'll discuss whatever you want tomorrow. We'll work through all of this tomorrow. Right now, I just want to be with you, without all of that mess getting in the way."

She'd thought of hardly anything else since they'd walked on the beach yesterday, but she'd tried to control those desires by reminding herself of her job, of Kitty, of the fact that she still needed to prove that she could commit. And now, thanks to Rose, she had an idea for making everything work, if she could control herself for five more days.

However, right now, Jeff was here, and he wanted her, and she knew she wanted him.

"Say yes, Babette."

She should wait, for five more days. But she'd been

waiting for a year already, and she simply wasn't willing
to give up another minute. "Yes."

His mouth was still near her ear, and he kissed it softly,
then smiled against her cheek. "A year is a mighty long
time to have gone without," he said, nibbling his way down
her jaw and to her neck, while Babette's eyes slid closed
and she relished the feeling of being with him again, of
finally having the man she'd never stopped wanting.

She twisted to face him, saw his eyes were even a
deeper blue with his arousal, and his pupils were dilated.
He wanted her and, Babette realized, she *could* read Jeff's
body language; she just couldn't read it for anyone else.

Because his desire was for her.

"I've missed you," she whispered, taking her fingers
to his temple and then tracing them along his cheeks, his
jaw, his neck. Back when they'd been together before,
they had always been in such a hurry, always frantic to
achieve their goal, to find sexual satisfaction. That wasn't
what she wanted this time. She wanted to enjoy being
with him. She wanted to enjoy loving him.

His eyes moved to her mouth, and even without her
knowledge for reading people, she'd have known he
wanted to kiss her. But again, the way he looked at her
now, as though she was exactly what he'd always wanted,
and the way he touched her now, as though she was something precious, told her that he was feeling the same surge
of emotions that she was feeling. And it told her she didn't
need body language to read Jeff. She just needed to open
her heart.

"Do you know how many times I've dreamed of kissing you again?" he asked.

Babette slid her hands behind his neck, tunneled them

in those soft curls as she slowly pulled his mouth to hers. "No more dreaming."

His mouth met hers softly, timidly, easing into what felt like their very first kiss. A shiver of desire, sweet and impassioned, flittered pleasurably through her, but she didn't rush the natural feeling. Rather, she treasured the gentle desire, building with the intensity of his kiss. His tongue was warm and gentle, parting her mouth and sliding inside.

Babette moaned approvingly as he lightly stroked her tongue, then slowly deepened the kiss, his lips pressing more solidly against hers, and his body shifting slightly, moving on top of her, exactly where she wanted him.

They let the kiss linger, his hand rubbing her side as their bodies aligned to each other, curving naturally, intimately, expectantly. Then his fingers found the top button of her blouse and slid it free. One by one, while they continued to kiss, he undid each button, then pushed the sides apart and ran his palm up her abdomen to the front closure of her bra and easily unclasped it.

Babette squirmed beneath him. She suddenly felt shy, a bit embarrassed about her shape, or lack thereof.

Jeff must have sensed her nervousness, because he eased his mouth from hers, and looked into her eyes. "Having second thoughts?"

"No," she whispered, then inadvertently glanced at her chest.

He shook his head slightly. "Babette, you're perfect." He lowered his head to her chest, brushed a tender kiss across her nipple. "You know, I've heard that a lot of women who have their breasts done end up losing all natural sensations there, particularly here," he said, running a fingertip around her nipple. "And to me, that's the sexiest thing about them. The way they're so responsive to the touch." He kept that wonderful finger circling one nipple, while his lips found the other and drew it inside his warm mouth.

Babette's hips lifted involuntarily, a direct response to the amazing things that his finger and mouth were doing to her breasts. Little or not, they *were* responsive.

"That's what turns me on more than anything to do with size, Babette. The way they respond to the touch. The way they respond to *my* touch. Babette, I want you, exactly the way you are. I wouldn't want you any other way, and I wouldn't want any part of you any other way."

His words touched her heart, because she had no doubt he meant them. She could see it in his eyes, hear the sincerity in his voice.

"Jeff."

"Yeah?"

"Make love to me." She should have thought about her words, should have told him something that didn't say so much, merely because she'd never said those words before, and because he knew it. This wasn't having sex; it was more, and she had no doubt they both knew that while this wasn't the first time they'd ever had sex, it was a first for them. They were heading into new territory, and Babette couldn't wait. Her heart was at the edge, and she was ready to let it fall. "Please."

He stood, slid his arms beneath her and scooped her off the couch. Then, walking toward her bedroom, he kissed her softly. "We're going to need more room."

Babette laughed, but her laughter died when he placed her in the center of the bed. She'd worn a black linen skirt, and he unfastened it, slid it down her legs and dropped it to the floor, then took a moment to stare at her, wearing nothing but a purple thong.

"You're beautiful," he said, taking his hands to her waist, then sliding his fingers beneath the tiny straps before moving them down her legs and dropping the satin panties to the floor. Again, he paused, looking at her boldly.

"This isn't fair," she whispered. "I want to see you too." Then she looked toward the windows, and the drawn drapes. "And I want to hear the waves when we make love, and see you in the moonlight."

He grinned, crossed the room and opened the drapes, and indeed, the moonlight cast him in perfect silhouette. Then he opened the doors and let the sounds and scents of the Gulf in, and Babette smiled, then reached for him. "Now, everything's perfect, except you're still wearing your clothes."

Another incredible smile spread across his face, and he pulled his white T-shirt over his head and tossed it aside. Babette felt her desire stir. His abdomen had always been impressive, lines of powerful muscles leading the way to—his pants and underwear hit the floor—and Babette's attention left his abs to focus on that part of him that would join them completely.

"*You're* beautiful," she said, and he was. Hard and bold and male and as perfect as anything she'd ever seen. Perfect . . . for her.

He climbed onto the bed, moving beside her, then running a palm down her stomach to where she burned the most. His finger passed over her clitoris, massaged it gently while her hips curved upward toward that blissful pressure. She was so close, and he'd barely touched her.

"I don't want to wait, Jeff. It's been a long time, and I want you so bad it hurts." She wasn't hiding anything from him now, wasn't about to act as though she didn't need everything he would give her, not only because she hadn't had a man in a year, but because she hadn't had him.

He leaned over her and kissed her, while his thumb moved over her clitoris, and his fingers dipped into her center. "It has been a long time," he said, "which is why I don't want to go too fast, Babette. I don't want to hurt you. Let me get you ready for me."

She knew what he was talking about. Jeff was no little man, but she *was* ready, had never been more ready. "Please, Jeff."

"As soon as you come, the first time," he said easily, his thumb and fingers moving rhythmically as he worked toward making that happen.

It didn't take long. Babette felt that building sensation, the press of a beckoning release, stirring deep within her, then he increased the friction, circling his thumb madly, while his fingers pushed inside.

"That's it, honey, you're almost there," he said against her ear, and Babette's stomach dipped in, her breath caught in her throat, and a hard, overwhelming climax claimed her completely, taking control, causing her to scream. And when she screamed, she screamed his name.

Her post-orgasm bliss was heightened even more when moonlight glinted off the foil packet in Jeff's hand. It'd been a long time since she'd had him inside her, but finally, finally, her dream was becoming reality. Without wasting time, he opened the packet and slid the condom down his length, then he moved above her, eased the head of his penis to her opening, still convulsing from the power of her orgasm, and guided the tip inside.

She pushed her hips forward, eager to have him where she wanted him. "Don't make me wait anymore. It's been too long. I've wanted you, for so long."

He kissed her, his mouth caressing hers while his hard length pressed inside, deeper and deeper, slowly pushing all the way in, while Babette felt her inner muscles stretching around him. His sweet kisses continued, his tongue exploring her mouth, brushing against her teeth, stroking her tongue, while his penis stroked her center, and while another spiraling sensation stirred within her.

He pushed in, then withdrew, pushed in, withdrew, and each time, Babette would swear that he was as far as he could go, all the way to the hilt, but then he'd give her more, and he captured her gasps of surprise and delight with his mouth.

The rhythm became faster, the sounds of their lovemaking combining with the sounds of the waves crashing against the shore. He broke the kiss and rose above her, bracing his hands on the headboard while his hips continued steadily thrusting, the tempo increasing, while Babette's imminent climax was also building, increasing, preparing to soar.

"Look at us," he said. "Look at us, Babette."

She followed his gaze to their joining, at his impressive length, retreating from her, long and hard and slick, then she watched him slowly push back in, all the way in, until there was nothing between them at all. They were together, completely. They were one.

Three more thrusts, and she couldn't control her response to watching them make love. This climax was even harder, even more powerful, causing her to tremble with the sheer force of it taking control. Her head thrashed on the pillow, and her mouth said what her soul was singing.

"I love you, Jeff. I always—always—have."

He thrust deep, his passionate growl of release dominating the night, while Babette took it all in, the man she loved losing control with her, because of her, for her.

# Chapter 18

Babette was sleeping better than she'd slept in years. It was so much easier to sleep soundly when snuggled up next to a man. No, scratch that; it was so much easier to sleep soundly when snuggled up next to Jeff. She smiled, snuggled closer, and attempted to drown out the obnoxious ringing that interfered with the peaceful sounds of the waves crashing on the shore and the man snoring beside her.

Then reality crept in, and she realized it wasn't a ring; it was a ding. And the ding sounding from her kitchen meant she needed to get up. "Oh, I nearly forgot," she said, climbing from the bed. She moved to the closet and switched on the light, found her robe and quickly tied it around her. Then she explained, "I've got to turn that out."

He made some very male grunting sound as he rolled over, leaned up on one arm and squinted at her. "Turn what out?"

"The bread dough. Don't you smell it?"

He inhaled, and apparently noticed that the entire apartment was filled with the sweet tang of yeast. "I do now." Then he laughed. "You're making your own bread now too?"

"Don't sound so shocked. I'm learning something new every day with my cooking lessons. So far, I can make four meals and two breakfasts."

She entered the kitchen and turned the bread dough onto the cookie sheet she'd already sprinkled with flour. Then she saw him sleepily crossing the living room wearing nothing but a pair of boxers. She laughed. "It's midnight. I can remember a time when your nights were just getting started at midnight."

"And then I grew up."

She laughed again, clapped her hands and then waved them over the big cream-colored blob. "Look at it! It looks just like when Hannah did it."

"You have a bread machine?"

"It was in the condo when I got here. And this is sweet dough, perfect for making cinnamon rolls. I used Hannah's secret recipe, and according to her, it's foolproof."

"Cinnamon rolls."

"The best cinnamon rolls, according to everyone at Sunny Beaches."

"Planning on eating them all by yourself?" he asked casually, and she looked up into those perfect eyes and saw that there was the slightest hint of curiosity to his look.

"I'd planned on taking whatever I didn't eat over to Sunny Beaches, but—"

"But?"

"If you'd like to stay and have some with me in the

morning, I'd like that too. I mean, tonight, us. Was that just one time, or did you—would you want more?" She'd kind of assumed they'd be together again, then she realized that she may have made a hasty assumption. Just because the thought of not having him inside her again made her miserable didn't mean he felt the same way.

"I want more."

There you go. Now, naturally, her mind was asking, *"More what?"* More sex, and only sex? Or more . . . everything. And did he realize that she was ready to commit now? Or had she blown the whole I-can-commit-to-something when she slept with the guy that she was supposed to be fixing up with someone else? And shouldn't the fact that she was in love with him, so he was different from any other Love Doctor assignment, enter into the equation?

"I suppose we're going to do something else to this before we move on to *more*, right?" he asked, indicating the bread dough, all fat with plump yeast bubbles popping out of the sides.

"You're going to help?"

"Why not? I like cinnamon rolls too. Maybe I'll learn to make them for myself. I actually think my condo has one of these machines, but I've never taken the initiative to learn to use it."

While she and Jeff had done lots of things together throughout their unusual relationship, cooking wasn't on the list, and the fact that he was interested in doing something so domestic with her pleased her more than she could imagine. She smiled. "It's really easy to use. You take the ingredients on the recipe, put them in the machine and select the DOUGH setting. When it's risen long enough, the machine beeps. Then you turn out the dough on the floured cookie sheet." She shrugged. "You're supposed to use a cutting board, but I couldn't find one in here, and the cookie sheet worked okay last time, when Rose and Hannah taught me. Actually, I could've probably left it in the machine until the next step, but this is the way Rose and Hannah did it."

"I'd follow what they did."

"Yeah, that's what I figured too."

"So now what do we do?" He moved closer, and the warmth of him nearly made her decide to forgo the cinnamon rolls, take him on to the bedroom for the "more" he'd mentioned and then head out for doughnuts in the morning. But he really did look excited, or interested, about working with the dough, and admittedly, cooking in the kitchen with Jeff excited her too.

"We follow the recipe," she said, pointing to the open book on the counter. "What does it say?"

He ran his finger down the page, got to the portion after the primary recipe for the dough and read, "Pour five tablespoons melted butter in the bottom of pan, then sprinkle with a half cup of brown sugar." He looked up. "Have you got melted butter?"

"There's butter in the fridge," she said. "I'll measure the brown sugar."

He found a stick of butter and cut it at the five tablespoon mark. Then he put it in a bowl, covered it with a paper towel, and popped it in the microwave, as though he'd been doing this his whole life.

Babette stared at him. "You cook?"

"I can melt butter."

She grinned, watched him grab a dish towel and use it to remove the heated bowl from the microwave.

"Where's the pan?"

Babette pulled the pan that Rose and Hannah had told her worked best for cinnamon rolls out of the cabinet and placed it in front of him, then he poured the butter in. She followed suit, sprinkling brown sugar on top of the butter.

"What's next?" she asked, because he was hogging the cookbook. He really seemed to be enjoying this.

"With a rolling pin, roll dough into an eight by fourteen inch rectangle." He looked at her skeptically. "Do you even have a rolling pin?"

Babette opened a drawer near her hip and withdrew the wooden rolling pin that Rose had found earlier in the week. "I learned how to make them already, remember? I just don't know the recipe by heart."

"Right," he said, and gave her the crooked little grin that told her what he was thinking—that she was cute, and that he wanted to have "more" with her.

Worked for Babette.

She poured a little flour on the counter, spread it out with her palm, then ran her floured palm up and down the rolling pin the way Hannah had shown her. "Okay, put the dough there." She nodded toward the floured counter.

"In the middle of it?" he asked, lifting the cookie sheet with the dough on it.

"Yeah."

He tilted the sheet and the big mound of dough plopped in the middle of the flour. Babette surveyed it; it seemed bigger than it had the other day when she made the cinnamon rolls with Rose and Hannah, but maybe she hadn't been paying attention that closely. Or maybe they had halved the recipe so they wouldn't make too many. Hannah had measured everything, so Babette wasn't sure whether they'd used the same measurements that she'd used on this batch. That could have happened. In any case, there was more dough here than Babette expected, so she sprinkled more flour on the counter and then picked up the rolling pin and began trying to convert a big, bubbly glob of bread dough into a neat rectangle.

After several minutes filled with a lot of grunting and huffing and puffing—it was harder than it looked when Hannah did it—she had a rectangle. It wasn't a neat rectangle, but it was a rectangle nonetheless. One side looked a little thicker than the other, but she couldn't seem to tame it, so she let it be. She'd always liked fat cinnamon rolls anyway; these would just be a little fatter on one side.

Jeff had stayed with her through the rolling, and had even sprinkled additional flour on the pin whenever the dough started to stick.

"Got the rectangle," she said. "Now we have to mix up the filling. I can't remember what all goes in it."

He looked back to the book. "A tablespoon of melted butter, a tablespoon of sugar, one and a half teaspoons of ground cinnamon and a tablespoon of brown sugar." He paused. "You mix it in a bowl, then put it on top of the dough. Want me to do that part, since your hands are floured?"

"Sure," she said, then watched admiringly as he melted more butter, then found the remaining ingredients, measured them precisely, and mixed it all up. Next thing she knew, Jeff was spooning the mixture over the top of the dough.

When the dough was covered and his bowl was empty, he looked at her and winked. "Every kind of cinnamon roll I've ever had was a round swirly thing. This looks kind of flat."

"Smartass." She nudged him out of the way and took control of the sugar-coated dough. "Watch this." Then she gently tugged one of the longer sides of the rectangle and started rolling it toward the other side, folding in the sugary filling as she went.

Jeff nodded approvingly as she completed the roll, then wet her fingers and pinched the seam to seal it. "So do you need a knife to cut it into individual cinnamon rolls now?" he asked, opening the drawers in the kitchen, then withdrawing a sharp knife.

Babette was extremely pleased that she was about to teach him something she deemed rather cool. "Nope, I need dental floss. Will you go get some out of the bathroom?"

He tilted his head and cocked a sandy brow. "Dental floss?"

"You'll see."

He left the kitchen while she made certain that the seams were sealed on the big roll. And it was a very big roll. Rose and Hannah must have definitely halved the recipe, because Babette's cinnamon rolls were going to be much bigger than the ones they'd made the other day. She smiled. Wouldn't Granny Gert be proud? And Clarise would absolutely freak.

Babette couldn't wait to tell them.

"Here it is," Jeff said, entering the kitchen. "But I can't imagine what you're going to do with it."

Following the example Hannah had shown her in her lessons, Babette took a nice sized piece of floss and eased it under the long roll to the point where she wanted to make the first cut. Then she pulled up both ends, criss-crossed them at the top and then gently pulled them in the opposite direction to cut the dough and make the first cinnamon roll.

"Okay, now I'm impressed," Jeff said, as she lifted the perfectly cut roll and placed it on the pan covered in butter and brown sugar.

"That's the idea." She cut the next one, while he picked up the dental floss container and got a string of it for himself.

"All right, you've had enough fun. Move over."

She did, then marveled at the muscled, gorgeous man in her kitchen, having a great time learning how to cut cinnamon rolls.

"Jeff," she said, as he skillfully cut the remaining rolls and put them all on the pan.

"Yeah?"

She covered the rolls with a clean kitchen towel. "These will have to rise a while now before we can bake them."

"Are we waiting until morning to bake them?" he asked.

"We can, or we can bake them later on tonight if you want. But either way . . ."

"Either way what?" he asked.

"We should think of something to occupy our time while that dough rises."

He started washing his hands, and Babette slid her

hands under the warm water with his, running her fingers across his, then sliding them to his palms, and all the while, moving against him and wanting to move even closer. "I can think of several things, and several places to do those several things," he said, turning off the water. Then he picked her up, put her on the counter and slid the sides of her robe apart. "Starting right here."

Babette woke up Saturday morning in Jeff's arms, where she'd spent the majority of the night, though in several locations. They'd made love in her bedroom, then they moved to the cove and made love there. On their way back to the condo, they'd had a very hot, very steamy encounter in the sauna. And then each time she'd rolled over in the night, he'd been waiting, hard and deliciously ready to go again.

"Morning," he said. He was propped on one elbow and looking down at her, and she suddenly wondered if he slept at all. Every time she'd awakened, he'd been awake, or had awakened right then. And now he was awake again, and looking at her the same way, like he couldn't wait to have her. She knew her hair was probably one big tangle, knew her eyes were undoubtedly ringed with black mascara smudges since she'd certainly never taken the time to remove her makeup, and she suspected that her face had a bit of razor burn, since his five o'clock shadow had become more substantial as the night had progressed, and he'd used that tingling stubble in all sorts of interesting ways. She had razor burn in several places, but it was worth it. Well worth it.

Even so, he was looking at her as though she looked

beautiful, and Babette couldn't deny that she felt that way. "Morning."

He ran a finger down her jaw. "I scratched you," he said, verifying the razor burn she suspected.

"I didn't mind." She inhaled and was welcomed with the tantalizing scent of cinnamon and sugar. "The cinnamon rolls?"

"I put them in the oven a half hour ago," he said, grinning. "I figured ten o'clock was late enough for you to sleep in, and I was getting hungry." Then he shrugged. "Plus, I wanted to see how we did cooking. They'd risen so much the ones on the side were hanging completely off the pan. I guess we did a good job. We'll know for sure after we taste them."

"A half hour ago?"

He nodded. "Which means they're almost done. You ready to see how good we were in the kitchen?"

"We were very good in the kitchen," she said slyly.

He winked. "Yes, we were, but I meant are you ready to see how good we did making the cinnamon rolls in the kitchen."

"I'm betting we were very good at that too." She climbed out of bed and slipped into a T-shirt and shorts. She didn't bother with underwear, since she suspected she'd be losing the clothing as soon as they'd eaten.

She entered the kitchen to find Jeff had already set the table with two glasses of orange juice and two plates filled with cinnamon rolls. And by filled, she meant *filled*. The rolls were enormous, at least three times the size of the ones she'd made earlier in the week with Rose and Hannah. The plates barely held them, and they were no tiny dessert plates; Jeff had used full dinner plates, and each of them was covered with cinnamon roll. "That's huge," she said, eyeing the one in front of her chair.

"You seem to be saying that a lot lately," he said, with that sexy smile and his turquoise eyes smoldering.

"Very funny. I'm serious. These are the biggest cinnamon rolls I've ever seen. Do you really think I can eat all of this?"

"I say you give it your best shot. I know I am." He picked up his fork and took a bite. "Man, that's good."

She couldn't resist and broke off a piece, then popped it in her mouth. The mixture of warm butter and brown sugar and cinnamon met her tongue and melded together to taste like pure heaven. She moaned her contentment. "We shouldn't have put all of that filling on the dough."

"Why not?" he asked, still digging into his, while she continued on hers as well.

"Because I can so see me licking this off *things*." She ran her finger through the warm center of the cinnamon roll, scooping out an excess of the filling, then popped it in her mouth and sucked it.

He stopped chewing and stared at her mouth, diligently licking and sucking the sugary mixture away. "We're making more of that filling tonight. Or maybe right after we finish eating," he announced.

"Okay." She ate more, licked more, and truly enjoyed the way his face tensed and his eyes grew darker blue as she did. Talk about power. Right now, she had it, and she enjoyed it to the max.

"You're cruel."

She continued eating, doing her best job to lick and suck on something every time he looked her way. "I try."

She giggled, ate some more, then knew she'd had enough.
"I'm done." She hadn't even eaten half.

"I could be, but it's too good," he said, still eating.
"And we've got a pan full of them in the kitchen."

"We can send them over to Rose. I know the seniors
would enjoy them. And it'll give them a chance to brag
about my cooking too."

"Our cooking," he amended. "But before we take those
over . . ."

"What?"

"I don't think it'd take me long to mix another batch
of that filling."

She laughed. It'd been a long time since she'd spent the
night with a man, a long time since she'd had breakfast
the morning after too. And, have mercy, she was having
fun. "I suppose I still have room for more . . . filling."

# Chapter 19

Gertrude pointed toward the White Sands entrance, and Paul turned his car into the parking lot. "I hope she doesn't mind the surprise," she said.

"I'm sure she'll love it that you've come down to see her," Paul said, reaching out to touch her hand on the seat.

That simple touch sent a frisson of desire skimming down her spine. She couldn't remember the last time she'd felt so right. And she could thank Paul . . . and Henry.

"Do you think I'm doing the right thing, though? I could be wrong about what I heard in her voice," Gert said, questioning her impulsiveness. Maybe her gumption shouldn't have been put into place, when it came to Babette and her relationships, or lack thereof. But Gertrude knew she had heard a hint of despair in Babette's tone last night, and she simply couldn't let that be without attempting to help.

"I know you're doing the right thing," Paul consoled.

"Besides, from what you said about his little deal with Babette, there's more going on than she realizes."

"You think the same thing I do, don't you?" Gert asked, really enjoying having someone to talk to about her thoughts and concerns. She could get used to that.

"That he bullied Babette into not flirting because he didn't want to see her flirt with anyone but him?"

Gert nodded.

"Oh, yeah. That boy still has something for your granddaughter, and he simply can't figure out what to do about it."

"Seems kind of odd that I'm down here trying to help her out with her relationship. She's the Love Doctor," Gert said with a slight grin, and Paul pulled into the resort.

"Trust me, doctors will take time to examine every ailment except their own. Maybe she's the same way," Paul said, and he sounded so smart, Gert thought.

"Physician, heal thyself?" she asked.

"Exactly." Paul stopped the car at the valet and got out.

"You think we'll be able to convince her that she needs to forget this getting Kitty back with Jeff thing and go after what she wants?" Gert asked.

"He may need some convincing too," Paul said, as they entered the White Sands lobby. "You did say that he has a problem believing she can commit."

"Yeah, but she *can* commit when she wants to. We've just got to make sure Jeff understands that, and I'm not leaving here until he does."

"I believe you." His mouth crooked up on one side, the way it did when she amused him.

Gert liked amusing him. She liked doing lots of things

with him, talking to him, confiding in him, laughing with him, being held by him.

As if he knew where her thoughts had turned, he brushed a soft kiss against her lips. "We'll take care of things here with those two."

"I appreciate you coming with me."

"Can't think of a thing I'd rather do." He stopped at the elevators. "Know her condo number?"

"Two fourteen."

Within minutes, they were standing outside Babette's condo, but there was no reason to knock. The door was open, and there was quite a commotion going on inside.

"What in the world." Gert entered to see three women older than Gert scurrying around in a tizzy and Babette moaning on the sofa.

She hurried in.

"Oh, who are you?" one of the women asked.

"Gertrude Robinson, her grandmother," Gert said, getting to Babette and dropping on her knees beside the sofa. "Honey, what happened?"

"I'm Rose," the other woman said, "and I'm trying to figure out what to do for something like this, but we're all not really certain. We were about to take her to the emergency room. Tillie's trying to find her identification and insurance information, and we need somebody to go check on Jeff. He went up to his condo to see if he had any Pepto Bismol, but never came back. And I think he ate more of it than she did, from what she said."

"Granny?" Babette asked, her eyes squinting in pain and her hands holding her stomach, which looked like she was in her third month of pregnancy. And Babette Robinson had never had a belly in her life.

"What, dear? What happened, honey?"

"I read the ingredients wrong," she said, then moaned out again and cradled her stomach.

"Three tablespoons of yeast instead of three teaspoons," Rose said, shaking her head. "We shouldn't have left her on her own in the kitchen yet."

"But she got the rest of it right," one of the other women said from where she was thumbing through Babette's wallet, probably searching for identification and insurance information.

"Jeff," Babette said between moans. "He's hurting."

"Where is he?" Gert asked Rose.

"He went up to his condo about ten minutes ago, but he should've been back by now. I could tell he was in pain, but I bet it got worse. I think he ate the whole cinnamon roll. Babette barely ate half."

Gert turned to Paul, standing nearby. He had his cell phone out and held up a palm. Then she listened as he talked to someone about delivering medications, then told them what order to place. She'd nearly forgotten his occupation. He'd been retired from his family practice for years, but evidently, he could still call in prescriptions, and he'd done that for Babette and Jeff. "Can you go check on Jeff?" she asked when he hung up.

"What's the number to his condo?" he asked, and Babette muttered, "Four twenty."

"What'd you call in for them?" Gert asked, as Paul headed toward the door. "Metoclopramide, or Reglan. With that much yeast in them, and as swollen as she obviously is, I think that's what they'll need."

"Will it," Babette started, then gripped her stomach, "work fast?"

"It should," Paul said. "And there's a local pharmacy that delivers, less than a mile away. They'll be here soon. Just make sure someone brings up the meds for Jeff to his condo. I'll be there. They're delivering them here."

"Thank you," Gert said, then watched Paul leave.

"Rowdy?" Babette asked.

"No, Paul," she said calmly, pushing Babette's matted hair away from her face. At Babette's furrowed brows, she added, "I'll explain later."

# Chapter 20

Gertrude's hand instantly tightened around Babette's cell phone, which she'd borrowed to communicate with Paul throughout the night, as Paul nursed the patient on the fourth floor while she nursed the one here. It'd taken more than one prescription called in, but he'd finally found the perfect combination to not only relieve some of the internal pain from puffing up like a blowfish, but also to allow Babette and Jeff—who was much worse than Babette, according to Paul—to sleep.

Paul and Gert didn't sleep at all, however, both of them staying up to take care of Jeff and Babette and talking to each other on the phone to help them fight the pull of exhaustion. He didn't suspect either of their patients to need anything, but Gert didn't want to risk Babette waking up in pain, and Paul had promised Babette that he'd make sure Jeff wasn't in any either.

And at some point in the middle of the night, while she and Paul had chatted nonstop like two teens, Paul told her that he loved her.

Now he was saying something similar. Three words, but they weren't about the two of them. "What did you say?" she asked, wanting to hear it again, for her granddaughter's sake. She glanced at Babette, still sleeping.

"I said he loves her."

"How do you know? Did he tell you?"

"Didn't have to. The guy was hurting more than almost any patient I've ever seen, and he hardly acknowledged it. Instead, he kept asking how she was."

Gert smiled. "She asked about him every time she woke up too. She's still sleeping, by the way. Is he?"

"Just woke up. He's a tough one, that boy. Got up and headed to the shower, saying he was going down to check on her. Personally, even with all the medications he took, I didn't expect him to be out of bed before tomorrow."

"He is tough, and determined," Gert said. Good qualities for a grandson-in-law, in her book.

"Jeff?" Babette asked, rolling over and peering up at her grandmother.

"No, this is Paul."

"Paul," she repeated, as though trying out the name. Then she nodded slightly. "Dr. Stovall."

Gert smiled. Naturally, Babette would remember Paul. True, he'd changed a bit since Babette had last seen him, but she would remember Paul and Emily as her grandparents' best friends. "Yes," she said. "Dr. Stovall."

"Good choice," Babette whispered, and Gert nodded.

"I think so."

"Me too," Paul said from the other end, and then he chuckled.

Babette's condo door rattled as someone knocked sharply against it. "Paul, I think Rose and her friends are back," Gert said. "I'll call you when they leave. I'm sure they want to check on Babette."

"Well, I'll come down with Jeff, as soon as he's out of the shower."

"Okay. I'll see you then. I may even try to brush her hair before he sees her."

Babette sat up. "Jeff? He's at the door?"

"No, I think it's Rose, but he'll be down here soon. You may want to clean up a bit, dear, if you can."

She nodded and then pushed herself to the edge of the bed. "I'll talk to Rose first. She was so sweet to come over last night, and so worried. Tillie and Hannah too."

"They're good friends," Gert said, glad that Babette had someone here watching over her before she arrived. She'd send them thank-you gifts when all was said and done. The door rattled as the knocking grew more intense, and Gert hurried to open it.

It wasn't Rose, or Tillie or Hannah. Kitty Carelle stood on the other side, the picture of rich beauty and determination in a pale blue pantsuit that matched her eyes perfectly.

"Oh," Kitty said. "I thought this was—wait; we've met, haven't we? You're the Love Doctor's, I mean Babette Robinson's, grandmother, aren't you?"

"Yes," Gert said, dismayed. She and Paul were trying to get Babette and Jeff to finally admit their feelings today, and this pretty blond woman was going to definitely throw a kink in their plan.

"Is Babette here?"

"Kitty?" Babette questioned, leaning against the doorway to her bedroom.

Kitty's arched brows climbed beneath her bangs, and her jaw dropped. "Oh, my! What happened?"

Babette frowned, and Granny Gert noticed that her eyes appeared to glisten instantly.

*Don't cry, Babette. Be strong, child.*

"I've had a little stomach problem," Babette said.

"A virus?" Kitty asked, taking a small step back as she spoke.

Babette paused, then said, "Maybe," and Granny Gert inwardly applauded. That was a good way to keep Kitty at bay.

"Is that why you didn't answer my calls this morning? I called several times on my way down to thank you. I got an e-mail from Jeff telling me he wanted to talk in person, and I came right down," she said, then smiled brightly. "You really are a love doctor, aren't you? Less than two weeks, and he wants me back. Well, I'm going to see him now. I just wanted to thank you, and tell you that you can still use the condo until your time is up. Take a vacation, have a good time. You deserve it for pulling this off. I can't tell you how happy I am! And you know, you may even see us around, *if* we ever leave the condo. He should be there now, right?"

Babette felt sick, and it wasn't merely the problem with the yeast in her stomach. Jeff had asked Kitty to come to Destin so they could talk things out. She swallowed past the threatening nausea that came from Kitty's statements. It'd only been sex, nothing more, just like always. Because he didn't believe she could commit. And because she couldn't wait to be with him, she'd proven him right.

"He is there, isn't he? Or is he at one of his stores this morning? Do you know?" Kitty asked.

"I believe he's in his condo," Babette said miserably.

"Thanks. I'll let you know soon how everything goes," Kitty said. She started to leave, then turned back toward Babette and Gert. "Not too soon, of course. We'll need some time to make up." She walked out and the door snapped shut behind her, then Granny Gert turned to Babette.

"You love him," she said, while Babette fell onto the couch, her hand still cradling her weak stomach.

"I can't talk about this now, Granny."

"Sure you can, and you will, child. You love that boy, and I have a strong suspicion he loves you too, and yet you're going to let her come in and try to take him away."

"Didn't you hear what she said? He *asked* her to come, Granny."

"Listen here, young lady. You are not the granddaughter I thought you were if you're going to throw in the towel now."

Babette looked up at her. "He knows how I feel. I told him last night. But—"

"But what?"

"But he wants her. I blew it. I was trying to show him I could commit to something, my job, and then I blew that by going after the guy that I'm supposed to be getting back with my client. Not exactly the best way to show him."

Gert huffed out an exasperated breath. "Not that long ago, you said that you wished you had the amount of gumption that it took for me to approach Grandpa Henry that day in the barn. Do you remember that?"

Babette nodded.

"Well, now's the time." Granny Gert grabbed Babette's hand and pulled her up from the sofa. "Go up there and stake your claim."

"I told him that I love him, Granny. Now it's up to him to determine what he wants, *who* he wants. Right now, I just have to wait."

"Sit back and wait? Child, you have no idea what I've been doing lately, just to have another chance at love. I've been talking to golf balls, for goodness's sake."

Babette's eyes widened, but Granny didn't offer additional explanation. Instead, she opened the door and nudged Babette toward the hall. "Let me know what happens after."

"After what?" Babette asked, bewildered by her grandmother's sudden surge of strength, or perhaps her own weakness. Granny had pushed her out of the condo.

"After you get up there and find your gumption, then take what you want," Granny said, slamming the door and locking it, and leaving Babette out in the hall.

Babette banged on the door. "Granny! I don't even have all of my clothes on!"

"Close enough," Granny said, her voice echoing from the other side.

Babette waited for Granny Gert to come to reason, but she heard nothing beyond her grandmother's footsteps fading as she walked away from the door, and then she heard the television volume kick up a notch within the condo. She banged again. The volume got louder.

Deciding Granny wasn't budging on her stance not to

let her back in, Babette turned and started down the hall, then met Paul Stovall getting off the elevator as she was getting on.

"Babette, where are you going?"

"According to my grandmother, I'm going to exercise my inherited gumption."

He smirked, and she thought he looked extremely debonair. No wonder Granny seemed so taken with him, and he was kind too, taking care of her and Jeff last night after she'd nearly killed them both with cinnamon rolls. Well, not killed, but she had prayed for death a few times during the night. She'd bet Jeff had too, since he'd eaten a whole roll. She hadn't even eaten half, and had thought her world was ending.

She realized she hadn't made any effort to get on the elevator, and Paul was still standing there, using his body against the frame to keep the doors open.

"Babette," he said.

"Yeah?"

"She's right. You need to use your gumption."

"Sure I do." She stepped into the elevator and wondered what in the world she'd say when she got to his condo and saw him with Kitty, the woman he *wanted* to see. Then the doors closed, and her reflection shot back at her from the mirrored finish. "Ohmigod."

Her hair was one big matted red mess, like a troll doll, but with more curls and less frizz. At least she wasn't a frizzy troll doll. Her eyes were puffy and swollen, her lips were uncommonly pale, and she was wearing a sleep shirt with "I'd give up chocolate, but I'm no quitter" printed on the front. She lifted the shirt. Good, she had on panties. But that was it.

And Kitty, as usual, had been flawless in a crisp pant-suit. Yeah, gumption was really going to do the trick.

The elevator dinged, and she stepped out. Her stomach clenched, and she wondered if it was still the after-effects of humongous over-yeasted cinnamon rolls, or nerves. Probably both.

She swallowed, decided that if her grandmother could proposition her grandfather in a barn at seventeen, then she could stand on her own against Kitty Carelle. She moved quickly down the hall, feeling the cool floor tiles against her bare feet. Granny could have at least offered some socks.

Then she got to his condo and knocked before she had a chance to reconsider.

Babette's stomach clenched again. "Please," she begged her queasy body. She didn't want them to open the door and find her hurling in the hall.

The door opened, and Kitty gawked at her. She looked mad, and Babette wasn't about to ask why. There were way too many possibilities.

"I need to tell Jeff something."

"Be my guest," Kitty said, opening the door wide and waving her hand. "I believe he needs to tell you something too."

Babette entered and immediately saw Jeff, sitting at the kitchen table, showered and dressed and sipping on something, while he peered at her over the edge of his cup. She glanced back at Kitty, still standing there and eyeing her. Her first impulse was to apologize for giving him a blow-up cinnamon roll for breakfast yesterday, but then she'd have to explain that to Kitty, and she really didn't want to go there. So instead, she said, "How are you feeling?"

"Okay." A single word. No more, no less. And he had barely moved from the cup to say it, so that Babette still hadn't seen his entire mouth.

"I'm sorry," she said softly.

"What was that?" Kitty asked, closing the door and stepping toward them.

"I said I'm sorry."

"Sorry for what, Babette?" Kitty asked. "What is it you're sorry for, because I'm definitely curious."

"I'm sorry for . . ."

"For?" Jeff asked, eyeing her. Thankfully he put the cup on the table. He was beautiful, and Babette's throat went dry.

"Yeah, Babette," Kitty repeated. "You're sorry for . . ."

"For telling you I could get you back with Jeff, when I knew deep inside that I couldn't." She turned from Kitty back to Jeff. "I couldn't, because *I* love you. I've been in love with you since the last time we were together, and I don't know why it took me so long to realize it." She shook her head. "But you want commitment, and I've been trying to prove to you that I can commit to something, to my job, so you'd see that I can, and that I want to commit fully to you. But then I couldn't do it, because committing to *this* job,"—she looked at Kitty—"meant helping her get you back. And I couldn't. Then you asked her to come down here, to come back to you, and that's the last thing I want. I don't want you with Kitty. I want you with me. And I thought—I mean, it felt like you wanted that too."

"I asked Kitty to come down here so I could end things the right way, face to face. And I told Kitty before you

came up here that I don't feel *that* way about her. I have
fallen in love, with a woman I do believe can commit."
He looked up, blue eyes drawing her in. "But I wanted to
hear you say that's what you want too," he added, smiling
slightly.

Kitty snarled. "I'll get back every penny of that money,
Ms. Love Doctor. Love Doctor, my ass. Your business is
history, Babette. I hope you enjoyed it while it lasted. And
you,"—she looked at Jeff—"If this is what you want,"—
she waved a hand toward Babette—"instead of this,"—
she indicated herself—"then you two deserve each other."
She turned and sashayed out of the condo, slamming the
door behind her as she went.

"Say it again." If possible, his voice was rough, demanding, and it sent a shiver of expectancy down her
spine.

"Which part?"

"That you want to commit fully . . . to me."

"I do. That's why I tried so hard to show you I could,
but—"

He held up a hand. "You did show me, Babette."

"How?"

"When you didn't have a third date since me." He
grinned. "For the Babette I know to go two weeks without
sex would be something for the record books, but you went
an entire year. Don't you realize what that said to me?"
he asked, standing and moving toward her. He kissed her
softly and smiled. "You've been committed to me, to us,
for the past year. Sex wasn't what you wanted."

She blinked, his words sinking in, and the truth flood-
ing her soul. "I *didn't* want sex. Not just sex, anyway," she

added with a smile. "I wanted love. But I only wanted it with you."

He kissed her again, tenderly, sweetly. Then he cleared his throat and said, "You do realize that your business in Birmingham is going to be toast, thanks to Kitty. She's a very vindictive woman, and I suspect she'll put the word out that you didn't deliver what you promised." He caressed her back as he spoke.

"Yeah, I suspect she'll do that," she whispered, her mind a little hazy due to the blissful realization that she was finally where she belonged.

"I think you need to bring the business down here," he said, and she straightened, suddenly completely alert.

"I'd thought the same thing!" she said excitedly.

"You'd already thought about moving here?" he asked, his words delivered laughingly.

Babette nodded. "And I think I need to specialize."

"Specialize?"

"The seniors. They obviously need someone to help them hook up with other seniors. And there are several of those types of condos around."

He laughed again. "I can see you doing that, and you could offer your services in exchange for cooking lessons, or whatever else you might like to learn. You wouldn't need to be paid beyond that."

"I wouldn't?"

"Not unless you wanted to," he said. "I can support what's mine."

"What's yours?"

"I nearly lost you one time because I didn't tell you exactly what I wanted. And you didn't tell me either. It's time to lay it all out there, and I'm going to start now, Babette. I want you, for today, tomorrow, forever. I want you to be my wife, and I want to have children with you, boys and girls that we can adore like we adore Little Ethan and Lindy. I want to grow old with you, have grandkids with you, be with you, every day, until I die. That's what I want." He paused. "What do you want?"

"I want commitment," she said, realizing that commitment of any type was the main thing that had always been missing in her life, and now, she realized why. She did take after her grandmother, and she did have Granny Gert's gumption, only wanting things when she could have them her way. So she'd tell Jeff now, exactly how she could have what she wanted . . . her way. "I want commitment," she repeated, "but I only want it if I can have it with you."

He gently pushed her hair away from her face, and that tender motion sent goosebumps down her arms, and an arrow of sharp desire to her center.

"Babette," he said, turquoise eyes looking at her as he eased, slowly eased, his hands beneath her shirt. His palms skimmed her skin, touching her, exciting her. "I want you now, but it won't be just sex. It hasn't been just sex in quite a while."

Her tears slipped free. He'd felt it too, the change between them that had occurred sometime over the past few days, or perhaps whatever had always been there, but they'd finally set it free. The emotional pull of one person to another that said that this wasn't merely mutual satisfaction, but a bonding of the souls.

"I know."

# Chapter 21

Babette had always suspected if she had a double wedding, it'd be with her sister. But Clarise had married six years before, so that wasn't a possibility. However, she was still having a double wedding, and a beach wedding, too.

The brides wore matching antique ivory dresses, except one of the dresses was altered for curves, and the other was altered for none.

Their rings varied as well, with the older of the two brides wearing a rock that would almost warrant a wheelbarrow to help her carry it down the aisle. Granny Gert held it up in the sun as they neared the preacher, and it made Babette (and everyone else around) squint from the glare. Paul was into big and flashy, he said, but Babette suspected he was merely trying to cater to Granny Gert's spunk.

The ring Jeff slid on Babette's finger was much, much smaller by comparison, but it meant the world to Babette to have it, and it meant the world to Granny Gert to give it to her. The tiny diamond that had adorned her grandmother's left hand for the majority of her life, the one Grandpa Henry had given her shortly after her day of extreme gumption in his barn, would grace Babette's hand now.

With all of their friends and family surrounding them, including the residents of White Sands and Sunny Beaches, the two couples married on the small strip of beach that centered the two resorts, which was only fitting, since they would all be residing there as soon as their honeymoons ended. Granny Gert and Paul had bought a condo at Sunny Beaches, and Babette and Jeff would live in his place at White Sands.

Babette had already set her Love Doctor business into place in Destin, letting all of the seniors at Sunny Beaches spread the word to their neighboring retirement condos that her services were now available, and that they could pay with cooking lessons (anything but cinnamon rolls).

When the last "I do's" were said, Babette accepted a hot and heated kiss from her husband, and it lasted nearly half as long as the one Dr. Stovall distributed to his new bride.

The crowd laughed and cheered with both sets of newlyweds, and Babette took the opportunity to whisper to the man that she'd loved for as long as she remembered, "I'm so glad I found my gumption."

"I'm so glad I found you," he responded.

Then she held her hand out and was tickled to see that it captured nearly as much light as Granny Gert's new rock. Undoubtedly, love made everything shine a little brighter. Babette's world was sure shining bright now.

*Dear Reader,*

If you're one of the many readers who sent the request for Jeff and Babette's story after meeting them in REAL WOMEN DON'T WEAR SIZE 2, thanks! I hope you enjoyed reading about their wild journey to love in FLIRTING WITH TEMPTATION.

And if you haven't read about Babette's sister, Clarise, you still can! REAL WOMEN DON'T WEAR SIZE 2 will let you in on how Clarise learned to stop hiding and start flaunting those Robinson Treasures at Tampa's Gasparilla Festival. Naturally, you'll learn a bit more about Babette, Jeff and Granny Gert along the way. So pick up a copy, and enjoy!

Happy Reading!

*Kelley St. John*

Kelley@kelleysbooks.com
www.kelleystjohn.com

# THE DISH

*Where authors give you the inside scoop!*

♥ ♥ ♥ ♥ ♥ ♥ ♥ ♥ ♥ ♥ ♥ ♥ ♥ ♥ ♥ ♥

*From the desk of Susan Crandall*

Dear Reader,

Oh, how I love to write a twisted villain, preferring the play of psychological tension to physical gore. Villains are so complex, for who in this world is completely good or completely evil? Hollis Alexander in SEEING RED (on sale now) provided a wonderful opportunity to explore the depths of darkness that can lurk in the soul, the evil behind the mask of physical beauty and agreeability.

I always like to center my novels on what I call an "everyman" story, one that could happen to any of us (although we certainly hope it doesn't). I like to make it personal, to delve into the emotions of my antagonist and my protagonist. Therefore, I rarely venture into the arena of irredeemable evil. Hollis Alexander is the exception. He's bad and that's all there is to it. He's smart and uses mental manipulation to its fullest—this, to me, is the scariest kind of villain. And if I admit that I really enjoyed writing him, does that make you worry about my mental state?

Well, I did. I loved it, even though the idea of a *real* Hollis Alexander gives me chills and makes

it difficult to sleep. Luckily, the idea of the *real*
Nate Vances, our real-world heroes, makes me
feel safe enough to turn out the lights and close
my eyes.

Thanks for coming along with me on this journey. May our real-world heroes always be there
when you need them.

Happy Reading!

*Susan Crandall*

www.susancrandall.net

♥ ♥ ♥ ♥ ♥ ♥ ♥ ♥ ♥ ♥ ♥ ♥ ♥ ♥ ♥

## *From the desk of Kate Perry*

Dear Reader,

Have you ever wondered what it'd be like to have
superpowers?

If someone gave me superpowers, I'd be stoked.
Or would I? Gabe Sansouci, the sassy heroine in
MARKED BY PASSION (on sale now), inherits
an ancient Chinese scroll that does just that, only
she finds out really quickly that having powers isn't
all it's cracked up to be.

Don't get me wrong—if someone tapped me

with a magic wand and said I could fly, I'd *so* be soaring through the sky. But there are a few powers I'd turn down:

## I Can't Go for That, No Can Do: Three Powers Kate Doesn't Want

1. Causing earthquakes.

I'm just being practical with this one. Like Gabe, I live in San Francisco. If I made the earth tremble every time I got upset, there'd be chaos. San Francisco is beautiful; it'd be a shame if it lay at the bottom of the Pacific Ocean.

2. Reading minds.

Shudder. The idea of reading minds is so horrifying to me that I couldn't bring myself to even torture Gabe with it. Imagine your Aunt Millie thinking about sex. I rest my case.

3. Killing by touch.

Gabe has the capacity to harm people through touch, but she also has the balancing ability to heal. Um, in theory.

Of course, Gabe's not alone in this thing. With the help of Rhys Llewellyn, man of mystery and all-around hot guy, she's sure to get a handle on her new powers. Eventually.

Hope you enjoy MARKED BY PASSION! And

keep an eye out for CHOSEN BY DESIRE, the second book in the Guardians of Destiny series.

*Kate Perry*

www.kateperry.com

♥ ♥ ♥ ♥ ♥ ♥ ♥ ♥ ♥ ♥ ♥ ♥ ♥ ♥ ♥

*From the desk of Kelley St. John*

Dear Reader,

One of the best parts of writing a novel with a multitude of passionate characters is learning that your readers want to know more of their story. That's what makes it so much fun to give you the "what happened next" portion of their lives, because, as you very well know, those characters continue to live in your heart . . . and mine. Thankfully, you can revisit several of your favorites, since they tend to find their way into my other books. For example, Lettie Campbell's sister, Amy, from GOOD GIRLS DON'T, is one of Rissi Kincaid's best friends in TO CATCH A CHEAT! And—you guessed it—if Amy's there, then that means her sexy cowboy Landon is also along for the ride. So if you didn't get enough of Amy and her sex toys or Landon and his famed massage oils in GOOD GIRLS DON'T, then you can have another delicious taste in TO CATCH A CHEAT!

And if you're one of the many readers who sent the request (okay, the demand) for sexy-and-sizzling Jeff Eubanks to get together with wild hellion Babette Robinson after meeting them in REAL WOMEN DON'T WEAR SIZE 2, I promise you that FLIRTING WITH TEMPTATION (on sale now) will give you exactly what you've been asking for—and then some!

Ever true to her impulsive nature, Babette is still changing jobs, addresses, and hair colors as often as possible. (And changing men just as frequently!) Even though she can't find a man who will stick, she's finally found a job that will: Birmingham's "Love Doctor," where she heals love that's gone wrong. Her business is—*until* Kitty Carelle hires Babette to get her back with her ex—none other than Jeff Eubanks.

Jeff believes that women—not men—are the ones who can't commit, and he has the power to completely ruin Babette's new career if he refuses to take Kitty back. So Babette is determined to make him see things her way, even if it means adhering to his ridiculous challenge of no flirting for a week. She can do it. She *can*. In fact, she could do it rather easily, if the no-flirting policy only applied to beach hunks who didn't have the last name of Eubanks. Because Jeff is looking mighty good, and Babette has been a long, long time wanting . . . everything he's tempting her with.

Have mercy, seven days never seemed so long!

Happy Reading!

*Kelley St. John*

Kelley@kelleysbooks.com
www.kelleystjohn.com